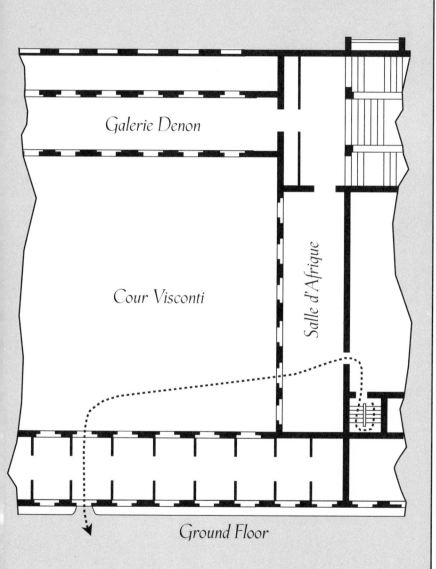

Galerie Denon

Cour Visconti

Salle d'Afrique

Ground Floor

Dotted lines indicate route taken by thieves.

*The Man
Who Stole
the Mona Lisa*

Also by Robert Noah

All the Right Answers
The Advocate (a play)

The Man
Who Stole
the Mona Lisa

Robert Noah

St. Martin's Press
New York

A THOMAS DUNNE BOOK.
An imprint of St. Martin's Press.

THE MAN WHO STOLE THE MONA LISA. Copyright © 1997 by
Robert Noah. All rights reserved. Printed in the United States
of America. No part of this book may be used or reproduced in
any manner whatsoever without written permission except in
the case of brief quotations embodied in critical articles or
reviews. For information, address St. Martin's Press, 175 Fifth
Avenue, New York, N.Y. 10010.

Design by Nancy Resnick

Library of Congress Cataloging-in-Publication Data

Noah, Robert, 1926–
    The man who stole the Mona Lisa / Robert Noah.—1st ed.
        p.   cm.
    "A Thomas Dunne book."
    ISBN 0-312-16916-7
        1. Leonardo, da Vinci, 1452–1519. Mona Lisa—Fiction.
    2. Art thefts—France—Paris—History—20th century—
    Fiction. I. Title
    PS3564.023M36   1998
    813'.54—dc21   —dc21
    [346.73'0668]   97-36510
                                                           CIP

First Edition: February 1998

10   9   8   7   6   5   4   3   2   1

For Peter, Patsy, and Tim

Acknowledgments

Invaluable help with the known facts of the theft came from several printed sources, principally Seymour Reit's *The Day They Stole the Mona Lisa*, Lawrence Jeppson's *The Fabulous Frauds*, Milton Esterow's *The Art Stealers*, and Karl Decker's *Why and How the Mona Lisa Was Stolen*. For background on Paris, New York, and Newport in the period, I'm grateful to *The Studios of Paris*, by John Milner; *New York 1900*, by Robert A. M. Stern, Gregory Gilmartin, and John Massengale; and *Newport Houses*, by Jane Mulvagh and Mark A. Weber, with photographs by Roberto Schezen.

And a special thanks to M. Vincent Pomarède, who as Conservateur, Département des Peintures at the Louvre, opened the Louvre's files to me and was kind enough to escort me on a special tour of all the sites involved, including the thieves' hiding place and the escape route that made the theft possible.

*The Man
Who Stole
the Mona Lisa*

In August 1911, the Mona Lisa *was stolen from the Louvre. It was missing for two years.*

In June 1932, The Saturday Evening Post *printed a story by reporter Karl Decker, in which a man calling himself the Marquis de Valfierno claimed to have planned the theft, and provided an astonishing answer to the question of why the painting had been stolen.*

His story may well be true.

1

In Buenos Aires, there'd been an apartment on the Paseo Colon. Not one that looked over the park, it's true, but a place that was airy and wide, with high ceilings and enormous windows, entered through a gleaming maple door atop a broad curving staircase of white stone that led up from the enormous lobby that swept visitors in off the Colon and surrounded them with elegant plaster copies of Roman copies of the marbles of Praxiteles.

Here in Mexico City things were modest. There were two reasons for this. First, modest living does not call attention to itself, and second, this was an unproductive period, during which their normally substantial income was not available. So the Marquis de Valfierno had trimmed their living standards several levels below what he, at least, had always found necessary, and they were making do with two small bedrooms, a windowless sitting room, and a kitchen so tiny it could barely accommodate the burly iceman who squeezed past its narrow cabinets to make his deliveries twice a week. The rooms were nearly a mile south of the Reforma, in a section that was struggling to keep its plain face scrubbed and was clearly doomed to lose that struggle.

The barber had been here yesterday, at which time he had made a solemn ceremony of shaving off Valfierno's beard and trimming back his flowing mustache. Now this same barber stood in the door-

3

way again, hat in hand, head bobbing in respectful nods as he reintroduced himself.

The Marquis smiled as he recognized the man. "You are back too soon," he said. "My beard does not return that quickly."

"Of course, Don Valfierno," the barber said, still bobbing in respect. "I return today because yesterday when I shave you I cannot help but notice, forgive me for saying this, that there may be another way that I can be of service."

The barber's gaze moved up, to the top of Valfierno's head, and Valfierno raised his hand to touch his hair as he realized what the man was staring at. It was the same absurd sight that continued to surprise Valfierno each morning in the mirror: half his hair was black, and half, the new half growing in, was white.

"Meaning no disrespect, I know this must disturb you," the barber said. "And I know now that I can make all of it the same." He was familiar with many dyes, he said, because he was often asked to alter nature. Of course, never in his experience had anyone asked him to turn black hair gray, or more precisely white, but it was simply a matter of mixing the pigments correctly. He had not thought it would be a difficult problem, and now he could demonstrate that indeed it was not.

Valfierno shook his head. He was not prepared to entrust the results he'd already spent weeks waiting to achieve to the hands of this neighborhood barber whose experience with dyes had surely been limited to the garish shades of red the neighborhood women seemed to find so attractive.

"Allow me, Don Valfierno," the barber said quickly. "Let me show you what I mean when I say I have proved what I can do."

Chaudron had appeared, still wearing the undershirt and work pants he'd slept in, the stale smell of alcohol almost visible around him, as it was every morning.

"Senor," the barber nodded in his direction. Chaudron acknowledged him with a closing and opening of his heavy eyes. Nothing else moved.

The barber turned back to Valfierno. "May I be allowed?" he asked.

"To do what?" the Marquis asked.

4

"To introduce my daughter."

Valfierno turned in confusion to Chaudron, who shook his head slowly. Chaudron had no notion of what this was about, but if it involved the introduction of a daughter it did not seem a good idea.

"Please," the barber continued quickly. "She is waiting downstairs. It would take only one minute, and you could see for yourself."

Without waiting for an answer, he turned quickly and ran down the stairs. The Marquis turned to Chaudron and shrugged. What was one to do? Chaudron stared at him and shut his eyes, then he turned and went back to his room and shut his door.

In no time at all the barber was back with his daughter, and when Valfierno turned and saw her in the doorway his eyes grew suddenly large at the impact of this unexpected, astonishing sight, this face of startling grace that looked at him uncertainly through large black eyes, set wide. An involuntary quiver went through the Marquis, but he was careful not to change his expression as he regarded the girl. She was of average height and slender figure, but it was that lovely face, dark, nearly round, perfectly textured, that arrested him. Her hair was completely wrapped in a bright yellow scarf that framed her in a sunrise glow. The Marquis stared, unprepared for such a sight.

"My daughter, Rosa Maria," the barber said, and the girl, with the uncertainty of her youth and station, smiled narrowly, unsure if smiling was appropriate.

"Enchanted," the Marquis said softly, and so he was.

The barber waited a moment, enjoying the reaction his daughter had produced. "She is sixteen, senor," he finally said, "and she is everything to me. I would not have attempted what I will now show you without being certain it would not mar her beauty."

With that he reached behind her and in one quick move whisked away the yellow scarf, revealing a sight that made Valfierno gasp. Her hair, which now reached to the middle of her back, had been dyed a dazzling white, a blinding white, a white as stark as sunlit snow. The girl smiled again as her hair was revealed, this time proudly, sure the Marquis would be pleased.

"You see what can be done?" the barber said.

Valfierno nodded.

"It will last a week, maybe two," the barber said. "Then it can be done again. And at any time, one can wash it clean." He turned to his daughter. "Is that not what I promise, Rosa?"

Still smiling, Rosa nodded.

"So you see," the barber said to Valfierno. "Your hair can be as I know you would wish it to be, one color again." He held up a small satchel he'd been holding in his hand. "I can do it now, at once. It can be done very quickly."

It of course would not be done at all, but Valfierno had no wish to treat the barber rudely, and certainly no wish to shorten this unexpectedly pleasant visit. "I am delighted, of course, at what you have done to try to be of service," the Marquis said. "Please, step inside for a moment."

But the barber's natural diffidence held him back. Unimposing though these rooms might be, the Marquis was clearly an educated man of significant background. The frayed surroundings notwithstanding, the gulf between the two men remained. Even having been invited, the barber knew where he did not belong.

"No, please enter," Valfierno urged, stepping into the cluttered sitting room. The barber looked at his daughter, then back to Valfierno. Then he touched his daughter's arm and moved with her partway into the room.

Valfierno turned to look at him. "This is most rewarding," he said, "to find in a city which is new to me a man so eager to be helpful. That is very pleasant. Your daughter should be proud of her father's kindness." The barber beamed.

"And of his skill," Valfierno said.

Rosa Maria looked at her father proudly.

"I think," Valfierno went on, "that for reasons of my own I will let nature color my hair in her own good time. But I think, too, that it is fortunate that you have chosen to come back to see me as you have."

The barber's face had darkened at the beginning of Valfierno's speech, but now it turned hopeful.

"Now that I no longer have my beard," the Marquis said, "it occurs to me that I will require shaving every second day. Perhaps more often, I am really not certain, it has been so long since I've kept myself clean-shaven. It has, in fact, been *so* very long that I am fearful of attempting to apply the razor myself."

The barber could see where the Marquis was leading. "Oh, yes, Don Valfierno, of course," he said eagerly. "I would be honored to shave you as often as you choose. Every day, if you like, for the price of every second day."

"We will set the price tomorrow," Valfierno said airily, "when we are alone." Gentlemen did not discuss money in front of a lady. Even the barber knew that, and was pleased that Rosa would receive this consideration.

"Tomorrow, then?" the barber asked, seeking to confirm what seemed very good news. Valfierno nodded.

"At what time, senor?"

"Eleven o'clock."

The barber nodded. "I will come then."

"Good. And if your daughter is not better occupied, she might accompany you," Valfierno said with careful unconcern. "I have some beautiful books that might interest her while you are at your work."

"She reads very well," the barber assured him. "Even some Latin. Yes, she will come with me. And Don Valfierno," the barber said slowly, "if I may suggest, you might think again about your hair. It can do for you quickly what otherwise will take many weeks. And allow me to remind you that if you do not like what you see, it can be washed clear."

"I understand," Valfierno said. "But I have reasons of my own." He looked toward Rosa Maria and smiled. "But I suggest that now that your daughter is no longer needed as an example, she would prefer her hair returned to its natural color, a color I know must suit her perfectly."

Even against her dark skin, the girl's blush was visible as she lowered her eyes.

"Indeed, Don Valfierno," the barber said, and bowed. And after more "thank you"s and other words of appreciation, the barber and his daughter left.

Let it be said quickly of Valfierno that even in a place and time that regarded a girl of sixteen as marriageable and therefore available in other ways, the Marquis de Valfierno had always set stricter limitations on his own behavior. No specific minimum number had ever been assigned to this, but as liberally as he might choose to interpret his self-imposed rules, a girl of sixteen would remain below the limit. None of that, however, would preclude an arrangement with the barber that would provide Valfierno with future opportunities to see the girl. There could certainly be no harm in that.

Care about his dealings with women was very much on his mind these days, since it had been the mishandling of a delicate relationship that had led to their quick departure from Buenos Aires.

The scheme itself could have gone on forever. It had been simple, effective, and easily maintained. It had depended for its success on the charm of its chief practitioner, the gullibility of his clients, and the considerable skills of Yves Chaudron. Since all three were in endless supply, only the fury of a powerful woman could have brought their activities to a sudden end.

The woman was Clara Teresa del Estero, wife of General Carlos del Estero, the Minister for Internal Affairs, whose government position had often been the source of much amusement in the frequent pleasurable meetings between his wife and her very close friend, the Marquis.

The Marquis Eduardo de Valfierno had met the general's wife in the place where he went two or three times a week for the specific purpose of meeting strangers, the Museo Nacional de Bellas Artes. She had been seated on a plush-covered bench in the middle of one of the darker but still more popular salons. In a city where elegant women style themselves in the European manner, there had been something about her dress and bearing that had made him mistake her for a North American. "I see you rest," the Marquis had said to her in his rigid but quite usable English.

"Only a little," she had replied, in English equally unsure, and in an accent that now made her origins clear. He had laughed and explained his mistake, and she had been flattered; not as flattered, perhaps, as if he'd thought her a Parisian, but pleased enough that he had imagined her to come from anywhere but here.

The fact that she lived here in Buenos Aires had made her useless to him for the business purpose that regularly brought him to the museum, but her lively manner was so thoroughly winning that he continued to pursue the conversation on its own merits, and very quickly the two of them were walking together through the many small exhibition rooms, and then out the back door and along the gravel paths of the garden.

She was open and friendly, and told him quickly who her husband was, information the Marquis received with considerable interest. It was evident that a woman so highly placed could be of great value at some time in the future; especially if that future were carefully built on a relationship strong enough to make her eager to please.

He found her charming, lively, and attractive, despite the barely visible lines that had just begun to etch themselves along the sides of her mouth. Her conversation was quick and edged with irreverence, and her knowledge of the pictures they'd seen together was at least as good as his own.

It was by playing on that knowledge that he arranged for them to meet again. She had mentioned Pueyrredon, whose work the Marquis had said he knew nothing of. That was mostly true, of course, for while he'd often seen the paintings, he'd never troubled himself to learn about the artist. There was no need to do so for a man whose customers were invariably interested in the works of the European religious painters.

So the following day they met and examined the gaucho scenes of the Argentinean master, and the day after that they had coffee at a quiet café, and by the end of the week she'd arranged to be free for a long midday meal at a restaurant run by Italians in La Boca, after which he took her for the first time to the apartment on the Paseo Colon.

Her enchantment with the black-haired, black-bearded Marquis was so complete that by the third such visit he felt secure enough to begin to amuse her with stories of his enterprise. At first she was unbelieving, unwilling to accept the fact that it could all be quite so simple. "Don't they suspect?" she asked.

The Marquis shrugged. "Not in fact," he said. "But just to be certain, I have ways to reassure them."

The Marquis then described his business in some detail, beginning with what he called the Factory, the large open loft to the north of town, on the river. It was here that the paintings were made.

Many were copied from the dozen or so master copies that Yves Chaudron had made over the years of the lesser known sacred works of Zurbarán and Murillo that hung in museums all over Europe. But others were what Chaudron called his originals: paintings whose style, technique, and subject matter echoed the two Spanish masters, but did not duplicate any preexisting work, and so could not be said, by Chaudron at least, to be copies. It was these latter paintings that the Marquis sold at the highest prices, because it was these that Chaudron signed with the greatest pride. (Though not, of course, with his own signature.)

At first their customers came only from the obituary columns—from the fine, large announcements of important deaths. Valfierno would learn where the widow lived and turn up at the grieving woman's door, announcing himself as a dealer with whom her late husband had been negotiating. It had been her husband's plan, he would say, to purchase a painting of the Annunciation by Bartolomé Esteban Murillo (always the entire name), and donate it to their joint place of worship, a place the Marquis could easily name, having read it in the death announcement.

The acceptance rate on the part of the bereaved was as astonishing as the gratitude that accompanied it. What a wonderful way to memorialize the man! What a perfect expression of a widow's grief, and of the devotion the two of them had shared; for each other, and for their faith.

And so all three parties to this transaction had everything to gain: the Marquis his substantial selling price, the widow her satisfaction at having perfectly expressed her grief, and the church its valued Murillo, a gift whose authenticity they would be far too sensible ever to call into question.

There were, of course, occasional weeks when no prominent men in Buenos Aires were considerate enough to die. It was during one of these longer-than-usual droughts that the Marquis had become bold enough to attempt a second plan he'd been considering for some time.

Since this new approach would involve a slightly more sophisticated customer, a group of paintings at the Factory now underwent an even more rigorous aging process. The fine-lined spider web of age was now produced more carefully, by hours of exposure to chill air streamed across the surface by electric fans. Fine dust was blown against the canvas by the nozzle of a reversed vacuum cleaner. Then pulverized coffee grounds were rubbed in by hand to represent the tiny fly specks that would have accumulated over the span of 240 years.

Experts might possibly (but only possibly) know the difference, but experts were not likely ever to judge them. And to the half-informed greedy eye, the carefully treated paintings were likely to be taken for what they were claimed to be. Especially when seen alongside the carefully prepared accounts of how they came to be here.

They found a print shop that would print to their specifications purported clippings from newspapers in Madrid. These reported the theft of this Zurbarán or that Murillo, the stories complete with full descriptions, and ending with appropriate expressions of official consternation and promised action by the police. The clippings were then themselves aged with facedown rubbings on tabletops, carefully spilled drops of wine, and many foldings with dirt rubbed into the creases.

Then it was time to create the market. To this end the Marquis spent two or three days a week strolling the salons of the Museo Nacional searching for likely prospects. These, of course, he told Clara, would certainly be men. (It seemed impolitic to confess that his initial approach to her had been nothing more than business.)

The men he was looking for were substantial, foreign-looking, and were in the museum alone. He had a distinct preference for North Americans, and if he could encounter them near the subject paintings, so much the better. If not, it was a simple matter to steer them in the right direction.

Depending on the result of the initial encounter, he either abandoned the effort or chose to pursue it. This further pursuit took place first in the museum, as the Marquis overwhelmed the prospect with his own enthusiasm for these particular artists, and then later over coffee at the same out-of-the-way café he'd taken Clara to. There he would learn more about the prospect's ability to pay, which often seemed to be considerable, and his desire to own a painting by one of the artists on whom Valfierno's skill had focused his admiration.

Finally, at what the Marquis sensed to be the crucial moment, came the prelude to the clippings.

What if, the Marquis would ask, the prospect could have the opportunity to own a painting by Zurbarán even finer than the ones he'd so recently seen?

Eyebrows would go up.

Valfierno would then reach into his breast pocket, take out his oversized wallet, and, letting several large bills flutter carelessly to the table, remove a clipping whose creases he'd then smooth out before passing it across the table. The prospect would read the story with growing surprise, then quickly put two and two together, lift his eyes, and ask the Marquis incredulously, *"Are you saying you are in possession of this painting?"*

From this point on it was simply a matter of getting past initial qualms, which rarely ran very deep, and then in another meeting or two settling on the price.

This was the business Valfierno described in complete detail to Clara Teresa del Estero after her first visit to the apartment on the Paseo Colon. When he finished his story, she sat up and cocked her head at him with a scolding look of admiration. He knew then that she would leap at the opportunity to become a part of the scheme.

She entered into the arrangement with the enthusiasm of an aristocratic woman whose daily life had become routine and who suddenly saw a chance to enliven that life through a scheme that was both daring and, since the Marquis had promised a percentage for each buyer she steered his way, potentially profitable enough to enable to her to squirrel away some money the General need never know about.

Visiting businessmen, as the Marquis had expected, were frequently in contact with her husband, and over the next few months she was able to introduce several of them to her friend the Marquis, who with surprising frequency was then able to work his magic. The arrangement might have continued for years, to their mutual profit, except for the unfortunate incident involving Clara's private box at the Teatro Colon.

The General had bought for his wife one of the "widow's boxes" that derived their name from the unusual privacy they afforded. There were five of them on each side of the sumptuous new opera house, and each was equipped with a heavy velvet curtain at the front, as well as the more customary curtain at the rear. With the front curtain drawn until after the lights went down, it was said that a widow still in mourning could attend the opera while minimizing her chances of being seen.

Whether or not these boxes had ever been bought with such a purpose in mind seems questionable, and it's certainly true that if General del Estero had been aware of what they were called, he'd never have bought one for his wife—no superstitious fossil such as he could possibly have done anything to connect the word *widow* with his wife. The box had simply been the best accommodation available at the hugely popular, elegant new opera house, and whether or not it had extra drapes or extra anything would not matter a bit to the General since he never planned to set foot in it.

But his wife did frequently. And her usual companion was the Marquis de Valfierno. There were many times when the front curtain was never opened at all. It made a pleasant change from their afternoons at his apartment, and provided occasional thrills when the musical crescendos were unexpectedly well-timed.

Toward the end of the year, the General had business in the south and insisted that his wife accompany him. She would be gone for three weeks and suggested to the Marquis that during that time he might still have access to the box.

Here things will begin to sound as gaudy and turgid as opera itself: the time away is cut short, quite unexpectedly; the returning wife is told by an unkind friend that her lover had twice been seen entering the opera house in the company of a beautiful young woman. A seething Clara goes to the theater one night and after the music has begun flings back the curtain to reveal an astonishing sight: a woman seated with her back to Clara, her hands on the hips of the standing Marquis, whose face has just gone soft in rapture.

Suddenly he sees the glowering Clara and his eyes widen and freeze in terror. *"Pendejo!"* she shouts, and she throws something long and shiny that spins past his head and slices into the heavy drape behind him. Then she spits in his face and turns and storms away.

The flashing knife having missed, a lesser man might well have allowed the scene to turn to one of comedy, but the Marquis was quick to realize that the potential for further disaster still hung in the air. He left at once with no thought for his distressed companion, and rushed back to the Paseo Colon where he awakened Chaudron, packed quickly, and had the two of them on a train heading north before midnight. Which was just as well because a troop of the Civil Guard showed up at the apartment the next morning, and when there was no one to arrest proceeded the few blocks north to the Factory, where they destroyed every painting in sight and then broke all the windows, just for the fun of it.

2

To the barber's deep embarrassment, the white did not wash out of Rosa's hair. And so Rosa Maria became the second member of Mexico City's most exclusive club: the club of people whose hair was two colors. The Marquis, of course, was the first.

As the weeks went by, each watched with great interest the progress of the other. The girl's hair, as you might expect, grew faster, advantaged as she was with youth. In two weeks, her shiny black hair had grown quickly enough to match exactly the growth the Marquis had achieved with his three-week head start. She laughed as he measured it solemnly with a piece of string he'd first held against his own hair. "It is fortunate for me," Valfierno said, "that in your case the line must travel so much farther. That alone may give the tortoise his chance in this unequal race."

The girl laughed again, and then with quick, deft moves neatly wrapped her hair in the yellow scarf she'd worn every day since they'd first met. They were alone this morning, the barber having left her there as he continued on to the small shop nearby where he rented one of the creaking, reclining wicker-backed chairs.

Rosa Maria had begun coming to the apartment as her father's baggage, but gradually the Marquis had made her presence necessary by creating special things for her to do. She was even paid a few pesos a week. Too much, both her father and Chaudron had separately complained; the one in embarrassed gratitude, the other in stern disapproval.

Her current assignment was the cataloguing and cross-referencing by salon and artist's name of the paintings in both the Buenavista Palace and the National Museum. Chaudron had argued that this endeavor was without purpose, but the Marquis had insisted that he would find it helpful. And, of course, he did; helpful in maintaining his relationship with the girl, and in supporting his representations to her and to her father that he was a scholar preparing material on the history of art in Mexico, both native and acquired.

Rosa generally stayed until after she'd prepared a small lunch for the two of them (or three, if Chaudron was at the apartment), then she would go home in time to prepare the evening meal for her widowed father. Valfierno never left the apartment. That was part of the plan—for him to remain in seclusion until his gray hair completely replaced the dyed black that would be noted on any official description. But on this day, an unusually pleasant one, when Rosa Maria turned to him as she was leaving and asked him to walk with her to her father's shop, he was too pleased at the invitation to refuse.

The walk would have created no difficulties if Chaudron had not appeared at precisely the wrong moment.

The strolling couple were within a few strides of the barber's shop when Rosa was suddenly greeted by two girls she'd been friendly with at convent school. There were happy squeals of recognition from the two young ladies, followed by joyful embraces and then Rosa's introduction of the Marquis, who doffed his hat and bowed in formal greeting. It was at this moment that Chaudron came around the corner.

Later, at the apartment, an angry, red-faced Chaudron erupted in sudden, surprising anger. Did Valfierno not realize the sight he presented, raising his hat in public for any passing official to see? All their work could be destroyed in a second by his having thoughtlessly turned a spotlight on his striped head!

Instead of hearing the justice of Chaudron's complaint, Valfierno heard only the insubordination. His back went ramrod-straight as he narrowed his eyes at the younger man. "Nothing I do can be challenged," he said in a firm, steady tone. "*Nothing!* Is that understood?"

Chaudron stared at him expressionless, aware of his lack of the quick tongue needed to trade words with Valfierno. Then, in resignation, he retreated to his small bedroom and closed the door.

The Marquis stood motionless for a furious moment, then stepped to the bedroom door and flung it open, letting it bang against the wall. Chaudron had lain down on the bed and in those few seconds had already slipped into a stertorous sleep. As the Marquis came close enough to wake him, the stale smell of alcohol was overwhelming.

"You've had wine—too much of it," Valfierno said when he'd shaken him at least partly out of his stupor. Among Chaudron's bad habits back in the days when he'd first met the Marquis had been an unquenchable thirst. But soon after his partnership with the Marquis had been formed (in fact, as a condition thereof) he'd made a solemn promise to drink nothing during daylight hours. Until now, that promise had been kept.

"Sit up!" the Marquis commanded, and with difficulty Chaudron propped himself up on one elbow.

"All the way up," Valfierno snapped. "Feet on the floor."

Chaudron cocked his head and looked at him with a crooked smile—the look of a rebellious child deciding whether to obey. Then he slowly swung his body around and raised himself to a sitting position.

"Hear me carefully," the Marquis said quietly. "Whatever I do is my affair. It may be wise, it may be foolish, but it can never be questioned. Is that understood?"

Chaudron nodded slowly.

"And you, my friend, for however long we remain together will stay clear of spirits until nightfall, or you will be back selling your charming deceptions to thieving dealers, who will once again cheat you as cruelly as they cheat their clients." He waited, his eyes locked on Chaudron's. "Are we agreed?"

Chaudron nodded again.

"Then go back to sleep," the Marquis said. "You're of no use to anyone the way you are."

And Chaudron lay back on his pillow and followed the Marquis' command to the letter.

17

Much later, when he awoke, Chaudron told the Marquis he had found the new Factory they'd been looking for; a large, sunny room in a section not far from the Zocalo. Its former tenants had been members of a religious cult whose name and beliefs were unfamiliar to Chaudron, but whose rituals stirred such deep passions that on one occasion an aroused communicant had actually taken an ice pick and murdered another on the premises. Word of the violent death had spread wide enough to discourage further occupancy, and after a lunch with Chaudron that had included the troublesome wine, the landlord had finally agreed that although Chaudron's offer was low enough to be insulting, it was probably the best he could hope for under the grisly circumstances.

"You're not afraid of bad luck?" Valfierno asked.

Chaudron shrugged. "Of course. But in this place, someone has already had it."

The new Factory had several things to recommend it. For one thing, it was closer to the center of things than its counterpart had been in Buenos Aires, and for another, the rent was less than half. The murder, of course, was one reason for the lower price, but so was the smaller size. Size hardly mattered this time, with the limited production they had in mind.

The scheme they were preparing in Mexico City would involve fewer but far wealthier customers, and one painting only: a large Virgin and Child that hung in the Buenavista Palace, painted in the mid-seventeenth century by the same artist who in Buenos Aires had served them so well, Bartolomé Esteban Murillo. They would sell it many times.

To Yves Chaudron fell the task of making the copies. To begin that work he appeared one day at the Buenavista Palace with palette and easel and introduced himself to the guard. He was a student, he explained, as he'd explained so many times in so many other such places, and wished to copy one of the wonderful Murillos he had heard were in the museum. The guard led him to the room that held the paintings and when Chaudron indicated which painting he wished to study, the guard looked at his canvas and satisfied himself that it was considerably smaller than the painting on the wall. That was the rule here, as it had been in Buenos Aires and in all museums: the student can make his copy, but only in a size that differed from the original. It was a sensible rule, the enforcement of which made exhibitors everywhere feel secure. Chaudron had always wondered why.

He set up his easel, studied the painting for a few moments, and then began. He forced himself to work slowly, as a student would work. He could not allow the skill he'd acquired over many years to reveal itself in the swift, confident brush strokes he would normally employ. And working at the slower pace gradually focused his attention on the subject work before him in a way that seemed to unravel the secrets of the master's skills, and slowly Chaudron's long-held contempt for the artist and his religious fervor softened into a grudging respect for the glory of his achievement.

In his real student days, copying the masters in the Louvre had seemed a futile exercise, so far removed was he from their techniques and their objectives. Finally, he had left the school, no longer seeing any reason to postpone the day when his real work could begin. He had imagined for himself the brilliant future that youth projects, his new work free of all restraint, recognized at once as the wave of the future, eagerly sought by the most important dealers. But if there was to be a brilliant future its arrival was tardy enough to make a problem of daily living, and when his model, who was also his mistress, became pregnant for the second time, the demands of routine living pressed more heavily. There were friends who urged him to turn his back, leave the country if he must. But the same act that future success might define as the artist's dedication to his work seemed simple cruelty to the young Chaudron, and so he found himself as trapped as if he'd been a stiff-collared clerk in some government office.

The only solution was to turn to work that brought at once the money that was needed, and gradually he sharpened his skills until it was as simple a matter for him to copy a style as it was to copy a specific painting, and the dealers who were less well known began to appreciate his impressive abilities. Of course, as it happened, the same mistress for whom he had sacrificed so much later formed an attachment to an older, unimportant Nabi, with whom she ran off to Provence, taking with her their two children.

It might seem that with the need to earn money thus removed, Chaudron would return to the kind of painting that had fired his early ambitions, but what had begun as bread-winning necessity had by now matured into easy habit, and so he continued doing the things that won him praise and other compensation.

"That is wonderfully done," came a deep, respectful voice from over his shoulder.

The sound had startled him out of his past. He turned and saw the guard nodding at the work he'd done. *"Merci,"* said Chaudron, surprised enough at the unexpected compliment to respond in the language of his thoughts.

It was the thirty-third year of the Porfiriato, and the numbing stability of the long regime of Porfirio Diaz had produced civil servants so comfortable in their jobs that bribery, never unknown, had become an expected prelude to the most routine transactions and the quickest, surest way for a modestly salaried civil servant to rise several rungs on the social ladder. Or so Emilio Cruz had been told.

His brother-in-law, for example, a customs inspector, had over the years gradually increased the subtle demands he made of the well-dressed visitors who passed through his station and had never once found a traveler unwilling to pay; or for that matter, one who was not in some perverse manner proud of his own sophistication in deducing with apparent accuracy the precise level of extortion that seemed to be expected.

But for Emilio Cruz, such opportunities did not arise. It was hard for him to imagine a circumstance in which a museum guard, which is what he was, might be the beneficiary of extra benefits. So when he finally heard the loud, unmistakable knock of opportunity, his only problem was not to reveal too quickly his eagerness to cooperate.

Opportunity had presented itself in the person of a wonderfully dressed and perfectly groomed older gentleman whose card identified him as the Marquis de Valfierno. How late would he be on duty? the Marquis had inquired. And having been told the museum closed at seven, Valfierno had asked the guard if he would be willing to join him at that hour for coffee or whatever liquid he liked at a small establishment not half a block away. The guard had forced himself to think for a moment, to cover a pounding heart that had immediately recognized the importance of this encounter, and then allowed as how, yes, that could be arranged.

Over coffee for himself and something stronger for his guest, the Marquis came quickly to the point. What he required, he explained, were periods of total privacy in the south wing of the Buenavista Palace. He would indicate these periods by asking as he entered how late the museum would be open. That would be the guard's signal to divert visitors from the area until the Marquis left the building. And this same arrangement would apply to another man, the Marquis went on, someone the guard had already seen; and he described Chaudron and explained that he, too, might occasionally require privacy and would ask for it in the same manner. The guard of course remembered Chaudron from Valfierno's description as the student whose copy he'd admired, and he nodded slowly several times, seeming to indicate, but not to promise, that such things might be possible.

Finally, the Marquis assured him, the guard could be certain that nothing that occurred during these solitary periods would in any way compromise the guard's position. Nothing would be removed, stolen, defaced, or disturbed in any way. The guard had his assurance on that score. And, indeed, the Marquis smiled, the guard had more than that—he was in possession of the Marquis' card, and could easily describe him to the authorities if he ever broke his promise. The guard dismissed that possibility with a wave of his hand, imagining all the while the wonderful moment when he would reveal to his brother-in-law this exciting turn in his fortune.

As if sensing that the time had come to discuss compensation, the Marquis now went on to say that he would not dream of making such a request unless the guard allowed him in some way to express his gratitude. What amount would the guard consider fair for each instance? The guard forced himself to pause, to appear to be considering his answer, but he had earlier established for himself the amount he would request—fifty pesos for each such instance.

The guard cleared his throat. *"One hundred pesos each time,"* he said with sudden boldness, and now it was the Marquis' turn to pause thoughtfully, so as to gather respect for his reply. In fact, the figure was less than half the amount he'd expected to pay, but if he agreed to it the guard would always wonder how high he might have gone. *"I had thought perhaps seventy-five,"* the Marquis said.

The guard pondered that figure for a moment. *"It is a most unusual request you make,"* he said. *"I think it must be eighty-five."*

Valfierno waited a few seconds, then nodded gravely. *"Done,"* he said, and the two men shook hands to seal what was for these two the perfect bargain: one in which each was certain he'd bested the other.

The Marquis had resisted the temptation to cut his hair short, to the length that had already grayed, and waited until the string told him his gray hair was now the same length his black hair had been in Buenos Aires. There was then a ceremonial final cutting by the barber, who trimmed off the last remnants of the black, and then moments later, at Rosa Maria's urgent request, shortened *her* hair by some ten inches to rid it of the last of the unwanted white. When it was done, a smiling Rosa turned to the Marquis and declared the contest a tie. But looking at her, neither he nor Chaudron nor the barber himself could laugh; with her hair now hanging softly to her shoulders, the girl had suddenly passed into a different time of life. All three stared at her, each in his own way astonished and shaken. Then finally Valfierno breathed deeply and forced his tongue to move again. Now, he said, there were things to be done. He had business with her father, he explained to the girl and Chaudron, and he and the barber would walk together to the barber shop.

The recruiting of new confederates was always a delicate matter and, as in the case of the museum guard, not nearly so difficult as might be imagined. Even a naturally honorable man could be persuaded that in a particular case the cooperation being sought, which would be well-rewarded, would not be so morally distasteful as to cost him his place in heaven. In the barber's case, this would prove to be especially true, because there was no need at this time to tell him any more than he had to know. If the barber was clever enough to see past the immediate proposal, he was also clever enough to know that too many questions can sometimes lead to burdensome answers.

Valfierno's suggestion was simple. He, Valfierno, would attempt to have him, Ramon (for that was the barber's name), installed in the elegant barber's salon at the Nacional, the finest hotel in Mexico City. That much, of course, pleased the barber greatly. Such a position would enable him to earn far more than he'd ever dreamed of. Then, the Marquis went on, the barber would serve an important function—he would, as part of whatever pleasant conversation accompanied his barbering efforts, recommend to his affluent customers while their faces were wrapped in towels that it would serve them well while they were in Mexico City to make the acquaintance of the Marquis de Valfierno, who might find many ways to make their stay more interesting.

That seemed simple enough, said the barber, careful not to question Valfierno's purpose. But how soon was all this to begin? There was future rent on his chair at the barber shop to be considered; and how certain was the Marquis that the position he described could be attained? Certain enough, the Marquis had responded.

In fact the arrangements were made in less than a week. All it had taken was a visit to the Nacional, an hour in a barber chair, and then a conversation with the short, round hotel manager in which Valfierno, at the height of his persuasive powers in this invigorating return to action, made it clear that he would frequent the hotel on a regular basis and recommend it to all his influential friends if it could be arranged that a certain barber of whom he was fond could be added to the staff. That afternoon, the manager visited the small barber shop and made the offer the barber had been told to expect.

And so the preparations were made for the playing of a scene similar to those that had been enacted in Buenos Aires, but different in one important respect: this time the subject would buy the painting that hung on the wall.

The curtain rises on the south wing gallery of the Buenavista Palace. No one is in the room. The Marquis enters, followed by a distinguished gentleman of roughly the same age, somewhere in his middle fifties. This man is in the banking business in Chicago, and wealthy enough to be able to support his newfound love of art.

The two men have previously ambled through other sections of the Palace, giving the guard, who had been asked what time the museum closed, the few minutes he might need to clear other visitors from the south wing, and remain at the entrance to that section where he could keep others from going in.

Valfierno has his guest deeply engaged in conversation as they enter the area. Yes, the man says, he knows well the paintings of Murillo, and is eager to see this fine example the Marquis has described.

They are in the room now, and the man spies the painting at once. Oh, yes, he says, this is a particularly fine example, although, he hastens to add, he does not pretend to be the last word on such things. His stab at modesty cannot conceal the self-confidence that in business had vaulted him over others and put him at the top of his profession. Valfierno is pleased to note this confidence, for it is the clever, certain man who is easiest to deal with. In the confrontation to come, Valfierno is counting on the banker's own intelligence to contribute to the deception. It was like the Eastern martial arts, where the opponent's own strength becomes the fulcrum that makes it simple for him to be flung to the ground.

"I imagine you would like to own such a painting," Valfierno says.

"What man would not?" responds his companion.

"What if I were to tell you this very painting might be for sale."

The other man is surprised. "The museum might be willing to sell it?"

The Marquis smiles and shakes his head. "No, not the museum. But if it were for sale, how much might you be willing to pay?"

The man thinks for a minute, then names the sum of sixty thousand dollars. Again Valfierno shakes his head. "Eighty thousand?" the banker inquires. Again a gentle no.

"We are negotiating," the man says, "as if such a sale were possible. I see no point in this."

Valfierno looks past the banker out into the hall, then steps in that direction and makes a great show of peering down the corridor to be sure no one is there. Then he turns back to the banker from Chicago.

"What if the painting were to be available for one hundred fifty thousand dollars?"

"But it's not available at any price."

Valfierno shrugs. "I am saying, if it were. Would you be willing to pay?"

The banker looks at him oddly, uncertain of the nature of the game but wanting it to continue. "Let's say I might be."

"Then I will say this," Valfierno says firmly. "The painting can be yours if you will agree to that price."

"Agree? You mean with *you*?"

Valfierno nods.

The banker stares at him for a moment, trying to understand. Then suddenly he smiles. "You mean, if I pay you a hundred and fifty thousand dollars, you will *steal* the painting for me?"

Valfierno responds softly. "For that amount, I will arrange to acquire the painting and deliver it to you in the United States."

The banker still seems surprised and amused, but his practical side begins to emerge. "How do I know you won't cheat me?"

"There are assurances we can arrange, but for the most part you know because you've spent your life evaluating men, and everything you've learned tells you I will do exactly as I say."

The banker stares at him. "Possibly," he says with a smile. "But please detail the assurances."

"They are simple enough," Valfierno says. "You will right now write me a check for the agreed amount, but you will date that check one month from today. If the painting has not arrived by three days before . . ." Valfierno shrugs.

"I stop payment, of course."

Valfierno nods, and the man takes out his checkbook and fountain pen. Then in a practiced banker's hand that hides the excitement stirring inside him, he begins to write the check for the amount agreed upon.

"But there's one more thing," the banker says before handing the check over. "How will I know the painting I receive is the one we're looking at, and not some worthless copy?"

"You're a careful man," Valfierno says admiringly, relieved that the important question has been asked. "Here's what we will do." He

25

leads the banker closer to the painting and asks him to take out his fountain pen again. Valfierno pulls the bottom of the frame away from the wall. "Here, on the back of the canvas, make whatever mark you like. When the painting arrives, look to see that it's right where you put it."

The banker nods and Valfierno starts toward the entrance to the gallery. "I will be certain no one comes to disturb you."

The banker pulls the painting farther from the wall and puts his initials on the back of the canvas. Then he thinks some more and draws a rectangle around the initials, and two diagonals through it that form an X. Then smiling at his own ingenuity, he takes a tiny pair of scissors from his pocket and cuts away a small section of the canvas that includes part of his design. He puts the small piece in his pocket. "All right," he says to Valfierno.

As the Marquis comes back into the room, the banker describes what he has done and shows him his scrap of canvas. "If the lines on my piece line up with the lines remaining on the canvas, I will know I've gotten *this* painting and no other," he says.

The Marquis looks at him in admiration. "Very clever," says Valfierno. "Indeed you will."

The next day, at approximately the same hour, Chaudron appears at the museum dressed in his smock and carrying his easel and covered canvases. He asks the guard how late the museum will be open, and after receiving his answer enters the Palace and, following Valfierno's instructions, takes several minutes looking at other galleries. Then he heads for the south wing, where the same guard nods as Chaudron walks past him.

Inside the gallery, Chaudron puts his materials down and goes quickly to the Murillo *Virgin and Child*. He lifts it from the wall, turns it around, and using a small pocket knife quickly pries free a *second* painting that had been set flat against the original, its canvas back seeming to be the back of the original, and now branded with the mark the Chicago banker had made.

Chaudron sets this second painting on the floor and admires again his handiwork. The copy is almost perfect. Still working quickly, he goes back to the materials he's brought with him and uncovers still another copy. This one is now set in place firmly against the original, just as the banker's had been. Now the double painting goes back on the wall, ready to take another's mark. And when, some fifteen minutes later, Chaudron leaves the Buenavista Palace with the copy he'd come to retrieve covered and tucked under his arm, the guard nods pleasantly and wonders at how little time he'd been in there. But instead of asking questions, the guard finds himself hoping that he will soon again receive a visit from one of these men or the other.

3

*I*s it dishonorable to steal if the theft will be only temporary, and if the purloined object will be returned almost at once, and in nearly perfect condition?

This question in situational ethics never so much as crossed the mind of the Marquis de Valfierno when his opportunistic eye fell on the colorful beaded purse sitting quietly in a corner of the empty dressing room. He grabbed it without a second thought and whisked it under his cloak, seeing at once how it might serve his purpose. Then he quickly left. No one had seen him come in, and no one saw him leave.

He had gone backstage to present himself to Signorina Duse. Her dressing room door was identified by her name, lettered in an unsteady hand on a ragged square of cardboard tacked at eye level. When he'd knocked, the unsecured door had slowly swung open and he'd stepped inside, into a sparsely furnished sitting room complete with makeup mirror. There was a second door to a more private inner room, and he'd been about to knock on that when he'd spied the purse and in an instant had formed his plan.

Outside the theater, he stepped quickly into a carriage and instructed the driver to drive around for half an hour. Then he sat back and snapped open the purse.

It contained very little money, which pleased him because even though stealing had not been part of his plan, having taken the purse he would now be obliged to extract whatever money he found in order to give substance to the story he planned to tell. He removed the few coins and notes and stuffed them into his pocket, and then was surprised to discover that the purse belonged not to the celebrated actress, but to someone named Valérie Rénard. This became clear when behind a packet of two tissue-wrapped thin black cigars he found first a letter addressed to this Mme. Rénard, and then her passport. At first he was disappointed, but then he saw that even though his plan might not now have quite the impact on Signorina Duse he'd hoped for, it could still be effective. Enough time having now gone by, he instructed the driver to start back to the theater.

Eleanora Duse had come to Mexico City to perform on alternate nights the title role in *Peer Gynt* (the first time a woman had ventured the part), and the title role in *La Gioconda*, a play that had been written for her by her inamorata, the celebrated soldier-writer, Gabriele D'Annunzio. The Marquis had been drawn to the theater by Duse's fame, of course, and also because in the back of his mind he hoped that he might somehow contrive to make her acquaintance, and then later, perhaps, direct her interest to the same patient Murillo that hung on its wall in the Buenavista Palace, waiting to charm new admirers.

As between the two performances he might have chosen to attend, Valfierno had selected *La Gioconda*, partly because it seemed ridiculous to gaze at one of the world's most beautiful women disguised as a man, and partly because a play about the art world's greatest masterpiece seemed almost perfectly appropriate. He was therefore surprised and at first disappointed to learn that D'Annunzio's play had nothing at all to do with the *Mona Lisa*. It was instead the modern story of a sculptor who is fascinated by, and ultimately enamored of, a model who has somehow and for no particular reason acquired the nickname of Gioconda.

Once past his initial disappointment, Valfierno had sat through the play as enchanted as the rest of the world had always been at the indefinable magic of Eleanora Duse. Later, his engraved and crested calling card in hand, he'd presented himself at her door as excited at the prospect of meeting this exceptional woman as he was by the thought of their possibly doing business. Then he'd spied the purse and moved quickly.

Now he was back at the dressing-room door, where the muffled shouting from within brought a smile to his face as he realized that his action was likely to have been its cause. He knocked loudly in order to be heard over the considerable din, and after repeated and increasingly more vigorous poundings, a maid finally opened the door.

Inside there was turmoil as Signorina Duse berated a mustached and bearded man who apparently had the misfortune to be the theater's manager. A second woman sat ignoring the noise around her, quietly writing what seemed to be a letter.

Her tirade finally finished, Duse gestured grandly toward the door. "Leave us!" she intoned in a sonorous contralto. "And if the police fail to find the thief, I shall hold your theater fully responsible!"

The manager nodded, miserable at this turn of events, but relieved to be dismissed. As he bobbed and backed his way to the door, all he could think was that finding the thief was not very likely, and that being held fully responsible to a woman like Signorina Duse was nothing to look forward to, even though the exact meaning of such a position was far from clear. At the door he stopped, bowed deeply from the waist, and quickly left.

"We never should have come here," Duse exploded in Italian. "South America is nothing but a land of thieves."

"Perhaps," said Valérie Rénard without looking up. "But we are in *North* America."

"It is all the same," Duse replied, dismissing the difference with a wave of her arm. Then she disappeared into the inner dressing room, having completely ignored, if indeed she'd ever seen, their visitor. Mme. Rénard turned to him.

"You wished to speak with Signorina Duse?" she asked in Spanish.

"In fact, it is you I must speak with, I believe," the Marquis responded in his serviceable French.

Valérie Rénard could not suppress the flicker of a disapproving smile at the, to her, abrasive sound his foreign tongue had given to the language he'd somehow perceived to be hers. When she spoke again, she put the conversation firmly back into Spanish. "How may I help you?" she asked.

The Marquis took the purse from under his cloak, and bowed slightly as he extended it in her direction. Seeing it Valérie Rénard gasped in surprise.

"I found this not five minutes ago," the Marquis said, "in the gutter, around the corner from the theater." He was back now on the solid ground of his mother tongue, his command of which marked his noble birth more surely than his title. "I had no choice but to look inside, for identification, and I found your name. I asked at the theater if they knew who you were, and they sent me here."

Mme. Rénard looked at him for a moment, as if trying to decide what kind of man this strange incident had unexpectedly put in her path. Then she took the purse and opened it, flipping quickly through the contents. "Everything important is still here," she said, lowering the purse to her lap. "The money, of course, is gone."

"I hope the amount was not large."

She shook her head. "Quite small, in fact." She looked up at him. "Someone must have taken it in the few minutes I was out of the room, then stolen the money and thrown the purse away. It's fortunate for me you found it."

The Marquis smiled.

"The loss of the passport alone would have been inconvenient, at the very least. And the purse itself has great value to me. It belonged to my grandmother."

"The purse is beautiful," Valfierno said.

"I am very much in your debt."

Valfierno smiled and bowed slightly. "It is my privilege to have been of service."

And so began the ever-deepening friendship that would one day lead to the theft of the very *Gioconda* whose name, by the purest coincidence, had been attached to the enterprise that had brought these two together.

The daily presence of Rosa Maria had begun to arouse feelings in the Marquis that he was no longer sure he would have the wisdom to control. The girl's fondness for the very much older man was clear; she missed no opportunity to be in his company. He was flattered, of course, but more than that, stirred by her interest to feelings that went beyond admiration. One day when the two of them were alone, as they often were, she'd asked him a question the answer to which he'd suggested they seek in his dictionary. As he'd turned the pages she'd stood so close that the slight distance between them was suddenly charged with a magnetic force so strong the Marquis knew that she must feel it. Finally she'd come close enough for him to feel her small breast against his shoulder and it had been all he could do to keep from turning and drawing her to him. When she pressed against him a second time, allowing her body's outline to settle against his arm, he lost whatever focus he'd had on the page before him. And when she touched her hand to his back and leaned still closer, he held his breath for a suspended moment, then turned and looked into the gentle, steady eyes and moved forward to kiss her. Her mouth had a welcoming softness and the lingering kiss soon warmed into the gentlest kind of passion as they slowly moved against each other. His hand found her breast; her hand settled over his.

The sudden sound of a creaking board on the staircase pierced the silence like a pistol shot. The two of them sprang apart, shame replacing passion in an instant. *"I must go,"* Rosa Maria had said quickly, and she'd fled.

The next morning, he wondered if she'd return. Their routine had changed somewhat since the days when he'd spent all his time in the small apartment, waiting for his hair to become fully gray. But the barber still came every morning, earlier now that he worked a chair at the Nacional, and Rosa Maria nearly always accompanied her father. Valfierno had undertaken the girl's continuing education, in part, of course, to encourage her visits, but largely because he'd seen in the girl the same kind of promise his stepfather had once seen in him.

The Marquis Eduardo de Valfierno had been born as Eduardo Something-else to a shabbily genteel family with no claim to any title and no reason to think that any of its members could possibly rise to any station beyond that of low-level clerk in the civil bureaucracy of Montevideo, where the family had always lived. Fortunately for the young Eduardo, his gentle, unimaginative father died of tuberculosis when the boy was very young, and his still-attractive mother quickly enchanted a minor scoundrel whose charm and skill at seizing opportunities had won for him the largely ceremonial title of Librarian of the National University. This Valfierno had with the stroke of a pen added the lordly *de* to his otherwise ordinary name, but lacked the daring of his bolder stepson who, in later years upon moving across the river to Buenos Aires, would add the title *Marquis* by means no more complicated than so describing himself to the engraver who printed his calling card.

The older Valfierno had never formally adopted the young Eduardo (such a bow to the legal niceties would never have seemed important), but there had been a kind of spiritual adoption almost at once. The young boy had been eight when his widowed mother had taken up with the dashing Librarian, and the bond between man and boy was apparent from the first. They even grew to look alike as Eduardo copied every detail of his stepfather's appearance: posture, walk, and attitudes at first, and then as the boy grew older, clothes and even the styling of his hair. Such things are significant, the Librarian had taught him; knowing how to rise in life is largely a matter of knowing who and what to imitate.

All of us, the older man had explained, are in some degree exposed to everything. The lower-class fool automatically apes the models close at hand, thus gaining for himself acceptance to the very world he should be struggling to escape. The people and customs that must be copied, the older man had said, are those of the only world whose gates must be unlocked: the world of wealth and power.

To set his stepson on the right path, Valfierno the elder arranged for him to be employed as a kitchen helper at the French embassy in Montevideo, instructing the boy to look sharp and work his way into the dining room at the earliest opportunity. This the lively twelve-year-old accomplished within two months, simply by being the best kitchen helper the staff had ever seen.

Livery having thus become his first uniform of acceptance, the boy next set out to overcome his dining-room ignorance, quickly becoming adept at setting the formal table without ever giving away the total ignorance with which he'd started. And later he learned to linger within those walls of elegance so as better to observe the usage of the various utensils he'd so carefully laid out.

But if manners were essential, they were nothing as compared with language. The elder Valfierno had insisted that language was the single most important element, the key to society's every door. And while it was true that the French embassy represented an opportunity to learn not only dress and manners, but also the language of diplomacy, knowledge of a foreign tongue was secondary to mastery of one's own. The elder Valfierno was forceful on this point. His own success in securing his sinecure as Librarian was based largely on the fact that his conversational skills and his ability to write the occasional letter his office might demand were both of such high order that the official who'd appointed him would have no fear about his ability to meet the demands of the office, minimal though those demands might be.

And so, when the opportunity arose two years later to find for his stepson a place in the University's prestigious preparatory school, the Librarian had insisted that the boy accept. It meant trimming his time at the embassy to weekends and occasional evenings, but so intent was the embassy butler on not losing his most skillful boy that those arrangements were quickly made.

How had the Librarian been able to obtain a place at such an important school? Eduardo was never told. But in later years his understanding of his stepfather's influence became clearer one drunken night when the older man had transmitted more than he'd meant to in one of his instructional generalizations. Sometimes one advances by displaying knowledge, he'd said, and sometimes by holding it back. He had been appointed Librarian, for example, not for his knowledge of books, but for his knowledge of a scandalous and possibly criminal fiscal transaction that had been entered into by the

Minister of Education and the builder of a rather large dormitory extension. The elder Valfierno and the Minister had discussed the matter, and Valfierno had given his oath that no word of the Minister's arrangement would ever be revealed. No word ever was, or needed to be.

But now to return to Rosa Maria. She did indeed come back with her father the following morning, settling at once into her usual routine as if nothing had happened. As the barber shaved him, the Marquis was aware of the girl's bustling about the apartment, putting things in order as she always did.

When the barber left the apartment Valfierno settled himself at the crude table that served as his desk and arranged some papers in front of him, but he found he could not keep his mind on the accounts. He was aware of every move the girl made around the apartment and kept wondering if she would come to him. When it was clear that she would not, he put away his notebooks, rose from the table, and walked to the shelf where he kept his folder of maps.

"Rosa Maria," he called, reaching up for the folder. She had begun to work in the kitchen, but hearing his voice came back into the room, carrying a small frying pan she was drying with a towel. She looked at him questioningly.

"I have been meaning to show you the new map I bought of Europe."

The girl smiled. "I know the map of Europe. My knuckles would have been reddened in school if I could not have named the countries."

"Forgive me," he said. "I know that you do. I will understand if you have no interest."

Her face turned sober. "My interest is that you want me to see it," she said quietly. She walked toward him and stood at his side, still drying the pan idly as he unfolded the map.

"I bought it because it's a new edition the bookseller was very proud of. It's printed in four colors, you see."

She nodded as she looked at the extended map. "Yes, I do see. Each country stands out very clearly." She looked up at him and smiled again. "Even Andorra."

"What do you know of Andorra?"

She put down the things she'd been holding and pointed to the spot on the map, on the border between Spain and France. "I know that it is here. I know that Sister couldn't answer when I asked her what kind of place it was. She was embarrassed not to know."

Valfierno dropped to his knees and spread the map on the floor in front of him. "I can't tell you, either," he said. "I know only that it is a country to itself, and yet it is not entirely so, because it remains under the rule of France and Spain."

She knelt beside him and watched as his finger traced the border between the two countries. "I know that along the Pyrenees nothing seems as clear as we might like. There is the Basque country, whose borders only its people really understand. And then there is this tiny country where the borders can be traced, but not the lines of governance. Perhaps that's why it has so often been convenient."

She turned to him and frowned.

"To those who wished to move things freely between Spain and France."

"Has that ever been your business?"

He shook his head. "No, but there are some I've known for whom it has."

She smiled at him and leaned closer. "You've told me a great deal about the country of Andorra."

He touched his forehead to hers. "I've told you everything I know."

"But tell me of the people. Are they Basque?"

He grinned at her—a young man's grin. "You are greedy to know everything."

"Then you must tell me. Are they?"

"I can tell you this, but then I swear I know no more. Not Basque, but Catalan."

She cocked her head, not understanding. "I don't know that word."

He said it again, but she shook her head. Then she put her finger to his lips and said, "Again."

Her finger held the iron smell of the frying pan and recognizing that he smiled again. Then looking directly in her eyes he whispered, "Catalan," and gently kissed the soft and pungent finger that had touched his mouth to tell him that yesterday had not been a dream.

4

*H*e lay on the bed with his back suddenly arched in a curve of resistance as the cold water ran down his face, trickled past his frozen look of surprise, and soaked itself into the pillow. His nude body was rigid with shock, except for the single part that no longer was. Expectation had turned in an instant to astonishment, confusion. His right hand clutched the bunch of carnations tightly, pointing them straight toward the ceiling.

He heard the rasping of a match and unsqueezed his eyelids enough to let in the sight of an almost unnaturally calm Valérie Rénard standing with her arm resting on the bureau as she puffed on her slim black cigar. She was as naked as he, but the slightly full figure was no longer the center of interest it had been only seconds ago.

"I suggest," he said finally in a low, steady voice, "that you refill the vase so I have someplace to put these lovely flowers."

"I am not concerned with where you put them," she said coolly.

"The vase," he said firmly. "Please fill it."

She stared at him for a moment, then picked up the red-and-green pottery vase from the night table, brought it into the bathroom, and returned with it filled with water. She stopped and regarded him. "I have half a mind to do it again," she said.

He smiled. "It will not be as surprising a second time, but the effect will again be unpleasant, if that's the result you're seeking."

She seemed to consider it for a moment as he looked at her unflinchingly. Then without changing expression she extended the vase toward him, inviting him to put the flowers in place. He did, with some relief.

"You are a filthy dog," she said.

He shrugged lightly. "It's an opinion you seem to have formed at an unexpected moment. It is disappointing to learn that at such a time your mind was on other matters."

She did not respond.

"Specifically, it seems, on the matter we spoke of earlier. I can only say that I would not have expected your feelings toward the Signorina to be so protective."

Valérie smiled and shook her head. "How little you know me. My employer, the Signorina, is a willful, selfish woman; a perfect Scorpio with never a thought for any life but her own. I despise her."

He propped himself up on one elbow and turned to her. "If you despise her, why are you with her? Does she pay you that handsomely?"

"She pays me well enough. But indeed, I am *not* to be with her much longer. She had my notice on Monday."

This news was unexpected—a fact that registered on the Marquis' responsive face.

Mme. Rénard cocked her head slightly, as if to be sure he understood the point. "I will be with her until the end of her engagement here two weeks from tomorrow. When she leaves Mexico City, she leaves without me. So you see, my anger with you has nothing to do with protecting the Signorina."

It had seemed, of course, that it had. He had come to the modest hotel room at two o'clock, as they had arranged. He had bought the carnations on the way because they had caught his eye as he'd passed the market, and flowers had often worked their wonders in the past. Although it must be said quickly that seduction had not been his intention—not, that is, seduction of the physical kind. His purpose had been to further the good impression he'd imagined he'd already made on this attractive woman who might prove to be the key to a prospective buyer.

The plan had been for the two of them to go to the Buenavista Palace, where the Marquis would show Mme. Rénard the remarkable painting he'd already described, and that, he'd hinted, might one day soon be available for purchase if some buyer found it sufficiently intriguing. That had been the plan, but they'd never gotten out of her room.

She'd seemed quite pleased when he'd presented the flowers, and after she'd placed them in the pottery vase, she'd expressed her thanks with a kiss of gratitude. So unexpectedly pleasant had that light kiss proved to be, that the Marquis had returned it more warmly, and then put his arms around Mme. Rénard, slowly pulling her closer, almost as if to see how far he might proceed before resistance was encountered. When none was, it was only a matter of moments before the embrace had increased in warmth to the point where clothes were falling to the floor and they had found their way to the plain wooden bed. Things had been progressing in the familiar sequence when suddenly Mme. Rénard had leaped to her feet, taken the carnations from the vase, asked him to hold them, and then flung the water in his face.

He had imagined that she had somehow divined his plans for Signorina Duse and the painting, and that the sudden insight had triggered her angry reaction. But now that she had denied that that had been the case, he was at a loss for an explanation. She allowed the puzzled look to remain on his face for several seconds before she spoke again.

"My purse," she said softly.

"Yes," he said slowly, trying to see how that could possibly connect with anything.

"The thief who stole it was you."

He was horrified. He had been so persuaded by his own invented tale that it had become as comfortable as sacred truth. "I *found* it," he said, with a feeling indistinguishable from genuine hurt. "In the alley beside the theater."

"In the gutter, you said that night. But the difference is of no matter."

"But don't you understand . . ." he sputtered.

"What happened is plain enough for all but a fool to see," she said crisply. "And I am embarrassed to have been that fool. You took the purse from the dressing room and then invented your story. If you deny it, I'll throw the whole vase at your head."

He started to protest further, but then suddenly stopped and lay his head back down on the soaking wet pillow. He smiled. "That would not be welcome. And since I have no doubt that you would do it, I have no choice but to confess."

"You thought the purse belonged to the Signorina."

He considered his answer for the briefest fraction of a second, then came down on the side of truth, for no better reason than it now seemed more practical. "It was in her dressing room. What was I likely to think?"

She stared at him for a moment, then bent down and in one swift move retrieved her clothes from the floor. He propped himself on one elbow, watching her get dressed.

"I suppose you would have me do the same."

She went on sliding things into place, tugging and adjusting. "I see no reason for you to remain as you are."

"I find that disappointing. I hope you'll see reason another time."

She shrugged. "Moments appear and disappear. One can never be sure." When she finished dressing, she turned and faced him. "I believe the plan was to see a painting."

"In due time," the Marquis said. "Sit down."

She looked at him for a moment, unsure that sitting was what she wanted to do. Then she sat stiffly on the edge of the bed, her head high, her back straight.

He reached out and took her hand, which she allowed him to do. His thumb gently stroked the hand, but she held it still and unresponsive. "Tell me about yourself," he said in an automatic purr. "What makes you suddenly aware of external events at a moment such as we were having?"

She looked steadily at him. "On what date were you born?"

"The third of August."

"In what year?"

He cocked his head. "I know little of astrology, but I've always thought the required information was the month and date."

"Please tell me the year."

"What if I don't wish to hear my horoscope?"

She looked at him firmly. "I don't intend to do a reading. I want to know how old you are."

He smiled. "Fifty-five."

"You are fifty-five?"

He shook his head. "You asked the year I was born. It was 1855."

"Then you are fifty-*six*."

He nodded.

"You look younger. My husband is fifty-two. You look five years younger than he."

He shrugged. "I never consider how I look."

Her face softened into a smile. "You? You cannot expect me to believe that. You are a peacock, a bird of splendor; as shamelessly vain as a beautiful woman."

"My sign tells you that?"

She shook her head. "*You* tell me that. Every word you utter, every move you make tells me that. But as it happens, vanity is consistent with your sign. You are a Leo."

"I know my sign. Even disbelievers know their place in the universe of stars."

"And you, of course, are a disbeliever."

"A practical man. One whose destiny is his alone to design."

She puffed on her cigar and then tilted her head back and exhaled slowly, sending a sinuous line of smoke toward the ceiling. "Doubters sometimes become the strongest believers."

He took the cigar from her fingers and rolled it between his fingers for a moment. Then he put it in the middle of his mouth and slowly drew in the smoke. He let it swirl inside his partly open mouth, and then discharged it gently.

"Very pleasant," he said approvingly.

"The cigars are from the Signorina. It's a habit I never had before."

He started to say something, but stopped.

"You were about to ask if she knows she keeps me supplied. And the answer is, she does. These were a birthday gift. And, no, you may not know which birthday."

The Marquis handed back the cigar. "You read my mind so skillfully I can only suppose that those are questions one might expect from a Leo."

She smiled. "Or from any other man."

And so the conversation continued—lightly, pleasantly, until the Marquis had regained composure enough to get back into his clothes without embarrassment.

Until now, our descriptions of the Marquis de Valfierno's efforts to sell some of the world's great paintings have centered only on success. But no seller, regardless of his skill, can offer his wares without encountering his share of "no"s. It was to the Marquis' great credit that such failures as occurred were quickly dismissed, always lightly, and always with at least a mental reference to an attitude he'd learned from his stepfather. The older Valfierno had, for a short period in his eventful career, sold life insurance. His commission on every sale was roughly a hundred pesos, and he had estimated that he was able to sell one policy for every ten men he called upon. Thus, he'd explained to his stepson, whenever a prospect proved disappointing, he would leave the scene of his failure telling himself he'd just earned ten pesos.

So the Marquis was not ruffled when Mme. Rénard failed to exhibit the kind of excitement in the Murillo that might lead to further business. Yes, she said, gazing at it with head-cocked appreciation, it certainly seems a wonderful example of the master's work; but, no, she quickly replied when he suggested that it might represent an opportunity for the Signorina. When it came to money, the Signorina remained a simple woman who would never fully believe in her own solvency. Whatever money she put by (a substantial amount, Mme. Rénard had reason to believe) was invested shrewdly and carefully tended. The buying of paintings would seem more like spending to her than investing, and as between the two activities she had a considerable preference for the latter. The Marquis had nodded and suggested they go for coffee.

And now, as they started on their second cup, the Valfierno charm reappeared at its fullest, centered in the warm, engulfing smile that could be broad enough to flood a drawing room, or narrow enough to focus brightly on the sole human being who occupied his universe. At the moment, Valérie Rénard had become that person, and worldly though she might have been, she felt herself slip under its spell. The friendship forged that day lasted longer than he'd imagined any such thing could ever last, and pressed him to exploits that his own lively imagination might never have devised.

The boy ran up the narrow street, moving with a rhythm and grace that seemed impossible. Chaudron had seen him often in the streets and had marveled at the way he swung his crutch in swift, perfect arcs—the short, rapid strokes of the carved left limb meshing perfectly with the short, rapid steps of the natural right.

The boy stopped when he recognized Chaudron, and thrust his face forward. "Keep this for me," he whispered urgently, and pushed at Chaudron a small paper-wrapped parcel tied with string. Then the boy turned quickly and was off again, racing down the street through the late afternoon crowd, which by and large failed to notice what should have seemed a remarkable sight.

As Chaudron turned back in the other direction, he saw the reason for the boy's flight: a puffing, overweight Civil Guard, who, though he was losing ground, seemed determined to continue the chase. As Chaudron watched, the Guard suddenly realized he had lost sight of his quarry and stopped to question a mustached flower vendor. "Which way?" he wheezed heavily. The vendor seemed not to understand and Chaudron stepped forward and asked if he could help. When the Guard repeated his question, Chaudron nodded and pointed to the left. The Guard thanked him and resumed his rumbling pursuit, unaware that each heavy step now put him more firmly in the wrong direction.

Chaudron smiled with satisfaction and reached into his pocket to touch the small parcel he'd been given. Whatever it was, the boy would certainly be back to claim it. Something stolen, of course. And if it was something that had been stolen in this neighborhood, it would be something of very small value. But of course the theft might well have occurred somewhere else, and Chaudron amused himself with an imagined chain of events that could have begun with an elaborate jewelry theft, the passing of a large emerald to this boy for safekeeping. . . .

So completely did the possibilities occupy his thoughts that he forgot the purpose that had brought him down from his workshop. And so when his thoughts were suddenly pierced by the sight of her, it was as if she had sprung out of nowhere, and the unexpected impact tumbled his insides.

She was here in response to his invitation, one he'd been sure she would not accept. But she'd seized on it with a delight that had surprised him, smiling eagerly at the pleasant prospect of learning more about his work. It would, she said, be a chance to see for herself the wonderful things he did with brush and paint, the fascinating acts of creation he wrought in the workplace he'd talked about that she could never imagine.

"Perhaps next Tuesday, at five o'clock," she'd said, *"if that is convenient."* Five o'clock would allow her to be less hurried. She would take the early afternoon to begin the preparation of her father's dinner (which is how she thought of it; *his* dinner, not her own) and would then apply the finishing touches to the meal quickly before he returned home at his usual half past nine.

Chaudron had written out the street directions in great detail, and promised that he would be waiting in front for her arrival. He had taken up his post a half hour before the specified time, and had been in a state of increasing agitation until the incident with the boy had provided its distraction.

He greeted her warmly, and then suffered some indecision as he debated whether to precede or follow her up the narrow staircase to the workshop. (It was Valfierno who still called it the Factory, not any longer Chaudron.) Finally he stepped in front and muttered, "This way," and clumsily led her up the steep, sometimes complaining stairs.

Once inside, it was as if he suddenly drew strength from this environment where he was master. Rosa Maria stopped in the doorway and gasped as she took it in.

The loft, small to Valfierno and Chaudron, seemed immense to the girl, and everywhere she looked there were canvases in various stages of completion.

45

"There are so many," she said.

Chaudron nodded. She walked to one of the five or six partly finished paintings set on easels. "You work on many before you finish one?"

"Sometimes. Sometimes I work to finish one before going on."

There were six identical Murillos stacked against the wall, all completed, all waiting to take their turns at the Buenavista Palace. Chaudron had meant to cover them with a cloth, but the girl didn't seem to be interested. She went instead to the nearly completed portrait on the easel directly under the skylight—something very different from Murillo.

"This," she said. "He is very handsome. Does he live nearby?"

Chaudron smiled at the question, because the young man on the canvas was meant to one day pass inspection as a nobleman of seventeenth-century Madrid. Still, despite the richness of his attire, despite the aristocratic arch the artist had so carefully given to his eyebrow, there was no doubt of who, in fact, he was. Chaudron nodded. "Nearby, indeed. He is a butcher's apprentice in a shop not five streets from here."

Rosa Maria stared more closely. "I think I might have seen him. But maybe not, because if I had, I would remember."

"Because he is so handsome?"

"Yes," the girl said.

"Perhaps in real life he is not so handsome as I have made him."

The girl looked at the picture again, thinking less of the boy's good looks than of the skill it must have taken to reproduce them, a skill so far beyond her own capacities that she could not comprehend it. She turned to Chaudron. "You painted him?" She knew, of course, he had. Chaudron nodded.

"You painted everything here?"

"Almost everything."

She turned back to the butcher's apprentice in his noble pose. "Who is he meant to be?"

"A Spaniard of noble birth."

"What was this Spaniard's name?"

Chaudron shrugged. Among the many promotional skills he failed to appreciate was the fact that the labeling of things was as important as their creation. He had not taken the trouble to bestow a noble name on his creature since such a step would require a trip to the cathedral library and a struggle with the written Spanish he'd largely managed to avoid. It would be something he would have to do one day. Unless, of course, he had a change of heart and included the Marquis in the current work he was doing.

Meanwhile he wondered what the girl would think if she saw this painting finished, named, displayed in a room with other works of the master whose style it so closely resembled. Would she accept it as belonging in their company? But this, of course, was the easy question. The more important question would be: could it, even signed with the magic name, be accepted by someone of taste and discernment? He thought it could.

But still, he could not resist the test.

He led her to a corner of the studio and reached into a bin and pulled out a painting of a young boy in regal clothes with a dog at his feet. "This painting is one I did not paint. I found it at a dealer near Chapultepec Park."

The girl took the picture, examined it carefully, and then gasped as she saw the signature. "Velázquez?"

Chaudron nodded.

"But what must it have cost?"

"Next to nothing," he said. "The dealer is an ignorant man."

The girl seemed unable to believe it, which was quite the right reaction, since the picture was in fact a copy Chaudron had made two weeks ago. But her disbelief was centered not on his veracity, for she would have believed anything he'd told her, but rather on his astonishing good luck. "It is beautiful," she said. "You will be rich when you sell it."

"Not rich," Chaudron said modestly, "but I will certainly earn a profit." And he carefully suggested that this might be a matter best kept between themselves.

He asked her to look closely at the painting and then led her, still holding the painting, back to the easel where the butcher's helper remained in his noble pose. "And now," he said, "look again at this handsome young man and tell me if he could not have been painted by the same hand."

Her eyes widened as she began to see what he'd suggested. "It is as if his spirit had guided you."

Chaudron nodded soberly. "I did not realize what was happening," he said modestly. Long exposure to the ways of the Marquis had made the lies come easier.

The girl studied the painting more carefully, her head slowly shaking in wonder. It was just the reaction he'd hoped for, but suddenly he was unable to enjoy it.

His pleasure was diminished not by the knowledge that he'd orchestrated her perceptions so carefully that her reactions were meaningless, but rather by a physical problem that had suddenly overtaken him: the urgent discomfort of an unwelcome bubble in his lower intestinal tract. The need to take this difficulty out of doors was overwhelming. "I think we must leave," he said quickly.

Rosa Maria looked at him in surprise. "So soon?"

"Yes, I must buy some brushes."

"But can't that wait?" The shops were open till nine.

"Tonight the owner leaves early," Chaudron said quickly.

The girl nodded and handed him the picture. He put it down quickly beside the easel and led the way to the door.

"May I come back another time?"

"Of course," he said in a voice strained with the effort of control. He preceded her out the door and led the way down the stairs. On the street he turned to her. "You must have a flower," he said with sudden inspiration. "Wait here."

And he ran ahead and bought her one.

5

Las Ursulinas was not a name that was known to Ramon, the barber, but the tone in which the Marquis de Valfierno referred to it was enough to make him suddenly light-headed as he felt the full impact of the remarkable offer that was being described. He lowered the razor to his side as his hand began to tremble.

"The finest school in Spain," the Marquis went on, lather still covering a small patch on the right side of his face. He turned to the barber. "Do you understand that?"

The barber seemed not to hear.

"Ramon?"

He heard the sound of his name filtering through his confusion, and he knew he must respond. "Yes, Don Valfierno."

"Do you understand? Perhaps the finest school in all of Europe."

But the barber could not for the moment continue the conversation. "I must sit down," he said, and he sank onto the stiff-backed chair near the doorway. There were dots of perspiration on his forehead.

The Marquis frowned with concern at his distress. "Would you like some water?" he asked.

The barber shook his head. "I am fine," he said. "I am just—what I mean to say is, this is nothing I ever expected."

"I understand," the Marquis said. "Sit quietly for a moment." The barber nodded and Valfierno touched his fingertips to his face and felt the remaining lather. "We have not finished my shave."

The barber nodded. "Yes, Don Valfierno. In a moment, if you please."

The Marquis rose from the chair and walked to the barber. "Give me the razor. I will finish it myself."

The barber was horrified—not at the potential danger in Valfierno's wielding his own razor, but at the prospect that he, Ramon Martinez, might be seen as a man who would leave his work undone. "Oh, no," he said quickly. "You must let me finish."

Valfierno looked at him and nodded. "As you wish," he said. "When you are ready."

"In a moment," the barber said again.

Valfierno turned and walked back to the chair. "I assumed you would be in agreement, so I have already posted to the school a year's tuition, with a request for them to inform me how quickly the girl may be allowed to start, and what clothing, books, and other things might be required." He sat again in the makeshift barber's chair. "There is also the matter of transportation, for which I will make arrangements. Now, much as I would like to be the one to tell her of our plans, I think she might be more comfortable hearing this from you."

"Oh, no," the barber said quickly. "I mean, I will do whatever you wish, but I would be happier if you would tell her yourself."

Valfierno looked at him for a moment. This was not news that he had any desire to deliver, but the barber's wishes were clear and it seemed awkward to discuss the matter further. He agreed to tell Rosa Maria what had been decided as soon as she arrived, and he hoped the barber would not have left by then.

To the barber, the impulse for Valfierno's startling offer appeared to have sprung from nothing more complicated than the generous feelings the older man felt for the girl. But while those feelings certainly existed, it would be only fair to note that there were other, more urgent, considerations. In fact, for Valfierno, his gesture served as the solution to two problems that had begun to press. The simpler one first.

Chaudron had become unhappy with Valfierno's closeness to the girl. He had expressed this disapproval several times, basing it, of course, on the obvious imbalance in their ages. But it had become increasingly clear that the painter's discomfort was in fact based on his own growing infatuation. Given the success the two men had enjoyed in their association, Valfierno was determined that any difficulty must be resolved.

Then there was the other problem—the matter of what the Marquis and the girl had come to refer to as their geography lessons.

It will be recalled that it had been a particularly handsome map of Europe that had been the catalyst that brought these two together. Ever since, whenever the Marquis and the girl had found themselves comfortably alone in the small apartment (which was several times a week), one or the other would suggest that it might be time for another geography lesson.

Warm as these lessons were, Rosa Maria would never permit them to reach what the Marquis had always assumed to be their logical conclusion. With the example of several disgraced young girls to point to, the barber had extracted from his daughter a promise that she would never give herself completely to any man outside of marriage, and either through fear or honor it was a vow she was determined to keep. It was a vow, however, that still left considerable leeway, and the ways in which she demonstrated her abundant affection for the Marquis were pleasant and, in their own way, fully satisfying. So much so that when the Marquis began a *second* close relationship, this one with Valérie Rénard, the increase in his romantic activity quickly went from doubled pleasure to potentially dangerous exhaustion.

It was clear that something had to be done, and since Mme. Rénard represented a blissful combination of future business and current gratification, a way had to be found to end his dalliance with the girl. Las Ursulinas was that way.

The future business with Valérie Rénard had begun to be discussed when she'd announced her plan to return to Paris. She had for some time thought of opening a gallery, and as she'd learned more of the Marquis' activities, she'd begun urging him to move to Paris with her. There existed a M. Rénard, of course, but for the present he would be no encumbrance, ensconced as he was in a prison cell on the Île de la Cité for having been caught in some financial dealings that had been found odious by both the authorities and his usually tolerant brethren on the Bourse du Commerce.

Valérie Rénard had suggested that if the Marquis would provide some of the backing for her proposed gallery, he might benefit both by finding himself in a profitable business and by discovering new ways to deal with the business that already engaged him.

As it happened, new ways seemed desirable. Chaudron had finally made the Marquis aware of his maturing skills in creating what the world would surely accept as newly discovered works by Velázquez. The painter had kept his new work secret for as long as he could, but he'd finally come to terms with his own lack of promotional skills and invited the Marquis to come to the studio to see what he'd been up to. The Marquis had been duly impressed.

And so all things seemed to be coming together.

Thursday was marketing day, so Rosa Maria was always late on Thursday, but this day she was even later than usual. When she finally arrived she was bubbling with her story of having been splashed with mud by a passing carriage and how long it had taken to find a cloth clean enough to do her skirt more good than harm. She was putting things away as she spoke, and the Marquis listened in silence. When she finished, the Marquis said he had something to tell her, and his grave tone seemed somehow frightening. She followed him into the sitting room.

After he'd explained it all, including the fact that her father had given his approval, she sat silently for a moment, staring straight ahead. He was unsure of what she was feeling. Finally, she turned to him.

"When will I be leaving?"

"In six weeks, or maybe eight."

It was a moment before she spoke again. "Madrid," she said quietly. "Will you show me where it is on the map of Europe?"

The Marquis looked at her, then nodded solemnly and rose to get it.

Chaudron now knew what was in the package. He'd known as soon as his eye fell on the newspaper headline. Normally, the newspapers did not interest him—world affairs were of no consequence to him, and besides, his ability to read the language he heard spoken all around him was even more limited than his ability to understand it.

But this day, the words had seemed to leap at him and he quickly bought the paper and rushed to the workshop, where he struggled with the sentences, slowly making sense of them.

The Archbishop of Mexico City had announced with sadness the theft of the ring of Juan Diego. It had been stolen from its glass case in the Church of the Virgin of Guadalupe at Tepeyac some time in the last few weeks. The exact date of the theft could not be determined because the thief had substituted an imitation for the genuine ring, and the substitution had been discovered only yesterday when a young priest, looking at the ring, thought it appeared different in some way and suggested to his superior that it be examined. The imitation being crude, it was quickly established that the real ring was missing. A reward was being offered for information leading to its recovery.

Chaudron put the newspaper down and went to the corner of the studio where he kept his supplies. From behind tubes of paint and clusters of brushes he extracted the crudely wrapped small package the fleeing boy had pressed on him. He wanted to open it, but somehow could not. The boy would be back for it and Chaudron felt obliged to keep it untouched until he came.

The ring of Juan Diego had a value that could scarcely be measured. Juan Diego was the Indian convert to whom the vision of the Virgin Mary had appeared on the hill of Tepeyac in 1531. She had instructed him to have a temple built on the ground where they stood and consecrated to her memory. But when the simple farmer had gone to the Archbishop Zumaraga with the story, the Archbishop had not believed him. The next day on that same hill, the Virgin appeared again to Juan Diego and made a cluster of roses suddenly bloom where none had ever grown before. She told Juan Diego to gather the flowers and take them to the Archbishop, which he did. When Juan Diego placed the roses at the Archbishop's feet, an image of the Virgin miraculously appeared on his rough cape, and the Archbishop knew it was a sign. The church was built and all Mexico worshiped at the shrine of the Virgin of Guadalupe.

Soon after the dedication of the Virgin's church, the Archbishop had presented a gift to Juan Diego: a gold ring nearly an inch wide and set with three tiny emeralds in a triangle. On Juan Diego's deathbed thirty-six years later, the peasant bequeathed the ring to the church, where it had been on display ever since.

For Chaudron, the small package in its hiding place was now a magnet. He came back to it several times a day, drawn by the wonder of what was certainly inside. He would set it on his table and stare at it in fascination, feeling the emanations flowing from the little package.

He waited for the boy, but the boy did not come. At first, he told himself he would wait two days. Then when nothing happened, two days more. And finally, he imposed upon himself three additional days so as to round out the waiting period to an even week.

The morning after the week had finally passed, he awakened in a nervous fever, quickly splashed some water on his face, and left the small apartment at an hour so uncommonly early as to astonish the suddenly awakened Marquis. It was still so early when he reached the workshop building that the iron gate was locked in place, something he'd never before arrived early enough to see. He had no key, of course—he'd never thought he'd need one. So all he could do was rattle the gate loudly until most of the neighborhood began complaining and the building's owner finally awakened and came down to let him in, grumbling at the hour.

Once inside the workshop, he shut the door behind him, leaning against it and listening for the owner's retreating footsteps, to be sure the man was gone. Then, as if to relish this moment of release, he took several deep breaths before slowly making his way toward the hiding place.

He stared at the hiding place, in his mind's eye seeing the image of the ring. Then he began to uncover it, slowly, deliberately. One by one the brushes were laid aside, and then the tubes of paint. Finally he reached into the recess under the bottom shelf, felt the tiny package, and drew it out.

He walked to the room's only table and set the package down. He scraped a chair into position and seated himself in front of it, unable to move for another moment. Then, astonishingly, he crossed himself and began to remove the wrappings.

The newspaper used for the job had been torn vertically in strips three inches wide, with each strip wound all the way around, and Chaudron unwrapped each strip carefully. He worked slowly, as if the wrappings needed to be saved. Gradually the package got smaller until finally he could feel something hard through the remaining layers. And suddenly, there it was, exactly as he'd known it would be: the ring of Juan Diego, a remarkable prize of whose existence he'd been unaware just eight days ago.

His lips parted as he stared at the ring. Its worth could only be imagined, but the thrill he felt came from an unexpected source: the wellspring of his long-forgotten childhood of unquestioning belief.

In a moment the spell was broken and a grin of simpler, more familiar pleasure spread across his face. This was good fortune of almost unbelievable proportions. He picked up the ring and held it straight out in front of him, still grinning wildly. Then he stood up quickly, put the ring in his pocket, and headed toward the door. He had just reached out to open it when two quick, loud knocks froze him as he stood. When the knocks were repeated he turned the knob and pulled the door open.

The boy was standing there.

Not all skeptics fall. But those who do fall hard.

The Marquis de Valfierno, having spent a lifetime believing in nothing he could not eat, drink, fondle, wear, or spend, had gradually over the last two months found himself slipping under the spell of Valérie Rénard and her heavenly mysteries.

In the beginning, of course, it had been with a certain canny patience that he'd flattered her with pretended interest in her charts and projections, her complex alignments and calculations. But as some of the things she foretold actually seemed to happen, he began to seek her opinion on the likelihood of certain business transactions coming to fruition, and he noted with growing respect that she seemed to be right amazingly often. (Was his bookkeeping in these matters wholly accurate? Did he value too highly the forecasts that proved even partly correct while ignoring those that didn't? If so, he would not have been the first to be less than precise in these evaluations.)

There was the matter of the Austrian nobleman. Ramon, the barber, had delivered this wonderful-seeming prospect in the usual manner, and the Marquis had escorted him on the customary tour of the Buenavista Palace, winding up at the usual center of interest. All had gone extremely well and the two men had agreed to meet again the following day to consummate the deal. But Valérie Rénard had been uneasy; something in the Marquis' chart had indicated this was a dangerous time for business dealings. The next day she accompanied him to the restaurant where the two men were to meet. The Austrian had been charming; he'd handed over his envelope with a gracious smile and left. As soon as he was gone, Valérie had shaken her head and said this man was not what he seemed. The Marquis had opened the envelope, examined the unexceptional check, and tried to show it to her. She'd pushed the check aside without a glance. Don't deal with this man, she'd advised.

Routinely, of course, the Marquis had no protection against bad checks. The checks he was given were always postdated at his insistence so as to reassure the buyer; the check could not be cashed until after the painting had been delivered. If the check then proved invalid, the Marquis would have no recourse. But astonishingly, in the time he'd been in Mexico City there had not been even one bank draft that had failed to clear.

That night, Valérie Rénard had referred again to her spiderweb charts, and when she'd finished she pressed her urgent warnings still more strongly. The following day the Marquis sealed the check in an envelope addressed to the Austrian, with a note explaining that complications now forced him to withdraw from their agreement, and left the envelope at the desk of the Nacional. Three days later Ramon reported that several uniformed government officials had called at the hotel to visit the Austrian and, so said a wide-eyed chambermaid, had suggested that if he agreed to leave the country at once the government would drop some eleven charges that had been brought against him based on the passing of fraudulent checks.

That had been two weeks ago, and had caused Valfierno's respect for Valérie Rénard's powers to rise still higher. No wonder, then, that he became extremely excited when yesterday morning she burst into the apartment with what she called the very best of news. She had been scanning Valfierno's charts, as she did nearly every day, and had suddenly seen that something extraordinary was about to happen. It could mean a great deal of money, and it would involve something far removed from his usual activities. Eager questioning from the Marquis elicited nothing further. What the nature of this opportunity might be she had no way of knowing, but whatever it was would occur very soon.

That is the background against which Yves Chaudron appeared with the ring of Juan Diego. No wonder that for a moment the Marquis felt faint.

Rosa Maria had certainly not *meant* to break down; she lacked the guile to stage such scenes for effect. But if she had schemed for a way to make the Marquis finally feel the depth of her pain, she could not have devised a method more effective.

No sooner had she appeared this morning, an ordinary morning, and received his cheerful greeting than she had unaccountably burst into tears. For a moment, he'd been too astonished to offer comfort, but when he'd finally put his hands on her shoulders she'd firmly pushed him away and run into his bedroom, slamming the door behind her.

Which was really just as well, for awkward as this moment was to explain, it would have been far worse if the Marquis' comforting gesture had accomplished its purpose and Chaudron and the boy had made their unexpected appearance at a moment that might have been more awkward still.

"She is unhappy about leaving her father," Valfierno said matter-of-factly, explaining the audible sobs from the other room. The boy had entered the room and sat down so quickly that Valfierno had not noticed the crutch until the boy extended it in front of him.

"This is Miguel," Chaudron said.

"Why is he here?"

The boy leaned forward. "To bring you good fortune, as you will see."

Valfierno turned to look at him for a moment with a stare that disapproved of his having spoken.

"You will see," the boy repeated.

"Be quiet," Valfierno said sharply. Then he turned back to Chaudron and repeated his question, this time in French. "Why is he here?"

"I will explain," Chaudron said, welcoming the chance to explain in the language in which he felt comfortable. The boy sat back, unhappy at having been excluded from the conversation, but reassured by the occasional glances his way that his role in the story had not been ignored.

When Chaudron had finished, the Marquis' flushed face revealed the extent of his excitement. He looked at the boy with something that was close to admiration, and when he addressed his next question to Chaudron, he asked it in Spanish. "You brought the ring?"

Chaudron took the package from his pocket. He'd rewrapped it in the cleanest cloth he could find at the workshop. He handed the package to the Marquis, who unraveled it, then held the ring up close to his eye. He frowned at Chaudron. "How do I know what this is?"

The boy jumped up angrily, positioning his crutch in one swift move as he quickly moved to within an inch of Valfierno's face. "Give it back, if you think it's nothing!" He reached for the ring, but the Marquis moved it away.

Valfierno smiled at the boy and spoke quietly. "I will ask again, this time of you. How do I know what this is?"

"It is the ring of Juan Diego," he said.

"You stole it?"

The boy shrugged.

"Tell me at once!" Valfierno said sharply.

The boy glanced at Chaudron, who nodded slightly.

"I was there when it was taken," the boy, Miguel, said. "I waited outside while another broke in and took it, leaving behind the ring he'd made to take its place. He gave it to me for safekeeping."

His confederate had turned the ring over because he was a felon known to the police and he feared that he might be suspected. Two days later the Civil Guards had come and searched his room. Finding nothing, they'd taken him to headquarters and submitted him to torture. He finally broke down and gave them Miguel's name and a full description. The crutch, of course, had made it easy for the Civil Guard to spot the boy on the street, and thus had begun the chase that had ended in his handing the ring to Chaudron.

"I suppose," Valfierno said, "you expect to be paid something if the ring is sold."

"The ring is mine," the boy said firmly. "It is mine until I agree with someone to divide the money it brings."

But he had not, Valfierno noted, reached out for the ring again. The Marquis smiled and offered it to him. "You're right, it's yours. Take it and sell it on the street to some dirty beggar for a hundred pesos. It's what you deserve."

The boy stared at him, his growing anger reflected in the flush that spread across his face. The tense silence hung in the room until it was suddenly broken by the sound of a hand slapping the table as sharply as a pistol shot.

Valfierno and the boy turned to Yves Chaudron.

"No more foolish talk," the painter said softly. "We are all here to profit from this good fortune."

"The good fortune is yours," the boy said sharply. "That I agree to share it with you."

"Sit down," the Marquis said firmly. The boy looked quickly at Chaudron, and when he nodded went back to his chair.

The Marquis waited until he was seated and then took a few steps around the room to gather his thoughts. Finally he stopped, put the ring in his pocket, and turned back to the boy. "Tell me your name again," he said.

The boy repeated his name.

"All right, Miguel," the Marquis began, "listen to several things. First, as you must realize, I am the man in charge here. That is something you must accept. It means, among other things, that when I ask you to do something you must not turn to another for approval, as you have done twice now; you must simply do as you're asked."

Almost involuntarily, the boy's eyes went to Chaudron, who was careful this time to give no sign. He looked back to Valfierno.

"That was the third time," the Marquis said coldly, "and it will be the last."

The boy waited a moment, and then nodded at the older man.

"Good," Valfierno said. "Now as for the ring. I will sell it for an amount higher than anything you've ever dreamed. And although you are undeserving of such generosity, I will deduct certain expenses and then give you one quarter of that amount."

The boy frowned. "One *quarter.* But there are three of us."

Valfierno shook his head. He turned to Chaudron. "Tell him," he said.

"There is a woman," Chaudron explained.

"A woman! But I haven't seen her!"

Valfierno shrugged. "Nonetheless, she exists. She is part of everything we do and you must accept that she will be part of this."

The boy seemed to think it over for a moment. "How much will my quarter be?"

"I cannot say."

"Will it be a thousand pesos?"

Valfierno threw back his head and laughed. "Will you right now accept as your payment an amount that is *double* that?"

The boy stared at him, trying to decide.

"And before you answer," Valfierno went on, "you may look this one last time to your friend for advice."

Miguel turned to Chaudron, who smiled and slowly shook his head.

6

*I*t was, of course, a kidnapped child. There was no other way to treat it.

The ring of Juan Diego could be converted into money in several ways, but it would clearly fetch its highest price from the grieving parent who had lost it.

That was the inescapable conclusion reached by the Marquis, much to the discomfort of Yves Chaudron. The painter, his forgotten faith unexpectedly revived by this providential contact with the ring, would have preferred to squeeze the money from some other source, but there was no disputing Valfierno's logic. And so it was agreed that a letter would be sent to the Archbishop of Mexico City.

That letter, of course, would be a ransom note. The ugly phrase was never used, but the thought of it disturbed Chaudron still further. And it seemed to disturb whatever watchful angel heaven had assigned to monitor their scheme, because not twenty minutes after the fateful decision had been taken the normally healthy Marquis de Valfierno was stricken with a pain so intense it bent him in two. Chaudron's eyes widened and his brow erupted in sudden beads of perspiration as he beheld what he could only read as a clear sign of divine displeasure.

The Marquis insisted it was a simple gastric disorder that would quickly pass, the result of his having eaten his excellent dinner much too quickly. But as the minutes went by the pain became more intense. Finally at the urging of Mme. Rénard, who had shared the meal with them, Chaudron went to find a doctor, although it seemed to the stricken painter that a priest might have been more in order.

He found a short, stout doctor just a few houses away and brought him back, his dinner napkin still tucked inside his shirt. A quick examination convinced the doctor that the problem was an appendix so inflamed it might be near to bursting, and he scribbled the address of a nearby surgeon and sent Chaudron out again to find him.

The dramatic operation was performed on the kitchen table with the Marquis gassed into blissful sleep. Afterward, the two doctors moved him into the bedroom and left instructions that he was to remain in bed for at least three weeks. The surgeon would call each day to change the dressings.

As soon as Mme. Rénard took her leave, the shaken Chaudron opened a second bottle of the Moulin á Vent they'd had with dinner and finished all of it within an hour. Ten minutes later he was so violently sick to his stomach that between retchings he prayed for the mercy of sudden death. But the spasms finally passed, and with his system purged his mind went slack and he was soon asleep.

And so the hectic night's events passed into the calm of a peaceful sunrise, and as Chaudron awoke in his cot alongside the bed of the sleeping Marquis, his fears had abated, and so had his unaccustomed scruples. He smiled at the deeply breathing Marquis and envied him his unwavering certitude. Never in the years they had been together had the Marquis Eduardo de Valfierno been nagged by doubts once a decision had been made. His quick mind functioned all the faster for traveling only in straight lines, leaping the distance between his thoughts by the shortest routes. No niceties pursued him, no crippling second thoughts. He was a man at peace with his nature, blissfully free to pursue his goals by any means that presented themselves.

But for now he was a man removed from any activity for what the doctor had said would be three weeks, and Chaudron slowly began to realize that, unexpectedly, there would now be time for him to put into action a plan that before the events of last night would have been impossible to execute.

* * *

It was to be his most faithful copy. And to make it so he set out to learn quickly the skills he would need to fashion the ring in precisely the right size and shape, and to reproduce its wondrous, almost reddish glow.

The goldsmith he chose as his unwitting tutor was located some two miles from the workshop. Chaudron described to the man a ring he would like to have made for his mother in Paris (there was no disguising his accent) and asked how he could be sure it would be just the color he had in mind. The goldsmith led him to the rear of the shop and showed Chaudron his molds and filing tools, and explained how the purity of the gold determined its hardness and color. Mixing three parts of gold with one part silver gave it the slightly greenish cast that was preferred for the finest jewelry. Mixing it with copper produced the warmer, burnished tone and harder finish that was used for coins. Chaudron thanked the man for his trouble and promised to return.

It had taken only a few minutes of observation for Chaudron to catalogue the materials and tools he'd need to do the job. In addition to his painting skills he had been born with an eye that saw at once how things went together, and with hands that were quick to learn and could deftly fashion all kinds of materials into useful shapes. Gold was just another metal that could be melted, poured, and shaped.

Copper it was that had given the ring of Juan Diego its radiant mystery. He unwrapped the ring and looked at it again. Copper. It seemed so evident now that someone had revealed the secret. But what were the exact proportions? He had no way to know, but if he began by adding only a tiny amount to the pure gold, too little to impart more than the slightest blush, he could then let the mixture cool and compare the colors. It could then be melted again and more copper added, and the same thing done again, as many times as might be necessary.

He slipped the ring on his little finger, where it fit him perfectly. (What a small man Juan Diego must have been.) He walked to the window and held his hand out to catch the light. The simple ring seemed more perfect each time he looked at it.

The following day, after tending to the needs of the recovering Valfierno, he dressed in his finest clothes and paid a visit to the jeweler's around the corner from the Nacional. The man behind the counter, dressed proudly in his shabby, too-large cutaway, leaned forward in a careful show of attentiveness as Chaudron described the tiny emeralds he required. The man then disappeared, to return several minutes later with the disappointing news that there was nothing that size in the vault. Perhaps the senor would be interested in some other stone? But no, they must be emeralds. In that case, we will find them for you, perhaps as quickly as tomorrow.

Not tomorrow, but three days later two dozen emeralds of various sizes arrived, and from them Chaudron selected three that seemed to match perfectly the emeralds in the ring. He thanked the salesman, paid what seemed an exorbitant price considering their size, and left with his purchase carefully wrapped in tissue.

It took him several more days to gather the things he needed. Mexico City was not Paris; tools especially were hard to find. He'd finally had to buy his loupe from a jeweler near the university who had an old one he was willing to sell.

Fashioning the ring itself was an act of devotion. He brought to it his considerable skill and his solemn determination that each detail would be crafted to perfection. When he finally finished he'd created a copy so perfect that he himself could hardly tell it from its model.

If indeed he could tell the two apart at all. The morning after he'd put the final touches on the copy he brought the ring of Juan Diego to the workshop for the final time. (He'd taken it home with him every night.) He brought the ring to the sunlight that streamed through the room's only window and set it down on the sill, on the black velvet he'd bought to serve as its wrapping. Then he got the copy and laid it to the right. He thought he could see a difference, but he was anything but sure. He examined each one carefully with the loupe, but was still uncertain that if he hadn't already known he'd be able to tell which was which.

He began to tremble as he seemed to be overtaken by a new and frightening possibility. His original plan had been simple: to keep for himself the copy he'd made and wear it around his neck, hidden beneath his shirt on the gold chain he'd bought for the purpose. But the temptation was suddenly strong to do the opposite: to keep instead the real one, the ring on the left. The fearful question was, would the Virgin of Guadalupe approve of such a decision? And he realized there was only one way to be certain—he would leave the decision to Her.

He looked around for the things he would need and his eye fell on the old newspaper in which he'd first read of the ring's disappearance. He reached for it and tore off two long strips of paper. He wrapped each ring separately, and put both into a dirty glass tumbler from which he'd first emptied the linseed oil. Then he covered the top of the tumbler with his hand, closed his eyes and shook the glass as a gambler shakes a dice cup. He shook it for several minutes, almost in a trance, and then finally stopped and set the tumbler down inverted on the table. With his eyes still tightly shut, he lifted the tumbler away, reached out blindly with his other hand, and grasped the first small package he touched.

The Virgin had made Her choice.

Thoughts tumbled and bounced through the Marquis' head every morning lying in bed in the moments just after waking—light, sparkling shards of seemingly random ideas that often evaporated before he rose, but that sometimes, as they did this morning, fell into perfect alignment, crystallizing as the solution to a problem he hadn't even known he'd been pondering.

What must be done with the ring had been clear from the start, but the precise steps to be taken had been less plain. Now those steps had presented themselves and were firmly locked in place.

The Marquis rolled over on his right side preparatory to getting out of bed, but a sudden pain on his left side reminded him that bed was where he must remain this morning, and for several mornings hereafter. He lay back on his pillow and reached for the bell Rosa Maria had thoughtfully provided, but his hand stopped when he heard the front door opening, and then the distinctive trochee sounds of crutch, foot, crutch, foot.

Rosa Maria had heard the steps, too, as she could not fail to in this compact living space, and in a moment she went to the front room to greet the boy, as the Marquis listened.

"Oh, you are here," the boy said, in some surprise.

"I am here every morning. It's when I can be most helpful."

"Is he awake?" the boy asked, and when there was no answer the Marquis assumed that Rosa Maria had shaken her head.

"Too bad," the boy said, disappointed. "Can you wake him?"

"Of course not, Miguel," she said sharply. And Valfierno was surprised to hear her use his name, although it was not unnatural that she should.

"I need the name of the surgeon. The one who did the operation," Miguel said. "I suddenly thought that he would be the one to tell me what I need to know."

"I'll ask the Marquis to write out his name for you."

Need to know about what, Valfierno wondered? But it was apparent that Rosa Maria understood. It was something the two of them had talked about before.

"No!" she said suddenly, whispering fiercely.

"Why not? He's asleep."

Silence followed; a long disturbing silence. Then he heard her mutter something, and there was silence again. And in his room, the Marquis suffered stabs of jealousy such as he'd never known. He imagined the boy's moving hand caressing her small, responsive body. He imagined, or perhaps he heard, her deeper breaths, her gentle cries. Valfierno's head was raised almost off the pillow as he strained to hear more clearly. But the sounds, if ever they'd existed, had now seemed to stop.

Suddenly, she spoke, quietly but firmly. "You must not do this again, or I will not be able to speak to you."

No answer for a moment. Then: "I thought that yesterday you didn't mind."

"You are young, Miguel," she said impatiently. "Too young to know anything at all of how I feel."

No answer. Then finally the trochee steps again. "What I need," the boy said, his voice now light again, "what I must have is the surgeon's name. Because he will be able to tell me who can make me the finest artificial leg."

"But how will you pay for such a thing?"

Valfierno could sense the knowing smile. "I will be able to pay." At least he had not bragged to her of the vast sum of money soon to be coming his way. The Marquis had been firm about the need for secrecy and he was relieved to hear his orders respected.

"When he awakes," the boy went on, "remember to get the name. I will be back tomorrow."

"All right," Rosa Maria said. She didn't say that she would not be here tomorrow; that tomorrow she'd be leaving on her journey to Madrid and might never see him or any of them ever again. It would have been too difficult to speak of all of that.

Valfierno heard the boy leave and then heard her footsteps approaching. His body stiffened in unreasoning anger and he pretended to be asleep. And for the rest of the day, each time she came in to see him his eyes were tightly shut. She left that night without ever having said goodbye.

Mme. Rénard wrote the note in a calligraphic hand she'd learned at convent school. Valfierno had scribbled it out beforehand and now read the words aloud as she copied them grandly in the thin-thick strokes that seemed appropriate for a letter addressed to an Archbishop.

Excellency, it began. *We possess the ring of Juan Diego and are eager to return it to its rightful owner. We will do so in return for the sum of one million pesos.*

As the Marquis intoned the amount, there were gasps from his co-conspirators.

"Too much," Chaudron said.

The boy shook his head. "They will not pay that much."

But Mme. Rénard's smile seemed to indicate that she'd recovered quickly from her initial surprise at the figure. "Perhaps they will," she said. And she went back to writing as the Marquis assured them all that indeed they would.

The note went on to describe in detail the steps the Archbishop must take. The money must be accumulated in paper notes no larger than 500 pesos each. They must be put into a cloth bag, tied securely, and banded with a black ribbon. Then on the night of November 3, the package was to be taken to Chapultepec Park, to a location marked on a map that Chaudron had drawn that indicated a remote spot in the park's northwest corner.

At that location there would be a metal box into which the package was to be deposited. Once the messenger had done so and left, and the area was determined to be clear, the undersigned would exchange the money for the ring.

To that point the instructions were routine, down to the standard warning of dire consequences if anyone was foolish enough to alert the authorities. But then the note took an unusual turn. *We insist also,* the note went on, *that after you have recovered the ring you tell no one the circumstances of its return or the amount that was paid. You are instead to announce that the ring was returned in exchange for the reward of twenty-five thousand pesos by a man whose identity you promised never to reveal.*

The reasons for this instruction were clear enough. If the ring had been returned for the reward, no further crime had been committed. No crime, then no investigation.

But why, the others wanted to know, would the Archbishop be persuaded to do this? Once he'd recovered the ring, they'd have no way to control his actions. He could say anything he pleased.

The Marquis smiled patiently. "He will say it because the suggestion will strike him as his wisest course of action. And for the following reasons. One," he said, holding up his index finger, "because he looks less foolish having paid twenty-five thousand pesos than a million. And two," a second finger went up, "because by making such an announcement he can avoid having to reveal the enormous sums of money his Church commands. It is hard to pass the collection plate after you're known to be rich."

Miguel frowned. "The Civil Guard will ask who got the reward."

"The Archbishop promised secrecy. Do you think they will press the matter?"

Miguel shrugged. "By then, it will be of no consequence to us."

Chaudron stood up as Mme. Rénard put the finishing flourishes on the letter. He walked to the streaked window and looked out at the fading daylight. "A million pesos," he said.

Miguel laughed. "A lot more than any of us will ever see. After it's divided, I mean."

Valfierno's eyes snapped to him. "If you'd been alone in all this, you couldn't even have claimed the reward. You were ready to sell the ring for a thousand pesos."

"I was," the boy said quietly.

"Instead," Valfierno went on, "you receive two hundred times that amount."

"Not so," the boy protested. "I must divide my share with the man who stole the ring and handed it over to me."

"Are you crazy?" Chaudron exploded. "He gave your name to the Civil Guard!"

"Because he was tortured," Miguel said. "That's the only reason. I must divide the money with him."

Mme. Rénard put down her pen and slowly folded the letter. "But even if you do," she said, "his share will come out to be small enough."

"I would not call it small," said Miguel.

Mme. Rénard put the last crease in the folded letter and then stared at the boy as if he were someone who had just arrived from another planet. "You'd have sold it for a thousand pesos. Give him his five hundred."

Miguel looked at her, not understanding.

"Exactly his half," said the Marquis.

Having laid the plans, Valfierno had no interest in their execution, and even late on the night of November 3 seemed detached from the enterprise when Chaudron and the boy returned from Chapultepec and Mme. Rénard joined the two of them in counting the money.

The others had assumed that Valfierno's frequent low spirits were part of his convalescence, but the truth is that he felt the absence of Rosa Maria more deeply than he'd expected to. The muffled sounds he'd heard coming from the front room on her last day had returned often to disturb him, and the jealous fantasies they spawned seemed to deepen his feelings for the girl. He would not have guessed that her absence would be this upsetting.

"Twelve thousand short!" Mme. Rénard pounded the table.

"It can't be," said Chaudron.

Valfierno turned toward them. "Count it again," he said.

They did, rather more quickly this second time, and once again the tally was short by twelve thousand pesos.

"The Archbishop has no honor," snorted Mme. Rénard.

"What shall we do?" asked Miguel.

Chaudron turned to the boy. "What would you suggest?"

The boy thought for a moment. "I don't know. Maybe send another note."

This time Valfierno laughed. "Yes, that's what we'll do. Another note, of course. Valérie, will you write it for us?"

Mme. Rénard held up her hand gently. "Don't mock him," she said.

Miguel's face had turned deep crimson. Valfierno rose and put his arm around him, then spun the boy around to face him. "What we will do, Miguel, is let the missing money make us even more grateful for the very large sum that remains."

Miguel nodded and sat down, and when Chaudron and Mme. Rénard began dividing the money into four equal piles, he turned to join them. It was true that a very large sum still remained.

A burden had been lifted from the Marquis de Valfierno; one whose weight he'd felt only after its removal.

He had not been aware of how completely he'd come to rely on the skills of Mme. Rénard. No recent decision had been taken without its first having been submitted for her approval. His dependence on what she called her science had entangled him in a snarl of unaccustomed restraints that, because he'd welcomed them, he hadn't really noticed.

The first crack in his faith had appeared one morning as he lay in bed recovering from his near-fatal attack of appendicitis and had begun to realize that this had been a dramatic event that had not been forecast by Mme. Rénard. Her skills were then called into further question in the matter of the assassination of President Porfirio Díaz; an event that had not occurred.

Mme. Rénard had made the dramatic prediction that the president would be shot to death by a political enemy before the end of the year. With the end of the year now approaching (it was mid-November) she had begun to claim another triumph for her skills even though Díaz was still alive and had been the target of nothing more lethal than the usual opprobrium.

"But you said *assassination*," the Marquis reminded her, with the elaborately patient tone he now used when discussing these matters.

Valérie Rénard waved away his comment. She was in bed alongside him, his recovery having proceeded to the point where certain limited pleasures had once again become possible. "If I used the word at all, and I really don't remember, I meant it of course in its general sense, to refer to his loss of political life. And we now see that reality coming closer every day. Madero will bring him down."

Valfierno persisted. "You did not present this as a matter of politics."

"But you see it *is*," said Valérie Rénard. "And once again the stars have been confirmed."

The Marquis saw no further reason to press the point. Instead, he took her hand and moved it to where it gave him comfort. His faith in her psychic powers might have diminished, but not his faith in her magic touch.

It was directly afterward that the moment occurred that was to affect the course of the rest of his life.

It was not announced by thunderclaps or rolling drums. It presented itself in the mild form of a playful smile that appeared at the corners of the mouth of the now comfortably supine Valérie Rénard.

"This seems the moment," she said, "to reveal a silly thought that keeps coming back."

"What a strange time for it to appear. I had hoped that at these moments your thoughts would be of me."

Her smile broadened and she reached up and touched the side of his face. "Of course of you. Always of you."

He returned her smile and waited for her to continue.

"The ring of Juan Diego. Perhaps its coming to us was providential. Perhaps there was something it was meant to suggest."

"You are being elliptical."

She sat up and raised her knees, resting her chin on them. "It was as if the ring had been kidnapped."

He shook his head. "We do not kidnap. The ring fell into our hands."

"But after we had it. We sent a ransom note. We collected ransom money."

The Marquis shrugged. "Similarities."

"If ransom can be paid for a ring, why not for a kidnapped painting?"

"But we do not kidnap paintings. We do not steal. We do very well by *not* stealing."

"True. But why should doing well keep us . . . keep *you* . . . from doing better? Instead of doing many things, why not one great thing?" She ran her hands down her legs as she leaned forward. "Suppose you could manage to possess the most famous painting in the world?"

His eyebrows went up and his lips jutted forward as he was struck by the boldness of the thought that had been behind that tiny smile.

"You are suggesting," he said, "that we *steal* this object?"

She shrugged in imitation of his shrug. "Is that so impossible?"

"I assume you refer to the *Mona Lisa*."

She nodded.

"And to whom do we address the ransom note? The government of France?"

"They are the owners. It is the owners who must pay the ransom."

He stared at her, incredulous. There were no complications in her vision of the scheme. He smiled and bent down to kiss first one nipple then the other, over which he lingered.

She pushed his head away. "I must go now. I cannot stay where I am not taken seriously."

She had not been taken seriously. But she had been heard, and to the Marquis de Valfierno no bold thought was ever totally ridiculous. And although he did not intend to go forward with such a plan, neither could he keep his otherwise idle mind from providing a devil's playground within which the thought, almost despite him, sometimes pranced and played.

If nothing else, it was clearly time for a change.

He'd resisted change since they'd been in Mexico City, clinging almost superstitiously to the too-small apartment long after their successful operations had made possible a grander scale of living. In recent weeks, the traffic through these tiny rooms had been brisk enough to be almost comical. Now new living arrangements were called for, and it suddenly seemed right that they be made as part of a new life in Paris.

The decision was taken quickly, and without discussion. All of them would be going. Ramon, the barber, of course, and also the boy. Miguel had attached himself to the Marquis in a way that the older man found flattering, and the boy's quick mind would always be useful. But at first, when Valfierno had asked him to come to Paris, the boy had been unsure. His leg; he'd found a craftsman who'd agreed to make an artificial leg. Valfierno had laughed. If such an artisan could be found in Mexico City, their numbers and skill would be many times greater in a city such as Paris.

And so the boy was reassured and eager for the move. As was the barber, who would thus be placed on the same continent as his beloved daughter. As for Chaudron, he could hardly believe the unexpected twist of good fortune that would return him to the city of his youth and dreams, and he put his hand inside his shirt to touch his ring as he gave thanks to the Virgin of Guadalupe.

The ring he'd kept was the real one. He was sure of that now.

7

A*rlette Valency* was the name that appeared on the freshly drawn lease. That same name would appear on the new passport the government clerk had promised to have in her hands within the month, and that name was the one she'd written a hundred times the night before as she'd perfected the slants and swirls of her new signature.

She picked up the crisp, official-looking document one last time to appear to be studying it carefully, and then with brisk strokes signed her newly minted name exactly as she'd practiced it, retaining the graceful backward curve of the V as that familiar letter had migrated from her first name to her last.

Putting down the pen, she opened her purse and extracted a fresh, white envelope. In the absence of established bank credit, she said briskly to her new landlord, she hoped he would accept this, and she handed him the envelope, which contained six thousand francs in crisp notes. She had, she explained, only recently returned to Paris after almost a year abroad, and there hadn't been time to arrange for a bank account; in the future, of course, payments would be made by draft. Yes, certainly, the plump little man replied quickly, as eager to oblige this attractive woman as he was to profit by his business with her. He handed over two sets of keys and promised to have his sign painter stop by in the morning to remove the old legend from the plate glass window and replace it with whatever name she wished.

Galerie Arlette it was to be. She would be called Arlette by clients, and addressed simply but formally as *Madame* by her assistants.

The change of name had been decided upon to guard against contact with the man whose name was being shed. Paul Rénard, so far as his wife knew, was still firmly locked in prison. But his sentence had been for only three years, and given the resourcefulness of his clever friends, that period could easily be shorter. If her nascent gallery were to prove as successful as she hoped, it would be far safer to have its fame accrue to a name that would not be recognized.

The location had been chosen only after considerable thought. The Left Bank had been ruled out at once, and so had the fashionable streets near the Madeleine, where Bernheim-Jeune and Druet flourished; too serious, too earnest—too likely to draw a too-knowing crowd. The spot they finally chose was a failed dress shop on rue de la Victoire, a few doors west of rue Laffitte, where the older galleries still prospered by dealing in the settled works of other centuries.

Arlette Valency (for that is how she will henceforth be known) had no greater knowledge of commerce than she did of art, but her quick mind soon mastered enough of both to guide her to sensible purchases both at auction and in the marginal galleries high up in Montmartre. Within six weeks she was ready to open her doors, and two days after that she sold her first painting, a Dutch landscape by Jongkind, for an amount nearly double the four hundred francs she had paid for it. She had one assistant, an adoring young girl named Nélie who was plain and plainly dressed, whose knowledge of their business was neither greater nor less than her employer's, and who seemed grateful for the opportunity to be underpaid in the service of this supremely confident woman who assured her that by so doing she'd be in at the beginning of what would quickly become an important enterprise.

"Madame is in the back," this Nélie said one day to the tall, figureless, wonderfully dressed, very much older woman who'd just stepped in out of the drizzle.

"Tell her Mme. Didier wishes to see her," said Mme. Didier in a firm voice that clearly expected to be obeyed.

Nélie stared at her for a moment, at the pale blue chiffon scarf wrapped loosely around her long neck, at the huge dark glasses that surely masked furrowed flesh and sagging pouches, at the proud stance that somehow overcame the reed-slim body, presenting it as regal instead of frail. Nélie curtseyed in automatic deference, then turned and disappeared into the back of the gallery, as convinced as their visitor that no further message would be needed to bring forth Mme. Valency. No further message was.

"Mme. Didier, how good to meet you," said Mme. Valency as she bustled into the room. Mme. Didier offered a royally arched hand in greeting, and Mme. Valency touched it respectfully as she bowed to the older woman.

"You've wrought wonders here," said Mme. Didier, indicating their surroundings.

"I've done very little," the younger woman said modestly, if not entirely truthfully. In fact, she'd done a great deal because much had been needed to be done, but Arlette Valency was careful to say nothing that might indicate previous neglect on the part of this woman whose name had only recently adorned the plate glass window.

Mme. Didier seated herself in the gallery's most comfortable chair and Nélie brought them both small glasses carefully half-filled with dry sherry. Within a few moments the two women were chatting as comfortably as old friends and Arlette Valency was being informed by Mme. Didier that the latter had surrendered her dress shop not for lack of clients, but rather because of a steady *increase* in the flow of business that had become more than she cared to handle.

"I concluded that I am at an age when it is time to slow down," said Mme. Didier. "I shall, after all, be fifty-three at my next birthday."

Mme. Valency gasped involuntarily. The scarf and the dark glasses had clearly been employed to cover much of the wreckage, but enough remained in view to place this woman close to eighty, if not beyond.

"You seem surprised," said Mme. Didier with a smile.

"As indeed I am," said Mme. Valency, recovering quickly. "I should have guessed no more than forty-five. Although I confess I always find it awkward to discuss such things."

Mme. Didier waved her hand to indicate that the discussion disturbed her not at all. "Forty-one or -two is the most common guess.

In any event, I am as old as I am, and can never again be young no matter what people seem to imagine. So I decided to give up the shop and restrict my future energies to serving a select handful of faithful clients."

That select handful, Arlette Valency understood as the conversation continued, had clearly been chosen on the basis of their unquenchable desire to keep pace with Mme. Didier's steadily rising prices no matter what improbable heights they attained. Those select few Mme. Didier had now begun to honor by allowing them to continue their patronage at the large apartment she'd taken near the Bois; an apartment she would use as both living quarters and workplace.

As may well be imagined, the mention of this distinguished clientele had stirred responsive ripples in Mme. Valency, and she immediately offered a second glass of sherry, which was happily accepted. It was clear that Mme. Didier represented the kind of opportunity that turns up all too rarely.

At the apartment on the rue d'Aguesseau, not far from the Elysée Palace, hardly a day passed without the arrival of a pale blue envelope addressed to the Marquis de Valfierno in an increasingly confident hand. On some days, there would be a second envelope, that one bearing the name of the barber, Ramon Martinez, who shared the apartment with the Marquis. Did the barber resent the greater frequency of the letters addressed to the Marquis? Not for an instant. In fact, it seemed to give him pleasure, as did every detail of his life in this newly adopted city.

And no wonder. In place of the cramped, airless quarters he'd shared with his daughter in the life that seemed so far away, he now found himself embraced and liberated by this cushioned paradise with its enormous ceilings and its labyrinth of corridors and rooms. His own bed chamber, while certainly not as grand as that of his employer, was so much more capacious than anything he'd ever dared imagine that each morning when he awakened it took him several minutes to reassure himself that the room in which he found himself was the room where he belonged.

It had been the Marquis' decision to settle the living arrangements in this manner: the newly created Madame Valency would inhabit an apartment of her own in the area near the gallery (and not, as she'd imagined, share living quarters with Valfierno); Chaudron would live and work on the Left Bank in a studio of his own choosing, sharing his quarters with the boy, Miguel. And the barber would be with Valfierno, thus providing the Marquis with someone who could be endlessly helpful without ever causing a moment's trouble. Ever.

About the letters: they were miracles. Each could be read as simple narrative—the description of an observant schoolgirl's day—or as a missive tinged with longing. As, for example, her account of her instructor's lectures on the topography of southern Asia, which she described as lacking in the fascination she had once found in the similar instruction the Marquis had once provided.

The Marquis replied only rarely, perhaps once every second week. And when he did his tone was careful, almost fatherly. He was pleased, he would say, to hear how much she valued her studies. He knew that when she was finished she would be ready to take her place in the finest company.

When she wrote to ask if she might spend the six-week summer holiday with them in Paris, he ignored the request, although (or perhaps because) it had stirred in him feelings deeper than he would ever acknowledge. She wrote and made the same request again, and he replied he would discuss the matter with her father. The following week, when she had not received a letter, she asked him yet again. And this time the Marquis agreed that yes, her visit would be convenient.

The knocking had been so loud, so vigorous, that Chaudron had expected to open the door on a brooding, angry Miguel. Disturbed behavior had become common with the boy these last few days; surprisingly, since he would seem to have much to be grateful for now that the date had been set for the operation that would enable him to throw away his crutch and move about on what he'd been assured would be a perfectly fitted artificial leg.

But instead of the boy, his visitor turned out to be a small woman with large eyes and arms folded sternly across her breast. "Is it Chaudron, the painter?"

He nodded.

She stepped past him and entered the room. "I am Sophie Perugia," she said in the deep, firm tones that he would later learn gave everything she said the timbre of importance. "I live across the way, in the flat on the ground floor. Not Perugia really; we are not married. But Perugia enough to be known by his name. You did this?" She was pointing to the still life on his easel.

"Yes," Chaudron said, relieved that the only painting he had left exposed was this one he'd been working on.

"It is masterful," came the crisp judgment of the almost-Mme. Perugia. Then she shrugged. "Not that I understand such things. Not that what I think makes any difference in this world." She walked over to the other canvases stacked facing the wall. "And these?" she asked, reaching for one.

Chaudron's hand shot out quickly to stop her. "Please," he said more firmly than he'd meant to. "I do not show my paintings."

She looked at him in surprise. "Then why do you paint them?"

"I do not show them," he went on more calmly, "until the time is right. Until I am ready, if you understand."

"I do *not* understand," Sophie Perugia said with careful emphasis. "But so be it." She was, her attitude seemed to say, accustomed to accepting behavior she did not understand. She turned back to the room.

"My husband is not an artist," she said in her normally aggressive tone, "but we are acquainted with every artist in this area, because we deal with them. He is a framer and glazier. His shop is across the way. I'm sure you can see it from your window." She took Chaudron's arm and led him to the window. "My God, we are higher than I realized. Yes," she said. "Just there. Beyond the baker's."

He looked obediently and nodded. She took out a piece of paper and handed it to him.

"This is the name. When you're ready to have something framed, come to see him. You'll find our prices most agreeable."

Chaudron nodded again. Sophie Perugia walked back to the

painting on the easel. "Yes," she said again, "I like that. Colorful. Harmonious. There will be a buyer for this painting."

"I hope there will be," said Chaudron.

"Of course," she said. "You love your work, but love puts nothing on the table." She walked to the door and turned back. "Take my advice: before you try to sell it, put it in a proper frame." And she was gone.

The rooftop studio Chaudron had chosen was on the Left Bank, on the rue Notre Dame des Champs, between the Luxembourg Gardens and the Boulevard Montparnasse. It might have been more convenient to be farther north, nearer the river, but this one small street contained so many painters that they seemed to provide a welcome sea into which he could disappear. And of course there was the name itself. When he'd turned the corner and seen the street name stenciled in faded letters on the side of the corner building, he'd involuntarily clutched the ring he wore on its chain beneath his tunic—the ring of Juan Diego. Our Lady had chosen the ring, and now she would choose the street where he would work and live.

Valfierno had decreed that the boy would share quarters with Chaudron, and it had never occurred to either of them to disagree. There was one small room with a door that provided privacy, and the boy was assigned to that. Chaudron slept in a corner of the skylit studio where surprisingly, given his former habits, he now found himself pleased to be awakened each morning by the new day's light.

The boy's assignment for now was to make himself generally useful, which meant that when Chaudron was ready to declare a painting finished, the boy carried it the nearly three miles to the apartment of the Marquis, or to the Galerie Arlette if that was its destination. When it was clear that the need for these trips would not be frequent the boy began to fill his idle time by sweeping and straightening their studio quarters, but Chaudron's impatience with the disturbance kicked up by that activity kept it to a minimum. So the boy, with Chaudron's permission, began spending more of each day at the gallery, where Arlette Valency found many things for him to do, including the running of an endless series of errands. When one day she marveled at his swiftness in performing these chores, he reminded her of her promise to find him someone who would fit him with an artificial leg. The next day she began a series of inquiries that finally led her to the surgeon who, she was assured by many (including the gentleman himself), could perform the orthopedic miracle the boy desired.

The news broadened the smile of Miguel. "Imagine," he'd said to Chaudron, "I'll have both hands as free when I walk as I do now only when I sit, or lie in bed."

The fitting of the artificial leg would require first an operation, described as minor by the surgeon, that would smooth the leg's uneven stump and contour it to accept the new appliance. Miguel wrote the details to Rosa Maria. He wrote to her often, and often received the same blue envelopes that went to the rue d'Aguesseau. It was after receiving one of these that his mood had suddenly changed. *I do not know*, she had written, *if I shall admire you as much in this new fashion. Will you seem more dashing as a young man who moves about with almost normal steps? Or will I remember with more admiration the boy I knew: an agile miracle, speeding along on a straight, unbending leg, attached to his body not at the hip, as with mortals, but in a manner that seemed perfectly suited to him and to him alone?* And so he began to wonder: might he be somehow diminished as an almost normal man whose unseen infirmity kept him half a step behind? Might he not be better as he was, a marvel whose artificial limb stood out for all to see; a master of his disability instead of its slave? And so his mood suddenly changed as he began to struggle with his decision, revealing to no one his uncertainty.

Miguel's deliveries from the studio to the Galerie Arlette were infrequent because Mme. Valency had communicated to Valfierno that it would be unwise for Chaudron to deliver as many canvases as he seemed able to. Newly discovered masterpieces could surface only so often, and so the wonderfully rendered, freshly imagined paintings of Velázquez were stacked up against the wall of the studio on the rue de Notre Dame; unneeded perhaps, but brought into being by Chaudron's delight in having found in the manner of the Spanish master a form of expression that seemed to him as effortless as breathing.

Fortunately for all of them, they soon reached the point where other paintings were once again required. And one other in particular demanded to be considered.

*   *   *

The Marquis de Valfierno paid a visit to the Lady at her home in the Salon Carré. It was the first time he had ever set foot inside the Louvre.

A few questions to a series of uniformed guards, some of whom knew the Lady's address and some of whom seemed unclear about the question, brought him finally to the room where she held court. As he entered, the Marquis was unexpectedly filled with a sensation he'd never felt before. Art had been his business, not his passion; but now he found himself standing in the presence of the one masterpiece that could erase the distinction between the two.

In the Salon Carré were Corregio's *Betrothal of Saint Catherine,* Veronese's *Marriage at Cana,* Titian's *Allegory,* and works by Raphael, Rubens, and Rembrandt. But large and powerful though these works might be, the room was dominated by the steady gaze of the dark, compact, supernal *Gioconda.* A modest thirty inches tall, she was the smallest painting in the room, but every eye was on her.

And the room was filled with eyes. It was a mild Sunday in early March and the crowds were here. The Marquis had chosen Sunday to become invisible in just this kind of crowd. He waited his turn to step closer and when he finally stood before the Lady, he examined her first with the worshipful stare she demanded, and then with the calculating eye of a carnival barker trying to guess her weight.

She was encased in a massive glass-fronted structure, exactly as Perugia had described. Perugia, the frame maker from the rue Notre Dame des Champs. Chaudron had brought him two paintings to be framed, and when he'd returned to pick them up Perugia had been lavish in his praise. *"I know fine work,"* the frame maker had said. *"I worked in the Louvre."* He had been part of the work crew that had built the protective glass-fronted frame for *La Gioconda;* the heaviest such frame he had ever seen. And looking at it now, Valfierno guessed it must weigh well over a hundred pounds (in fact, it was over a hundred fifty), and that it would take the strength of two men to lift it from the wall.

". . . against vandals, is that not so?" That was all he'd heard of the question, but when he turned to its source it was clear what the rest of it must have been. The young man standing beside him with his pale and earnest wife was the one who had spoken, in an accent that sounded German.

"Yes, of course," the Marquis responded. "The glass was installed in January because there'd been an incident. In fact, in this very room. Someone dashed India ink against the lower right-hand corner of the Veronese," and he pointed to it. "A madman, of course, but all it takes is one such. Destruction is always a simple matter."

He had fleshed out the story with his own invented details. It was true that a painting had been vandalized somewhere in this vast museum, but assigning the crime to a painting in this very room gave presence to the story. The couple nodded with interest and stepped to the Veronese to examine it closer. In a moment the young man was gesturing and pointing to something in the lower right-hand corner.

A week later the Marquis returned again to the Louvre, this time to see for himself certain features of the area around the Salon Carré that had been described to him by this same Perugia at a meeting Chaudron had arranged; a meeting at which the Marquis had taken care to be introduced as Colonel Carlos Almazàn Zamora of Seville. The Colonel had begun with the pointed question: *"Do you know what a secret is?"* Perugia had frowned for several seconds, then shrugged and said that everyone did. The Colonel from Seville laughed at that.

"Everyone? I think not. I will tell you what a secret is." And the stern Colonel's stare now reached for Perugia's eyes and snapped them to his own. *"A secret is something that must never be spoken. Never. Not to anyone on earth. Can you agree to such a secret?"* Perugia frowned again, still staring at the man he knew as Colonel Almazàn, and then agreed that yes, he could. Valfierno leaned forward and touched his hand to Perugia's. *"Your word then that what is said today is said in secret."* Perugia nodded, and Valfierno smiled. *"For now I promise nothing,"* he'd said, *"but one day you may earn more money than you have ever imagined."* That had made its intended impression and the Marquis had then gone on to question the man for nearly two hours; that length of time reflecting not so much the thoroughness of the interrogation as the difficulty of extracting even simple information from this Perugia, especially after half a bottle of red. One fact Perugia kept repeating, still unable to

believe it himself: *"Four times. Four times we built it before they were satisfied."* But finally Valfierno managed to move him to other matters and coax from him the information he'd wanted. Now he was standing here to see for himself the things Perugia had described.

It did not daunt the Marquis that he had never planned such a thing before, that there were people who devoted whole lives to this sort of activity and still failed. Nor was he disturbed by the fact that at the present time he had no notion of how to proceed. He took it for granted that when the moment of need drew closer a workable plan would present itself, and that no other person on earth was better equipped to devise such a plan than he. For now the only problem he explored was the matter of egress.

He stood in the Grande Galerie, adjacent to the Salon Carré, where Perugia had described a door behind which a stairway led down to an exit. But there was no such door in sight. Not surprising; details were likely to be fuzzily recalled by Perugia. He moved through to the Salle des Sept Mètres, and suddenly there was the door, unframed and flush against the wall. There were other people in the room, but he strode quickly toward the door with the confident manner that kept him always in harmony with his surroundings. He touched the small door handle lightly, pulled the door open, and stepped inside without anyone turning his way. He shut the door behind him, turned, and looked down the narrow wooden stairway that descended in an oblong spiral. As he started down he reached into his jacket pocket and took out a small cardboard container the size of a bar of hotel soap.

At the bottom of the stairs he came up against a heavy wooden door with a large brass knob. The door was locked, as Perugia had said it would be. And the lock was as he'd described it. *"A plain lock,"* he'd said with a shrug, *"as you might see in a schoolhouse."* Later Chaudron had said it sounded like a simple affair; turning the key would slide the bolt. All that was needed was a key that would fit the keyhole.

The keyhole itself was a zigzag affair that resembled a small lightning bolt. The plate that held it hung at a slant because the bottom screw was missing.

Valfierno twisted the plate into alignment and from his cardboard container he extracted an oval of soft wax and as one hand held the plate firm, the other gently pressed the wax against the zigzag keyhole so that half an inch slid in. After a few seconds, he withdrew the wax and returned it to its container, careful not to disturb its new shape. He retraced his steps up the stairway and let himself back into the Salle des Sept Mètres. From across the room a guard who had just entered expressed surprise at seeing him come through the doorway and came to question him.

Valfierno glared at him. "There is no exit that way."

"Sorry, monsieur," the guard said retreating apologetically. "That stairway is only for the staff."

"They might mark it so," Valfierno said impatiently, and he turned and strode from the room.

He found his way downstairs in more normal fashion and asked for directions to the Salle d'Afrique. Once there he located the outside of the door whose inside he'd so recently faced. No eyes were on him, so he tried the door. Locked, of course.

He turned and followed Perugia's directions to the Cour Visconti, and then, smiling broadly, he passed through an open door and into the street.

He needed more details, and Perugia was not the man to provide them. It would have to be Chaudron. For Chaudron to be able to come and go freely at the Louvre would be a simple matter; all he would need would be permission to copy *La Gioconda*. No request would be treated as more routine.

But the plans for the theft of *La Gioconda* refused to snap into place because the most significant piece was missing: how to dispose of the prize once it was in his hands.

The notion of holding the Lady for ransom had appeared sensible at first, but further thought had made it seem unlikely that any government would humble itself by paying a huge ransom for a national treasure its own ineptitude had allowed to be lifted from the wall. If a vast sum was to be realized, its source would have to be a private buyer whose yearning for the unattainable was as great as his ability to pay. Who that buyer would be he had no idea, but he would know him when he appeared.

For now it was time to begin exploring other sources of income, more modest but more certain. And just at this time an unlooked-for opportunity presented itself from out of the blue, where so many good things come from.

Mme. Didier and Arlette Valency had become good friends. The seeds of that friendship had been planted at the end of their first meeting, when Mme. Didier had mentioned in passing that she found great significance in the alignments of the sun, the moon, and the stars. Mme. Valency, who had lost her own interest in these matters since coming to France, had seized on Mme. Didier's as a way to become better acquainted with this woman who might prove useful, and both agreed that they must meet again. And they did, often. Mme. Didier, having for so many years made her way daily to the familiar address on the rue de la Victoire, now often found it pleasant to traverse that same route. And she in turn urged Mme. Valency to visit her still-new apartment on the rue de Montevideo, just east of the Bois.

It was on her second such visit that Mme. Valency was introduced to Jacqueline Privas.

Jacqueline Privas was the widow of André Chateauroux, who late in life had married the much younger woman and thus combined the fortune he had made in textiles with the already substantial Privas fortune she had inherited from her banker father.

At the moment, Mme. Privas was too preoccupied to pay much attention to her introduction to Arlette Valency; she was totally absorbed in the new afternoon frock being pinned into place by a frowning Mme. Didier. Mme. Privas found that frown disturbing, for while she was totally confident in the complex worlds of business and of art, she had never felt secure in the far more mysterious world of fashion.

Mme. Didier removed some pins, rearranged the simple but mysterious folds of silk, then deftly pinned things back in place and stepped back to reevaluate her work. This time she smiled and nodded, and when Mme. Privas turned to look in the full-length mirror, the women's eyes met, and they both nodded in agreement.

Later, over high tea, which Mme. Didier set daily in the English fashion, Mme. Privas' interest in this third person whose name she'd already forgotten was aroused when she learned that this was the owner of the new Galerie Arlette that had replaced her old friend's shop. She had, she explained excitedly, passed by often and admired what she'd seen. She was, she explained, something of a collector herself ("The most important in France!" Mme. Didier later insisted). Perhaps Mme. Valency would like to come by one day and see her children?

"Her children" were the astonishing canvases that covered every inch of every wall in the house on the Boulevard Haussmann through which Arlette Valency was escorted by her proud hostess the following week.

The collection had begun when André Chateauroux had started to acquire fine tapestries on the theory that tapestries were textiles, and textiles had made him rich. Later, with the help of his wife, he had expanded his collection to include paintings, and very quickly their home had become a showplace for much of the best of eighteenth-century French painting (his love), and several astonishing works of the Italian Renaissance (hers).

Then, with the death of her husband two years ago, Mme. Privas had moved more heavily into religious art and had begun to acquire the work of the seventeenth-century Spanish and Italian masters, including, *mirabile dictu!*, a handsome work by Murillo.

The familiar voice of Ramon came from behind her. "I must ask you to put that down."

Mme. Valency ignored the request and went on reading.

The voice spoke again, quietly. "I must insist, you know."

Defiantly, she put the pale blue envelope on the hall table while still holding the matching blue letter in her hand. She turned to face him.

"You will insist on nothing where I'm concerned. And we are in my country now. You will speak to me in French."

"I am comfortable only in Spanish," Ramon replied in that language. "Please put the letter down."

"When I have finished," she replied in French, and continued reading. Ramon struggled with the notion of wresting the letter from her, but it was clear that whatever damage there was in the situation had already been done. He stood by uncomfortably and waited.

"Charmingly written," Mme. Valency said in Spanish when she'd finished. She folded the letter along its creases and returned it to its envelope. "Las Ursulinas has already worked its wonders."

Ramon was pale with anger. "Not even I would presume to read that letter, and I am the girl's father."

"You seem quite certain of that," said Mme. Valency.

He shook his head unhappily. "Why do you insult me?"

She smiled at him. "I am here to see the Marquis de Valfierno. Tell him so, please."

Ramon turned and left. Mme. Valency stepped into the broad parlor and sat stiffly in a corner of the divan. She was more shaken than she'd allowed herself to show.

Moments later the Marquis appeared. His changed appearance surprised Mme. Valency each time she saw it. The face she knew in Mexico City was the face she imagined when she thought of him, and their encounters in Paris had not been so frequent as to alter this image. But since coming here he had allowed his beard to grow. Ramon kept it clipped to a consistent three inches long, and shaved it just below the cheekbones every other day so that it curved against his face in an elegant combination of steel-gray strength and foppish artifice.

"I did not think Arlette Valency would read mail addressed to others."

"Meaning that Valérie Rénard could have done so easily?"

"Valérie Rénard was a woman alone. She had need of her cunning, of her manly side."

"Not cunning—strength."

Valfierno smiled and settled himself on the arm of the divan. "We will not argue the point."

But she went on. "May I point out that in Mexico City you seemed more aware of the feminine side than you have been here in Paris."

"But nonetheless the still-new Mme. Valency seems softer," the Marquis persisted.

"You mean I no longer smoke cigars?"

The Marquis shrugged. "Rather more the entire change."

"But still this new person, more feminine though you say she is, no longer seems to hold your interest."

"That is not something I wish to discuss," the Marquis said firmly.

The old Mme. Rénard might have plunged forward in spite of his resistance, but Mme. Valency after a moment leaned back against the soft cushion of the divan and smiled. "Does her father know?"

The Marquis' expression did not change. "Was there some other purpose to your visit?"

"I shall get to that in a moment. First let me say this: Despite the careful, secret language of that letter, language designed to have no meaning to anyone but you, the girl is innocent. You were not meant to become entangled with this kind of innocence."

The Marquis nodded. "And now you must tell me of your other purpose."

She stood up and stepped toward the window. She stared out for a moment, seeing nothing in particular. Then she turned back and told him of her visit to Jacqueline Privas.

8

A charming picture," the Marquis said of the Murillo. "Warm, respectful; full of mystery and devotion. Charming, indeed. But this," he said, turning back to the painting on which he'd already lavished praise, an Annunciation by Giovanni Bellini. "Never have I seen this glorious moment so perfectly conveyed. This piece would be the cornerstone of any collection anywhere in the world. With this in the room, Mme. Privas, it is difficult for the eye to move elsewhere."

Mme. Privas beamed. "Yes," she said. "Yes, that is my feeling exactly."

And so the misdirection had been accomplished.

The Marquis had been furious when Arlette Valency had told him of her astonished gasp on seeing the Murillo. "What possible good can this painting do us now that you've turned the spotlight on it!" the Marquis had stormed. "Do you think I can perform my magic when the whole world knows exactly where to look?"

But later, after some of the fury had evaporated, he began to consider ways to repair the damage. "This old woman," he said. "The one who introduced you to Mme. Privas . . ."

"Mme. Didier."

"Yes. This Mme. Didier must learn from her friend, Mme. Privas, which of her many valued paintings is the one of which she's proudest."

90

Arlette Valency nodded hesitantly. "I'm sure that question can be asked. But how will the answer help?"

Valfierno smiled. "Misdirection," he said. "The very heart of magic."

The information was easily obtained. And as with most collectors, her current favorite was of course her most recent acquisition: the Bellini. Fortunately for the Marquis, the consonance of its theme with that of the Murillo had led her to hang the two works on opposite walls of the same room, where each seemed to reinforce the other.

In that room, the Marquis continued to study the Annunciation, first from several feet away, then from very close. Then this vain man, who never used his spectacles in public, pulled them from his breast pocket and examined more closely something that seemed to have caught his eye at the picture's lower right. He frowned and touched the frame lightly.

"Is something wrong?" asked a suddenly concerned Mme. Privas.

Valfierno removed his spectacles and turned to the collector. "Certainly not," he said. "Not wrong at all. At least not yet."

"What is it?" Mme. Privas persisted.

"Probably nothing worth mentioning," said the Marquis. "Might I see the back?"

"Of course," the disturbed woman said.

Valfierno returned the spectacles to his pocket so as to free his hands, and then gently lifted the picture from the wall and turned it back to front. He stared at it for a moment. "Yes, as I thought," he said.

Mme. Privas turned questioningly to Mme. Valency, who seemed puzzled, then back to Valfierno as he lifted the picture back into place. When he'd finished he said, "There is just the beginning of some warping in the stretcher. You did not reframe this picture when you acquired it?"

"I did not. The dealer did not recommend it. Nor did my Adviser."

Adviser. The word rang with possible unpleasant overtones. "Is that Adviser someone whose name I might have heard?"

"Perhaps," said Mme. Privas, and she mentioned an Italian name that was not familiar to the Marquis, although it is not likely that any name would have been; Valfierno's expertise in the world of art tended to be slimmer than his attitude suggested. "He died just before Christmas," she went on, "at the age of ninety-one. I find it very difficult without him."

"I'm sure you do," said the Marquis sympathetically.

"Why did you ask about the frame?"

The Marquis turned to Arlette Valency. "You understand, of course."

She smiled knowingly and nodded, having no idea what he was talking about.

"There are, Mme. Privas," said the Marquis, "newer techniques in the craft of framing that can strengthen the backing and keep the stretcher from becoming warped. The framer Mme. Valency uses is, of course, adept at this sort of thing."

Mme. Valency nodded again. "Quite so," she said.

Mme. Privas looked quickly from one to the other. "Could he reframe this for me?"

The Marquis turned to Mme. Valency. "Madame?"

Mme. Valency nodded. "He is busy, of course. But if the request were to come from me, I am sure he would do the work."

Mme. Privas was effusive in her gratitude and Mme. Valency promised to send her boy around to pick the painting up.

"We must, of course," the Marquis said, "examine all the others. The problem is not uncommon."

His help in the matter would be appreciated, said a grateful Mme. Privas, and the Marquis indicated that he would return another time for a thorough examination of every piece in the collection. Then, on the way out of the room, he stopped suddenly in front of the Murillo, his eye arrested by signs of similar trouble.

"Should it be reframed, too?" frowned a worried Mme. Privas.

Valfierno nodded soberly. "I think that would be prudent."

Mme. Valency promised that her boy would pick up both.

Perugia stared at the painting expressionless: the kneeling angel, the attentive Virgin, the porcelain glow of both their faces, the central marble column belonging to the background but rendered so flat it seemed to come between them.

Sophie Perugia turned to him. "Two hundred twenty-five francs to reframe it," she said crisply, having just added half again to the figure she'd had in mind. Perugia nodded in agreement.

"There is, of course, one requirement," Mme. Valency added quickly. "The work must be done right here in this room." They were standing in Chaudron's studio. "We cannot allow the painting to leave this room."

Perugia looked at Sophie, who said to him quickly: "You can measure the canvas now, and then make the pieces in the workshop; the final assembly you can do here." Perugia nodded again.

"Oh, and one more thing," Mme. Valency said quickly, as if she'd just remembered. "There is a second painting also to be done. I assume the price will be the same."

"If the size is similar," said Sophie. "May we see it?" Chaudron brought the Murillo from where it had been leaning against the wall. Sophie looked at it for a moment. "Yes," she said. "The same."

So all was settled and Arlette Valency left with Miguel, Mme. Privas having asked for the boy to be brought around so she might speak with him. Perugia and Sophie stayed behind to measure the two paintings with lengths of string he always carried in his pockets. When they'd finished and left, Chaudron slammed the door behind them and allowed the fury he'd been holding back to roar out of him all at once. He kicked an empty turpentine bucket the length of the room while bellowing a primal sound. He picked up a half-full bottle of wine and smashed it against his work table, a piece of the flying glass nicking his left hand and starting a trickle of blood. *Valfierno should have been here!* Then he licked the blood from his hand and wrapped the hand in a dirty cloth and clattered out of the studio, not bothering to secure the heavy lock Arlette Valency had insisted on having installed. *Valfierno should have been here—not this woman!*

To say that Sophie Perugia knew that something was amiss would be to endow her with a prescience she didn't have. But things either seemed right to Sophie or they didn't, and this thing clearly didn't.

The first question that had nagged at Sophie Perugia was whether or not there really existed such a place as the Galerie Arlette.

A brisk walk to the Right Bank and a few inquiries along the rue

Laffitte pointed her toward the rue de la Victoire, where she quickly found herself staring at the handsome gold lettering that proclaimed the gallery's existence. She pushed open the door and walked inside.

The tinkling of the front doorbell brought a flustered Nélie rushing from the back, a small napkin clutched in her right hand. There were rarely customers this early, which was why she'd formed the habit of eating an early lunch.

"May I speak with Mme. Arlette," asked Sophie.

Sophie was not at all the sort of person Nélie had expected to see. Her thick boots and black muslin dress made it clear she was not a potential customer.

"Mme. *Valency*," Nélie corrected her. "Mme. Arlette Valency," she explained.

"As you say," said Sophie. "May I speak with her?"

"Madame is not at the gallery this morning. If you would care to leave your card, I will tell her you called."

Sophie thought for a moment, then shook her head. "No, it's not important."

"I can give her any message," the eager Nélie said.

Sophie shook her head again. "It can wait for another time. I had some questions about the new paintings; the Bellini and the Murillo."

Nélie frowned. These were not names with which she was familiar.

"You don't know them?"

Nélie shook her head.

Sophie shrugged. "Ah well, it doesn't matter. As I said, I shall be back another time." And Sophie left without leaving her name, confident that Madame's assistant would not remember the paintings she'd asked about. And not really caring if she did.

If Vittore Giacinto had lived to be ninety-six as his father had, instead of expiring peacefully in his sleep at the age of ninety-one, it would have been necessary for the Marquis de Valfierno to devise some other means of gaining constant access to the Chateauroux-Privas mansion. But as it was, the position of Adviser to Mme. Privas was open, and it became a simple matter for the Marquis to slip into the role almost before the woman realized he'd taken it on.

A surprisingly few sessions at the same public library available to any charlatan had made him glib enough on the few subjects that interested Mme. Privas to be able to comfort her with the apparent vastness of his knowledge. She began to seek his company eagerly, almost greedily, as she daily grew more dependent on his confident pronouncements. Within a very few weeks she was so completely in his thrall that when he suggested it might be wise for him to review everything in her collection with an eye toward possibly selling certain weaker examples and replacing them with more important works, she agreed to the project at once and furthermore insisted that he feel free to come and go as often as he pleased, and of course to bring with him anyone he chose at any time. The staff, she said, would be so instructed.

This was to be considerably easier than bribing the guard at the Buenavista Palace.

Easier still when it became clear that Mme. Privas' interest in Miguel had ripened into fascination.

Since that first day when she had requested an interview with the boy, Mme. Privas had on many other occasions asked that he be sent to see her. There were, it seemed, many odd jobs that no one seemed able to perform as capably as he, and it soon became routine for him to appear shortly after noon and remain for several hours, with much of that time being spent on work that needed to be done above the first landing. There was soon a splendid new wardrobe for Miguel that attested to his favored position, and almost overnight the boy was transformed into a confident young man. But what mattered to the Marquis was that Miguel was now able to enter and leave the mansion freely.

All that remained was to create a flow of customers. To that end, the Marquis arranged, with surprisingly little effort, for Ramon to be installed in the barber shop at the Crillon, where he would perform as he had in Mexico City. That would be one source. The second, of course, would be the Galerie Arlette, where it had always been assumed that those customers who expressed interest in the murky provenance of some newly discovered Velázquez might also be interested in other unusual items.

The third source was to be the exceptional client list of the talented Mme. Didier, whose coming birthday would be celebrated by a lavish party in her honor at the rue d'Aguesseau.

The frantic buzz of preparations had just been punctuated by the thundering crash of two dozen dinner plates when Ramon was informed that the Marquis wished to see him. The message was conveyed by the butler, who, like the dinner plates, had been borrowed for the evening.

Ramon frowned because even if the dinner plates had not fallen this would have seemed an inappropriate time for such a summons. "At *once*," the butler emphasized. Ramon put down the seating chart he'd been studying after Valfierno's hundredth reorganizing of his guests, and started upstairs through the bustle and confusion, unable to imagine what might be required. When he reached the open door of Valfierno's chamber he saw the Marquis standing in his dressing gown, smiling warmly.

"Come in, my friend," he said.

This was not the style the barber was accustomed to. Valfierno was not a rude or overbearing man, but neither was he one whose conversation was cushioned in politesse.

"I know you must be overwhelmed downstairs, with our guests due to arrive in, what? Less than three hours. Sit down, Ramon. I will be brief, I promise you."

The barber sat, still puzzled.

"I have watched with admiration these last few days," the Marquis said, "the skill and vigor with which you have assumed increasing responsibility for overseeing the arrangements for this evening. And suddenly, tonight, two things struck me, and have led me to a decision."

The Marquis paused and seemed to be waiting to be prompted.

"Yes," Ramon said dutifully. "And what decision is that?"

"It is clear to me," the Marquis said, "that tonight's event will be the first of many such. It is time for you to assume a new position in this household."

Ramon felt a certain panic grip his stomach. The direction of this conversation was now clear and its consequences could prove uncomfortable in view of certain arrangements he'd already made, and about which he had not yet informed Valfierno.

"As I said," the Marquis continued, "it became suddenly clear that this was the direction in which our future lies. Twenty contacts can be made on an evening such as this for every one turned up in the barber shop. *This* is what we must be doing, my friend."

My friend. A second time.

"Which means there is a new position for you to occupy, with of course financial compensation consistent with the increased importance of your duties."

Ramon shook his head slowly. "I am not at all sure I understand," he said.

"I mean a future income that will enable you to provide for yourself and your daughter for the rest of your life. Would you like a glass of champagne while I describe our new arrangement?"

Ramon looked around and saw the bucket in the corner, with two empty glasses nearby. He shook his head slowly, still confused at being addressed in this warm manner by a man he'd always placed several planes above him, with the gulf between them having nothing to do with noble birth, and everything to do with the natural order of things.

The Marquis' explanation was brief and clear. He, Ramon, would be put completely in charge of running the household; he would hire the staff, including a permanent butler; he would arrange for the purchasing of food and household supplies. And from this day forward he would no longer be paid a salary, but would receive instead ten percent of everything their efforts produced.

Ramon was overwhelmed by the prospect of what could clearly be enormous sums of money, and also by the importance of this new assignment. Valfierno assured him that a man of his abilities would learn quickly whatever he needed to know.

The scale of this dramatic change in fortune had set Ramon's head spinning, and he only half heard the Marquis when he said they must drink to their new partnership. Out of the cloud of his confusion he saw the Marquis extending him a glass.

"Only a sip," the Marquis said, "to seal the bargain."

Ramon nodded and took the glass. He wet his lips with the sip that seemed to mean so much to Valfierno, then he rose and mumbled some awkward words about needing to go downstairs. As he set his empty glass on the dresser he suddenly realized the Marquis' real reason for wanting to make this incredible change. And it had nothing to do with him.

9

*L*a Terre, the bar was called by everyone. Short for La Terre Ferme, the name on the wooden sign over the front door that swung crookedly on its one unbroken chain. The words had been painted in an arc above a geometric camel whose humps were two long isosceles triangles rising from a trapezoidal body. The sign had been the offering of a neighborhood artist who'd submitted it as payment for a hopeless bill. The camel was a nod to the owner's native land.

Farid was his name, though whether his first or last no one seemed to know. Farid at fourteen had signed on as a cabin boy on a French freighter that had stopped at Port Said, where he had come from his native Cairo in hope of just such an opportunity. For the next six years he had sailed the world; first as cabin boy, then as apprentice to the ship's carpenter, and finally as carpenter himself. But having achieved the goal that had seemed so distant when he'd started out, he was immediately faced with the dead-end reality of his new situation. And so, with nothing further to which he could reasonably aspire, he began to hate each rolling, pitching moment and vowed to save every penny of his wages against the day when he could set himself up in a carpenter's shop on the now longed-for terra firma.

But a nasty shipboard brawl had suddenly made it prudent for him to make the change at once, before he'd had time to accumulate the sum that had been his goal. He'd jumped ship at Le Havre (forfeiting some two months' pay), made his way to Paris, and taken the only job he could find: sweeper-bartender at the small place he would later own. The bar had been called Le Cheval Blanc, and was the property of an old drunk who died penniless some five months later. The man from the bank came to survey his unwanted new property and was persuaded by Farid, who was as glib in French as he was in his native tongue, to accept two thousand francs, which was everything he had, as a first payment on the place. The name was changed, the establishment was revitalized through the considerable woodworking skills of the Egyptian, and it quickly became if not a gold mine, at least a source of dependable income for its unlikely owner.

It was late afternoon and there were four customers in the place, all regulars, all sitting in solemn isolation at separate tables. Toward the back sat Sophie Perugia, a jug of deep-red wine in front of her alongside a nearly empty tumbler. Sophie spent much of every day at La Terre now that Perugia had moved out for what would likely be several weeks. Perugia had been called back by the company he'd worked for earlier in the year that had made and installed the new protective glass covers with their heavy wood frames for some dozen paintings in the Louvre. The same company had been hired again to work on several dozen more, and Perugia was grateful to have been remembered; regular wages, even low ones, were better than the insufficient work that came his way as the least patronized of the three framers competing for work on the rue Notre Dame des Champs.

The hours on his new job would be long and taxing, and his employers had agreed to provide a dormitory bed for him in a large room they'd rented for several workers across the river from the Louvre. So Perugia would be gone for a while, and Sophie had taken it upon herself to try to persuade those few in the neighborhood who had used his services in the past to hold what work they had till his return.

Chaudron had been one of those she'd gone to see, just this afternoon in fact. The door had been open and she'd walked in (those elaborate locks were almost never used), surprising him at work. Surprising herself, too. For there on his easel she saw the same Murillo that Perugia had so recently reframed. Strange. Why would it be back here? And why would Chaudron be working on it? What work was it that he really did?

Farid cooked a little for regular customers, and Sophie planned to stay again this evening; it was easier than shopping and cooking for herself. Besides, for Sophie there was never a bill. Farid was aware that Sophie would return to Perugia when his job was completed, but meanwhile the Egyptian was content to provide her with whatever meals she wanted in return for the comfort she provided every night.

In the open kitchen at the back, Farid was just tasting the stew he'd prepared when he heard the front door swing open. He wiped his hands on his apron and stepped forward, to see the most unlikely visitor who had ever entered La Terre.

Unlikely not in her appearance, but in the fact that she was here. For this was a woman whose lightly worn elegance marked her at once as a person of consequence who carried her status with such total comfort that young as she was, every move, every gesture seemed to declare her certainty that no matter where she was, she had only to express her wishes to have them instantly fulfilled.

Not even the stray wisps of deep-red hair that had been blown across her cheek could lessen her confident appearance, and when she spoke it was in brisk, clipped phrases designed to minimize the number of words between her question and its answer.

"Sargent," she said. "The American. Can you tell me where he lived?"

Farid looked at her blankly. It was not a name he had ever heard. He shook his head.

"Perhaps someone else," she said looking around, her head turning smoothly, like a camera on a tripod. But then she stopped suddenly and her nose raised up as she became aware of the wonderful odor drifting out from the kitchen. She sniffed, and asked what she was smelling.

Farid shrugged. "Potatoes and meat," he said, "and some vegetables."

The woman's eyes went bright. *"Pot-au-feu?"* she asked. The Egyptian nodded.

"You are serving that tonight?"

"I am cooking my dinner," Farid said cautiously.

"It is for you alone?"

Farid shrugged. "For me, and a few others."

The woman seemed delighted. "We will be among them," she said.

The plural form took meaning when the front door swung open and a distracted man entered quickly, stopping in relief as he saw the woman. "Mme. Sinden," he said. "I wasn't sure where you had gone."

"Just here, as you can see," the woman said impatiently. Her accent marked her as not being French. The man was.

"I am relieved to see that," he said. "It is not safe to rush ahead like that."

"I do not feel unsafe," the woman said with a pleasant smile, but in a tone firm enough to close the subject. "We will be stopping here and having dinner."

"At this hour?" It was not much past six.

"I am hungry at this hour," she said. "But if you find this hour inconvenient, there is no need for you to join me."

The man bowed. "I shall, of course," he said. "With your permission," he added quickly.

The woman nodded and Farid led the pair to a table near where Sophie sat. The woman was no more than twenty-five, the man some twenty years older. As it happened, he was a man unaccustomed to the servile posture his present position put him in, but recent circumstances made him grateful to have the association. He held the chair as she sat down.

"*Bon soir,*" the woman said pleasantly to Sophie as she was seated. Sophie nodded in return.

"Do you live near here?"

Sophie nodded again.

"I wonder if you could tell me if it's true the American painter Sargent once lived in this street."

"I am sorry," Sophie shrugged, meaning she didn't know; that she had no knowledge of such a person. But the woman thought Sophie had not understood. She turned to her companion questioningly, seeming to ask if her French had been inadequate.

The man tried to ask the same question, but in his more confident local accent. Sophie shrugged again.

"Perhaps, then," continued the man, "Carolus-Duran?"

At that Sophie's face broadened into a grin of recognition. "Oh, yes," she said, and she repeated the name. "He is famous here. On this street."

One of the old men sitting alone at a table stirred in his chair. "Fifty-eight," he mumbled.

Mme. Sinden turned to him. "What was that?"

But her companion understood. "Carolus-Duran lived at number fifty-eight?"

The man nodded and Mme. Sinden's face lit up. "And the American, Sargent?" she asked.

The old man shook his head.

"You don't know?"

"He never lived here. His studio was on this street. For a while it was. I don't know where."

Mme. Sinden clapped her hands in delight. "But it was *here*," she said. She turned to her companion. "We might have walked right past it!"

Two months ago at a dealer in London, Clara Sinden had been shown a small panel, ten-by-thirteen, of a study John Singer Sargent had made of his teacher, Carolus-Duran, in 1879. She hadn't bought it that day, belonging as she did to that strain of acquisitive people who must intensify the joy of any purchase by first teasing themselves with the lovely agony of delay.

But during this period of waiting she discovered the existence of a second work, a full-scale portrait of the same subject that had been painted later that same year. When she investigated the possibility of acquiring the larger painting she was told it had been sold to an American collector.

The existence of the major work had lessened her desire for the small panel, and she so informed her dealer. That gentleman was understandably crestfallen, but then he recovered sufficiently to suggest that in many ways the panel at hand was the more important piece, representing as it did Sargent's first impressions of the artist who'd influenced him so profoundly. That argument had been enough to rekindle Clara's enthusiasm, and when she left the gallery that day, it was with her new purchase tucked under her arm.

She had bought the painting because of her interest in Sargent, and having acquired it that interest now burgeoned. She asked the dealer to arrange for her to meet the painter, but Sargent, the dealer explained, was currently in America and was not expected to return for at least another month. The dealer did, though, put her in touch with a short, bearded, unpleasantly pungent young man who could and did show her the building where Sargent had his studio. She found seeing it incredibly satisfying, and decided on the spot that before her next visit she would ask her husband to write ahead and arrange for an introduction to the artist.

Research in other London galleries quickly made her knowledgeable about Sargent and Carolus-Duran, and the Paris leg of her tour now had these two men as its focus. As soon as she'd arrived in Paris she made inquiries about both of them, quickly learning that both had once worked on the rue Notre Dame des Champs.

Clara's husband had been unable to accompany her this year. Thomas Sinden did bold things on the Exchange that very few people understood, but those things had been wildly successful. The extent of his fortune was not really known, but even the lowest estimate placed it at a level that made it unsurprising that he had last year given the go-ahead to building plans for a cottage in Newport; *cottage* being the glaring misnomer so firmly fixed in the language of Bellevue Avenue (and Fifth) as to no longer reflect the arrogance of its self-conscious understatement. Sinden's preoccupation with the finishing touches to this magnificent residence had kept him at home while his wife made what had been for the two of them their annual pilgrimage to England and France. They had friends enough in London to assure her of companionship in that city, and he wrote ahead to an associate in Paris asking him to recommend someone suitable to accompany her there. The man recommended was the man who was with her this evening in La Terre, a reliable businessman named Paul Rénard.

Farid set two bowls in front of them and asked if he might bring them wine. Clara pointed to Sophie's table. "What is her wine?"

Farid shrugged. "Red wine."

"We'll have that," said Clara, who then turned again to Sophie: "Would you be willing to join us?" she asked.

Sophie was surprised enough by the invitation to glance in confusion around the room, as if seeking either advice or permission. When neither was forthcoming she made her own decision, picking up her jug and tumbler and moving to the woman's table.

And the woman's table it was. The man who sat there sat at the pleasure of this regal presence, who now introduced first him and then herself. She then began to ask Sophie a series of questions specific enough to draw from even the reticent Sophie more facts than she might normally have divulged.

Conversation was not a familiar experience to Sophie, and she found it pleasant to be the center of this impressive woman's curiosity. And when Clara Sinden asked if she could name some interesting galleries in the neighborhood, Sophie suddenly felt she might have something to contribute.

"Not here. Not near here," Sophie said quickly. "In these places you see only pictures of no importance. The places you want are on the other side."

"Of what?"

"She means the Right Bank," said Paul Rénard, and Sophie nodded.

"Yes, of course," Clara Sinden said, showing her disappointment. She was well aware of the usual places.

Sophie went on. "Do you know the Galerie Arlette?"

Mme. Sinden shook her head. She turned to Paul Rénard. "Have you heard of it?"

He nodded without hesitation. "Oh, yes, madame. Most interesting, indeed."

Clara's eyebrows came together. "Where is this place?" she asked.

Paul Rénard frowned, as if trying to remember.

"On a small street near rue Laffitte," Sophie went on eagerly. "I cannot think of the name."

Rénard nodded gravely. "Near rue Laffitte. Just so."

"Rue de la Victoire," she said, remembering.

"Exactly," said Paul Rénard. "We will find it tomorrow. If that suits you, of course," he said quickly.

The early light pressed against the heavy crimson drapes, turning them into warm translucent panels whose glow drew him slowly out of sleep. Things could be done, he'd been assured, to eliminate the intrusion of the morning light, to keep his room a perfect midnight black for as many hours as he wished, but he'd chosen instead to leave things as they were. There were worse ways to awaken.

The Marquis de Valfierno lay with his eyes closed and his mouth widened into a small, pleasant smile; the same smile that began every morning as the day's first thoughts took hold, reminding him of who and what he was, and where he was. Today that smile was wider still as the morning's return to consciousness brought its reminder of who he would see alongside him as soon as he opened his eyes.

Everything about last night had been surprising. At dinner she'd sat at the end of the table as if presiding in a long-familiar role. When they'd finished she'd calmly picked up the tiny servant's bell as if she'd done such things all her life, and when the butler came she informed him that they would be having coffee in the other room.

There had been just the three of them at dinner: the girl, her father, and the Marquis. Rosa Maria on this, her first night, had been full of questions about Paris and their life here, and about this wonderful apartment, so huge compared with the flat her father had taken for the two of them around the corner on the rue Montalivet. The Marquis had answered her questions quietly pleased with the manner in which she spoke, with the changes the year had wrought. Ramon had been silent.

Later, when they'd finished their coffee, she'd risen and announced to her father in a firm but pleasant tone: "I shall be staying here tonight." Then she'd walked to him and kissed him good-night, as simply as if she'd been unaware that in that one brief sentence she had foresworn forever the obedient posture of childhood. With her hand still on her father's shoulder, she'd turned to the Marquis and announced that she would wait for him upstairs. Then she'd left the room.

It was several minutes before either man had been able to speak. Finally the Marquis, in a businesslike tone, asked the barber to please have the new invitation list ready in the morning so that he might see it. The barber promised to do so, excused himself and left, to make the short walk around the corner to the now-pointless flat he'd taken to preserve his daughter's honor.

The Marquis sat still for a moment, then got up to pour an Armagnac, thought better of it and poured himself another coffee, which he drank quickly. He took note of the time and let a precise fifteen minutes go by before setting his cup down firmly and starting upstairs to bed.

The fact that she'd been a virgin was confirmed by the usual evidence, but she had loved him with the skill of a royal courtesan. "I shall not go back to Madrid," she whispered finally in his arms.

"No," he'd said, and she pressed against him again.

Now his gaze seemed to awaken her, and she turned to him and kissed him gently. "Am I really here?" she whispered. He smiled and nodded, and then with a minimum of gentle movements she was in his arms again and the day had its real beginning.

10

*P*romptness was a habit with two of the three people who were scheduled to meet at 9:30 A.M. in the lobby of the Chanticleer on the Place Vendôme. Sophie had arrived some fifty minutes early and sat quietly in a cushioned corner beside the tall ormolu clock, trying not to watch the heavy pendulum slowly arcing through the seconds. At 9:28 Clara Sinden appeared and seemed pleased to see her. The two women spoke for a moment and then Clara asked at the desk if the carriage she'd ordered had arrived. She was assured it was waiting outside. At 9:45, an impatient Clara announced she would wait no longer and the two women left on their short drive to the rue de la Victoire.

Promptness was not completely beyond Paul Rénard. He had managed to arrive punctually for all his previous appointments with Clara Sinden, but the persistent pressure of deep personality traits must finally prevail against even the most determined efforts to keep them down, and this morning his demon had wriggled free. His being late was simply a matter of oversleeping, but it was clear that such an explanation would never do, so as he walked briskly toward the Chanticleer he reviewed several more acceptable excuses. He finally settled on one involving a shirt that had been scorched in ironing, and his man's subsequent difficulty in finding another that could be made ready on short notice. By the time he arrived at the Chanticleer at 10:30 he was so comfortable with this story that he could not himself have distinguished it from the truth. But it seemed the telling of it would have to be postponed because, the desk clerk told him, the women had left nearly an hour ago.

To the clerk's question about whether or not he should summon a carriage, Paul Rénard smiled a pleasant no, noting that the day was fine and the distance agreeable. He convinced even himself that his decision to walk had been for the pleasure of it and not to save the few francs.

Rue Laffitte was familiar to him, but not so the rue de la Victoire. As he turned onto the street, he stopped and appraised it, concluding that although the Galerie Arlette was the only gallery in view, its location was likely to reflect the luster of its famous neighbors around the corner.

He stepped closer to the plate glass window and looked inside. There were Clara Sinden and Sophie, engaged in animated conversation with the woman who appeared to be the proprietor, who was standing with her back to him, holding up a small canvas for Mme. Sinden's approval. As the woman turned the picture to show it in a more favorable light, he saw first her profile and then in three-quarters view that suddenly familiar face, the sight of which struck him with such force that he was propelled a startled half-step back. He stood frozen for a moment, then turned quickly and hurried away, his mind instantly trying to imagine ways in which he might be able to derive some advantage from the fact that he now knew what had become of her, while she still had no idea of what had become of him.

It was as if the trembling of his hands atop the cherrywood case resting in his lap had been the worst of his rage shaking its way out of his body, leaving Ramon with an anger that, though still intense, was at least back under control. In this more normal state he was suddenly clear on two points: he did not have the stomach to kill, and certainly did not harbor a wish to die.

One or the other would have been the likely result of the plan that had brought him here to the Marquis' apartment at five in the morning.

When his hands finally held completely still he opened the lid of the polished case and stared hard at the pair of pistols. In his mind he heard again the description the dealer had recited: matched Colt .45 revolvers; single action, gold-plated cylinders, ivory handles with the coat of arms of the Count de Palikao carved on one handle and the same gentleman's portrait bust worked into the other; the pair was thought to have been the gift of the Empress Eugénie. The dealer had insisted they were in perfect firing condition and had loaded the pair himself and then nestled them back into their velvet lining. The barber had paid nearly four thousand francs.

Ramon touched his finger to the likeness of the Count and lightly traced its outline. Then he lifted the pistol from its case and held it out in front of him. Single action, so the hammer must be drawn back and clicked into place. He pulled the hammer back and held the pistol at arm's length, pointing toward the bookshelves that lined the far wall. He moved it back and forth slowly, and finally stopped as he saw just above the front sight the three-foot-long tropical fish tank the Marquis and Rosa Maria had giggled themselves into purchasing one recent afternoon. He held the pistol steady and then, largely to his own surprise, jerked the trigger.

The blast was deafening. His right hand flew high in the air and the pistol sailed out of his hand, falling to the floor and spinning halfway across the room. Miraculously, he had hit his target and the tank had exploded, sending water, glass, and desperate fish tumbling down the front of the bookcase and slithering all over the floor. By the time the Marquis appeared, thoroughly startled in his rumpled night clothes, the air was so dense with black powder the barber could barely be seen.

"Ramon," the Marquis shouted when he finally made him out. "What has happened?"

The barber stood up and set the wooden case on the table beside his chair. He put the pistol back in its cushioned nest and closed the lid. Then he turned to the Marquis, took a deep breath, and stood very straight. "I have come to take my daughter home with me."

Valfierno frowned at him in considerable confusion. Then he looked toward the bookcase and the floor, and finally walked to the bell rope near the door and pulled it several times. "Someone will be here in a moment," he said. "We will use that moment to compose ourselves."

The only person in the servant's quarters whose sleeping state did not resemble death was apparently Lisette, the fiftyish parlor maid, because in a few seconds it was she who scurried into the room adjusting her nightclothes and looking every bit as dishevelled and confused as the circumstances warranted. The Marquis turned to her. "Bring two bowls from the kitchen, filled with water. Some of the fish may still be alive. The rest of this can be cleaned up later."

Lisette seemed frozen, uncomprehending.

Valfierno shouted at her. "Two bowls filled with water. At once!"

She curtseyed mechanically, turned, and hurried out.

"Now," said Valfierno very calmly, "I will speak quickly because she will return in a moment. In these few seconds, I have come to an important decision. I have decided that my affections for your daughter have reached the stage where, if she will have me, she and I will be married. If, of course," he added hurriedly, "you will grant your permission. The wedding will take place as quickly as it can be arranged, and until that time your daughter will reside either here or with you, as you decide."

The barber's eyes went wide. He could hardly believe the Marquis' words. This was a result he would never have imagined. For a moment, he could not find his voice, but finally he spoke. "You have my permission," he said.

Then Ramon picked up the hardwood pistol case and turned back to the Marquis. He clearly had something to say and the Marquis waited until he was able to say it. "The Count de Palikao was a general the Empress appointed to head the cabinet during the time her husband was away at the front, near the end of the war with Prussia. Or so I was told. When the Count accepted the post, she presented him with these American pistols, which are very beautiful as you will see. You must have them." And the barber extended the case to Valfierno. "Be careful," he said. "They are loaded."

In the beginning, Arlette Valency's morning walk from her small apartment on rue Provence had been straight up rue le Peletier, then left on rue de la Victoire the few steps to the gallery door. Later a sense of community led her to stroll the slightly longer route up rue Laffitte, where she could gaze into the gallery windows along the way, and occasionally step inside. She soon became a familiar sight along the street and regularly gathered a morning bouquet of greetings that ranged from the ragweed of grunted nods to the bright blossoms of cheerful waves. There was one particular old gentleman with an enormous goiter and an even bigger smile who always seemed to be raising or lowering the awning in front of Galerie Picard-Roth as she passed. She stopped each morning to exchange a few words with him, delighted by the way he swept off his cap and beamed his pleasure at seeing her. He knew who she was, as the entire neighborhood seemed to know, but she knew him only as Alfred, having no idea that this was Alfred Picard, father of Lionel, the reigning Picard, who was one of the two or three most important dealers in Paris.

On this particular morning as she stopped to chat with the beaming Alfred, she was suddenly aware of a tall, slender man standing perhaps a hundred feet away at the next cross street. He was looking in the other direction, so she could not see his face, but there was something in the line of his body that seemed familiar, and then more familiar still as he leaned back against the building. He seemed to be waiting for someone, and without knowing why she had the uncomfortable feeling it was she.

"One day when you have time, you must come inside," Alfred said. "We have some wonderful new things. I still say we, you see, although of course these days it is my son Lionel who makes all the acquisitions."

The distracted Mme. Valency had only a rough idea of what he had said. "Yes," she said. "I would like that, of course." Then quickly: "I am sure I will see you again tomorrow morning."

Alfred smiled and bowed slightly. "That will provide a pleasant beginning for another day."

She smiled in return and left quickly, heading up rue Laffitte toward the spot where the man still leaned against the building. As she walked her skin began to tingle and as she got closer, she realized why.

It had been a speck of flour in her eye that had caused the tears to stream down the right side of her face, the waitress explained, they should please pay no attention. She looked from one to the other as they gave their orders for what seemed a modest breakfast. Then she dabbed at her eye and scurried away.

"Arlette Valency," said Paul Rénard slowly, rolling his tongue around the sound of it. Then he frowned and shook his head in disapproval. "It does not suit you. My tongue cannot pronounce that name."

It was said in the cold, contemptuous tone she'd almost forgotten. Her stomach tightened at the sound of it, but there was no question that she had now become the person she'd designed. She sat up very straight. "I shall answer to no other."

He looked at her for a moment in some surprise, and then, with an effort, softened his expression.

"Please understand," he went on. "It is not easy for me to think of you bearing a name other than mine."

She stared at him without changing her expression. "I have very little time," she said finally. "You had something you wished to say to me."

He shifted in his seat. To business then. This was clearly not the woman who, while far from timid, had never challenged him. More than just the name had changed.

"All right," he said, "I will explain." Where to begin? His release from prison, he supposed. That had been arranged, he told her, by some influential friends just two months ago. And life had been hard since then: no decent income, no prospects of anything in sight. Then suddenly a turn for the better when someone had recommended him to Clara Sinden.

Her eyes widened at the name.

He smiled. "Yes, the same Clara Sinden who was in your shop on Tuesday."

The word *shop* did not sit well. "Recommended you as what?"

Paul Rénard shrugged. "Knowledgeable companion. Guide. Escort."

"And more, perhaps?"

He shook his head. "I was employed by her husband, recommended through a chain of friends."

"Why would that matter?"

He smiled. "I am as I described, and nothing more."

"All right," she said. "And you seem to imagine that has something to do with me."

"I imagine only that there are ways in which I might be helpful. To her, as I am paid to be, and possibly to you."

Paul Rénard had waited in the street this morning for the woman who was still his wife because he had determined that if anything was to be gained from this unexpected turn it would only be through revealing his connection with the very rich American woman who had wandered into his wife's establishment, and who could, as he now began to explain, be encouraged to do so more often.

He had stopped speaking and it was clearly her turn to respond. She fought back the impulse to tell him to leave at once and forever keep his distance and instead composed herself sufficiently to suggest that they meet again at this same place on Monday (this being Thursday), when she would have had a chance to consider what he'd proposed.

"As you wish," he replied. "But I ask you not to underestimate the ways in which I might be helpful to you."

"We shall speak again on Monday," she said firmly. "And now please go."

There was no mistaking her tone, and he rose and left quickly.

It was as if a disturbance had been removed, and she felt the sea of turbulent air slowly begin to settle. She took the last sip of her coffee and rattled the cup back onto its saucer, surprised by her unsteady hand.

She looked around this tiny pastry shop, aware that although she must have passed it every morning she had never noticed it before. Then from the kitchen there was a shouted oath in an ugly male voice and the clatter of a saucepan being thrown. A moment later the waitress reappeared and busied herself wiping tabletops. Mme. Valency called her to the table and settled the bill. She looked up at the girl as she snapped her purse shut, and then she opened it again and took out two hundred-franc notes and pressed them in her hand.

The girl stepped back, astonished. "But why, madame?"

Mme. Valency touched a spot on her own cheek. "Leave him," she said.

On Monday, he made sure to arrive on time, even a few minutes early. He slipped into the seat at the table they'd occupied on Thursday and took some papers out of his pocket so as to seem occupied when she arrived. But he could not keep his eyes from drifting toward the front door to look for her. At quarter past he decided to order something and tapped his spoon on the table. The burly owner (he seemed to be the owner) came out from the back, and Rénard was aware that the waitress he'd seen last time was not here this morning. When he asked about her, the apparent owner shrugged off the question with a surly, "She is gone."

"Where to?"

Another shrug, and silence.

Paul Rénard reached into his pocket and took out a ten-franc note. "I would like to talk to her."

"About what?"

Rénard smiled. "Nothing to do with you, I can assure you."

"Of course not. I know that."

But still he did not respond. Rénard took out another ten-franc note and Léon took them both. "Not far from here. She lives on the rue d'Hauteville. Number seventeen, I think."

"Her name?"

"Durtal. Louise. Don't say I told you."

Rénard nodded. By now he was certain Arlette Valency (as he must begin to think of her) was not planning to appear, but he was hungry so he ordered a roll and coffee and when he was finished found his way to the rue d'Hauteville and very quickly located the young woman, who answered the door timidly but then recognized him when he reminded her of where they'd met and let him in.

He stayed for an hour and his pleasant ways slowly made her more comfortable. She'd been to see Mme. Valency, she told him, and would next week begin working for her as a domestic, with some hope of a more responsible position in the future. By now he was seated beside her on the small couch and although her posture was rigid she did permit him to touch her hand. He thought it wise to attempt no more. As he rose to leave he said he would like to call on her again. She gave no response except to say good-bye.

How little effort it takes to stay ahead of the uninformed.

Having assumed the role of Adviser to Mme. Privas, the Marquis de Valfierno had done the minimal research required to keep him one step ahead of his enthusiastic but not terribly curious employer and was adequately armed for his encounters with amateurs and dealers. He was now secure enough in his own abilities so that it seemed only natural for him to nominate himself as the authority Arlette Valency was looking for.

"You!" Mme. Valency had been pacing the enormous library of the flat on the rue d'Aguesseau and turned now to face him. "But you of course," she said, lowering herself, somewhat stunned, to the edge of the enormous sofa. It seemed so obvious she could not believe she had not thought of it. "I will arrange for Mrs. Sinden to visit Mme. Privas. Each will be charmed at the notion of meeting the other. And once Mrs. Sinden has seen the collection . . ."

"I will appear."

She raised her hand in a grand flourish. "The man without whose advice Mme. Privas never makes a purchase. The man willing, nay eager, to be of service while Mrs. Sinden is here in Paris."

The Marquis bowed at the waist and clicked his heels. "Your servant."

She shook her head slowly and smiled. "It seems too perfect."

Suddenly her head stopped moving and her eyes locked on to something just over his left shoulder. He turned in the direction of her gaze but saw nothing unusual. "What are you staring at?" he asked.

"Isn't that different? The aquarium?"

"Yes," he said. "It is new. The old one proved unsuitable."

The sound of approaching footsteps raised Mme. Valency's eyebrows over the rim of her teacup and she smiled at the sight of the familiar figure striding down the long hall toward them. He seemed more confident than ever, reflecting, she was sure, his relish at the prospect of meeting the two people she had brought here today. But while his high spirits certainly included that component, the truth was that his steps were generally livelier these days, since he had suddenly determined to marry Rosa Maria. The possibility of marriage had never occurred to him; not until the early-morning pistol shot had blasted the notion into his head. And now that the decision had been taken, it seemed astonishing he had not thought of it before. With the predictable exception of Miguel, all in his circle had been delighted with the announcement. They were certainly aware of the unbalanced life-arithmetic involved, but all seemed too pleased to give but a moment's thought to numbers. With such positive reinforcement shoring up his decision, and with the prospect of a fairy-tale wedding in his very near future, of course his step was light and strong.

The planning for the Marquis' entrance this afternoon had been devised for maximum effect as to both time and place. The time was to be four o'clock, allowing just an hour for the Sindens (Thomas Sinden had surprised his wife two days ago by joining her in Paris) to be overwhelmed by the splendors of the Privas collection; the place would be the broad statuary hall on the upper floor of the Privas mansion, with its small sitting area some fifty yards from the head of the staircase. Here the group would be served afternoon refreshments, and here promptly at the appointed hour the Marquis would appear at the top of the stairs and parade the length of the hall, growing larger and more grand with every step as he came to greet them.

Introductions were made. This, said Mme. Privas, one of Europe's supreme collectors, was the man whose advice and judgment she valued to the point where no decision was taken without him. As tea was poured it was immediately clear that the large, ebullient Thomas Sinden and his wife, Clara, were immediately taken with the charm, intelligence, and knowledge of the man who had joined their group. As to the Marquis' reaction to Thomas Sinden, it was one of considerable surprise. He had expected the bright, darting eyes, the confident manner, but not the rumpled appearance. Thomas Sinden's clothes were of the finest material and were surely the product of the most skillful hands, but they looked as if he'd spent the night in them and were marked in several places by gray smudges of carelessly managed cigar ash. The tea cake he was eating seemed to generate crumbs at an exceptional rate, to the point where his wife, in a casual, practiced move, reached out with her napkin every so often to tidy things up.

There was routine conversation about the paintings the Sindens had just been privileged to see, with lengthy elucidation from the Marquis on those works whose creators' backgrounds were best known to him, and then a question from the Marquis (to which he already knew the answer) about whether there was some particular artist the Sindens meant to explore while they were in Paris.

"A particular artist! Oh, yes indeed," roared Thomas Sinden in something between a bellow and a laugh. He turned to his wife and asked with a broad smile that softened the booming voice: "You mean you have not made it known that you've come to Paris to pursue your passion for an American painter who lives in London?"

Clara Sinden turned to the Marquis. "My husband sees humor in many of my activities," she said good-naturedly.

Thomas Sinden roared again at that. "Yes, of course. Of course."

"And the object of this collector's passion of yours?" the Marquis asked the young woman.

"John Singer Sargent," she said.

The Marquis nodded thoughtfully, as if he were absorbing the information and thinking of how he might be helpful, but in fact he had fully prepared himself on the subject. "Mme. Sinden shows remarkable taste," said Valfierno, nodding in her direction. "But you must be aware that while there will certainly be works by Sargent to be found in Paris . . ." He shrugged.

"Oh, yes, I know," nodded Clara Sinden. "There is very much more in London; but wheels are already in motion in London and I want to explore his Paris days."

"Yes, of course," said the Marquis. "And quantity will not matter if we can discover something to your liking. I shall be pleased to make inquiries on your behalf, but may I suggest that your interest in Sargent might also be served by exploring the work of another man."

"Carolus-Duran?"

Valfierno smiled. "I see you are indeed quite knowledgeable."

Mme. Privas rustled in her seat a trifle peevishly. "But I fear that *I* am not."

Valfierno turned to her. "Carolus-Duran was the American's teacher."

Mme. Privas nodded.

Clara Sinden turned to the older woman. "John Sargent took a studio near Carolus-Duran on the rue Notre Dame des Champs. I have visited the street and plan to go there again." Her husband's strained expression reflected his struggle to understand; not the facts of the conversation, but more basically, the language in which it was being held. His knowledge of French was much inferior to his wife's. In English, he asked her to explain and Clara took his hand and repeated what she had said.

When she'd finished, the Marquis said, "Then if you would like, I will inquire in general what might be available by both men. With Carolus-Duran, we are more likely to have more to choose from."

"We should be grateful to see whatever you might find," Clara Sinden said.

Indeed you will, the Marquis thought, more grateful than you imagine. And much more eager to buy.

11

*A*gain!" Rosa Maria commanded, her brows drawn together to im-
prove her concentration. From the end of the room, Miguel turned
toward her sharply, not pleased to be ordered about this way. But he
did as he was asked and crossed the room again, his back very
straight, his hands stiff at his sides. When he reached the other end,
he turned to measure her reaction.

"Yes," she nodded in approval. "That is excellent."

He scowled at her. "I am pleased to have passed the test."

"Then you would do well to *look* pleased."

The boy laughed and started toward the couch where she was sitting. "Stop!" she said suddenly.

He stopped where he was, puzzled but obedient.

"There," she said. "You were more natural then. More natural
when you were no longer trying."

He laughed again. "Then I must never try," he said, and he sat beside her and leaned forward to kiss her, surprised when she turned
and offered her cheek. "I am then to be your brother," he said quietly.

"You are to be my friend, as you have always been."

"Friend, of course; but not as I have always been."

She did not answer. "Is there pain? When you walk, I mean."

He shook his head. "There is no pain. But it feels strange. As of
course it must."

It had been Mme. Privas who had insisted that he be fitted for the artificial limb and had found the surgeon to prepare his leg. He had not written about it to Rosa Maria because he did not want to hear her objections again. He did not share her affection for the crutch that had been part of him since the day the runaway water wagon had taken his leg when he was three years old.

He reached out and touched his hands to her face. "Are you aware of these?"

Her body had stiffened slightly at the contact, but she did not withdraw. "Aware of my cheeks, or of your hands?"

"Suddenly both my hands are mine to use all of the time. Not only when I am sitting, but also when I walk. Both hands are *free*. Do you know what that means?" He lowered his hands. "How can you? You cannot appreciate what has always been yours."

She wanted to cover his hands with hers, to kiss the sweet face that asked for understanding. But she feared that any show of affection might be misunderstood. "I know I am glad you are pleased."

"Yes, *pleased* is the word," he said. "I am pleased. It is nice to know that if I am noticed, it will not be for the one skill that never brought me pleasure: my deftness with the crutch that kept me bound. From now on if I am noticed it will be for myself."

She laughed. "Such vanity!"

They were in the apartment on the rue Montalivet, to which she had moved at the insistence of the Marquis de Valfierno. She was to live here with her father until the wedding day. Appearances during these prenuptial days seemed to mean a great deal to the Marquis and even his frequent visits to the small apartment occurred during hours he considered appropriate; hours that conveniently coincided with those times when the girl's father was busily occupied at the rue d'Aguesseau. Living in the small rooms on the rue Montalivet was not an arrangement Rosa Maria would have chosen, but having had it imposed upon her gave her one more change of status to look forward to as part of the coming event.

"Now," she said with sudden animation. "You must tell me more about where you are going and who you are to be!"

He drew himself up with mock pride. "I am to be the second son of the Argentinean branch of the most important family in Seville."

He recited his role with theatrical perfection, having learned it well. "I have been traveling modestly in Europe, and have recently taken a small cottage in Clichy where I am to remain until I have been able to complete certain business; specifically, the disposition of some valuable pieces from my uncle's collection. Among these pieces are several paintings of unusual value, including one exceptional work by Diego Rodríguez de Silva y Velázquez, which has been in the family for generations."

"But which your family's reduced circumstances have made it essential for you to sell."

Miguel cast his eyes down, playing the game. "We are proud people. We do not discuss such things."

Rosa Maria clapped her hands and laughed. "But why Argentina? Why not from Seville, where the main branch of this nonexistent family has always been centered?"

"My accent, of course. My attempts at the Castillian affectation have not had the ring of authenticity, says Don Valfierno. So I will speak my language as I have always spoken it, and these unworldly Americans will not know the difference between the sounds of Mexico City and the sounds of Buenos Aires."

"And Mme. Privas? She knows what you are doing?"

Miguel shook his head. "Surely you know the Marquis' most important rule."

"*Each* of his rules is the most important."

"But this is first and foremost: No one is ever to have one scrap of information more than is absolutely necessary. So Mme. Privas has been told that I will be traveling to Rouen for several days, to examine for the Marquis the work of a local restorer of old paintings."

Rosa Maria smiled. "I am sure Mme. Privas will be pained by your absence."

The boy shrugged. "Certainly she will."

She laughed. "How willing you are to accept your importance. You are vain indeed."

"I am who I am."

"You are who you have *become*."

He nodded at that and looked at her. "And you are who you are *about* to become."

* * *

It fell to Mme. Valency to accompany Miguel to the secondhand shops in the Marais to search out the proper costumes for the boy's upcoming charade. Two such would be needed: one for the first meeting, where he would show the painting to the Sindens and, when requested to do so, tell them the price; the other for the meeting three days later when he would reluctantly agree to the lower figure the Marquis would have advised the Sindens to offer.

Two appropriate examples of worn finery were found in two separate shops, and Mme. Valency suggested they pause for a citron before starting back. In addition to the cool drink, Miguel ordered two large pastries, and when it all arrived Mme. Valency was appalled to note that while much had improved in the boy's dress and bearing, he still attacked his food in a manner more suited to the barnyard than to the role he was about to play.

"Is food to be served at this meeting with the Sindens?" she asked.

Miguel stared at her, anger slowly reddening his face. Then suddenly his hand pounded the tabletop so hard heads turned toward them from every table. "I will hear none of this from you. You are not to play the role of Mme. Privas!"

Nor would I choose to, thought Mme. Valency. And then she smiled despite the vehemence of Miguel's response. "You still call her that then? *Mme. Privas?*"

"I call her what I call her," he said firmly. "And as for my behavior at the table, I take my food as I always have: with relish, with pleasure. If you find that offensive, I will say to you what I say to her: leave the table."

Mme. Valency restored her face to a properly sober look. "If I have rubbed a sore spot, I am sorry."

"You have. A spot that is very sore. I have allowed myself to be changed in every way: my clothes, my language, even my leg. *Still* she is not satisfied. I cannot be the perfect gentleman she wants me to be until I change the way I eat, and this I will never do. Not for her, not for anyone."

And as suddenly as his anger had risen, so was it spent, and he leaned forward and devoured the remainder of the pastry. Then he buried his face in his napkin as he wiped his mouth almost clean.

"Now," he said. "I must tell you that I am less worried about how these people will see me than I am about whether they can be made to believe the painting is genuine."

Mme. Valency shrugged. "There are two things you must never underestimate: first, the skill of Chaudron, and second, the remarkable ability of a charming, well-credentialed man to encourage even the most worldly of human beings to allow free rein to their deep-seated need to believe."

"No *doors!*" the Marquis bellowed; so loudly, in fact, that a concerned Ramon looked up and down the rue d'Aguesseau to see if they were being stared at. They weren't. The street was empty. Empty, that is, except for the shiny, sleek Panhard-Levassor motorcar in which the nervous barber had just been driven here from the company's head-quarters west of the Bois. The driver, who was sitting impassively be-hind the wheel, had explained that he did not normally do this sort of thing, but since no regular driver had been available he was fill-ing in. It was clear that his company viewed as more than normally important the two potential clients to whom the car was being lent today.

"Watch me," Ramon said, and stepped first onto the discreetly placed footrest above where the normal running board might be and then over the low side and into the back of the car, making the move with the grace he'd acquired in ten minutes of prior prac-tice. "See?"

But Valfierno did not. "I see that a man can do it easily. But how can we ask a woman to manage such a thing?"

"Women do not mind at all."

"Is that what you were told?"

"By Labourdette himself. He insists that women love his motor-car. He calls it the Skiff."

"Indeed," the driver nodded. "It is the Skiff."

Valfierno shook his head. "Of course. Because a skiff has no doors."

"No," said the driver. "Because it is light as a feather and fast as the wind."

Valfierno looked again at the long, unbroken line and smiled as he began to see it differently. It did indeed look as the driver had described it; so much so, in fact, that he began to find himself hoping that the women would want to leave the top down, as it was now, so as not to interrupt the sculpted sweep of this handsome new machine. He set his foot on the footrest as Ramon had done and swung himself into the front seat. "Whatever it is," he said, "it is ours for the day and too late for it to be otherwise."

The Marquis was a man who believed in his own good luck; whatever chain of apparently random events had put the Sindens in his path was really just another instance of the many ways in which fortune smiled on him. Thomas and Clara Sinden had been precisely what his current situation required, so fate had delivered them— richer and more needy than even he could have dared to hope for.

Their candidacy for the role of Ultimate Buyer had been clear at their first meeting, but that was a decision for a later time. For now Valfierno's considerable skills were focused on the objective at hand.

The cottage they were heading toward belonged to Mme. Didier, who had lent it, she'd thought, to Mme. Valency, to allow that hardworking woman to spend a peaceful few days away from the bustle of her gallery. This same Mme. Valency was now seated, along with Clara and the Marquis, in the back of the Skiff, while Thomas Sinden, as befitted his considerable bulk, sat in the front of the open car as it headed toward Clichy. The wisdom of this move (arranging for the car) had seemed doubtful for the first few moments when the enthusiastic Thomas Sinden had seemed more interested in the car itself than in the treasure waiting at their destination.

"That bonnet!" Sinden had roared, pointing to the car. "See how the line flows into the windscreen? Perfect. *Perfect!*"

"An elegant design," Clara had agreed.

Thomas Sinden had thrown back his head and laughed, then quickly turned sober. "When we get back home we must arrange to exchange the Packard for one of these."

Clara's long practice in dealing with her husband's enthusiasms kept her voice level. "We should certainly give it some thought."

"You think me foolish since we only just bought the Packard."

Clara smiled. "I think you must have what you admire."

He nodded soberly. "It's something I shall consider."

Another man's enthusiasm for the car might have dimmed somewhat when, after a half hour on the road, the beautiful machine coughed several times and died just past Porte d'Asniéres, but Thomas Sinden had seized on this as an opportunity for a closer look at the engine. He'd leaped out as soon as they'd stopped and watched eagerly as the right side of the hood went up.

"What must it be?" he'd asked the driver.

The driver poked around for a minute or two looking to find the trouble, and then Sinden, who'd suddenly spotted the loose wire near the distributor, firmly pushed the man aside and snapped the wire back into place with a "There, that should take care of things." It did, and in a minute they were rolling again.

The rest of the trip was peaceful and necessarily quiet, conversation being impossible in the open car, but the contented smiles around him made it plain to the Marquis that his guests were enjoying their outing, and when they finally stopped at the cottage the Sindens confirmed as much.

"I've seen so little of the countryside," said Clara, climbing out of the Skiff. "It's every bit as lovely as I've been told."

Thomas Sinden patted the swooping fender as he debarked. "I've decided we'll keep the Packard," he said.

Clara laughed. "Well, I'm relieved to hear that. It's really quite suitable, you know."

"Yes. And this would be right for Newport. It would feel more at home near the sea. Yes, old boy?" he asked the Marquis, who nodded.

The driver smiled.

Thomas Sinden took Valfierno's elbow and started him up the path. "Your Argentinean friend owns this house?"

The Marquis shook his head. "In the family's current circumstances he could not afford even so modest a place as this. He has rented it for a short time. Until he accomplishes what he came here to do."

The Marquis had primed his guests so carefully that he was surprised that the American had forgotten even this unimportant detail.

But unimportant it was, and there was no doubt that both Sindens were fully aware of the facts that had brought them here. The Argentinean they were about to meet had made inquiries into the local market and had been referred to Mme. Privas; it had been his contact with her that had led him to the Marquis. And as soon as the Marquis had learned that a Velázquez was among the items the young man had for sale, he thought at once of his American friends. Why? Because both John Singer Sargent and Carolus-Duran had worshiped the Spanish master. Both had traveled to Spain to see everything that could be seen; Sargent had spent endless days at the Prado copying Velázquez as he tried to fathom his secrets. And while Velázquez had not been the subject of the Sindens' quest, the Marquis had reasoned that they might well be interested in acquiring, or at the very least examining, a painting that he would describe as a work of unusual interest.

Clara Sinden's excitement had been instantly apparent, and her husband, whose enthusiasm for collecting was at least as strong, quickly agreed that this might well represent an unexpected opportunity.

The Marquis' knock on the door was answered by Miguel. He was dressed in the first of the two costumes that had been bought for this occasion, and he seemed every inch the impoverished young nobleman he'd been described to be. Greetings were exchanged, Miguel said he knew why they were here, and he invited the group in to see what they'd come to see.

It is not unusual for the right things to happen for all the wrong reasons, and in the case of Chaudron's visit to Madrid that was certainly the case. The trip had been undertaken with an objective he failed to achieve, but if he had not gone he would never have produced the startling work called *Maribárbola*.

The chain of events had begun some four months earlier on a night when he and Miguel had been eating their dinner at La Terre Ferme and drinking a quantity of wine that was beyond their usual portion. The combination of wine, familiar company, and the pain and pleasure of shared memories propelled the young Miguel down a path of mournful confessions, each exploring further the depth of his feelings for the incomparable Rosa Maria. Soon tears were streaming down his face and his ability to speak was curtailed by spasms of painful sobs.

But youth being endlessly resilient, the next morning Miguel awoke refreshed and cheerful, the deep sleep of the young having worked its wonders. He hummed and whistled his way through his morning splash and sailed off to his duties at the Privas mansion. (These were the days before the boy was living there.) But Yves Chaudron, his memories of the same Rosa Maria having been so unexpectedly aroused, could not so easily put them aside.

Chaudron had not thought of her this way since Mexico, but now he could not rid his mind of that radiant face, still pictured in its frame of swirled yellow turban that for so many weeks had covered her black-and-white hair. Perhaps if there had been pressing work on which to refocus his thoughts he'd have been able to put this torment behind him, but his quick, facile brush had advanced his output well ahead of either Valfierno's or Mme. Valency's ability to sell, and so he was free to harbor thoughts he might not otherwise have had time to entertain.

The following morning, after a largely sleepless night, he shook Miguel awake and told the boy that he would be leaving Paris for a time; Miguel was to tell no one of his absence unless the question arose, which it almost certainly would not. Miguel nodded dully and went back to sleep, and Chaudron gathered the few items that seemed essential and began the journey to Madrid.

At Las Ursulinas Rosa Maria proved to be less accessible than he'd imagined she would be. He'd appeared at the school on a Sunday morning and asked to see her, but the sisters seemed suspicious. Finally they agreed to produce her for a brief conversation late in the afternoon—supervised of course.

Rosa Maria was surprised and delighted to see him and asked what on earth had brought him to Madrid. He'd come to explore the treasures of the Prado, he explained, something he'd never done before. He would be doing that tomorrow, and he thought it would then be pleasant if she would join him afterward for dinner.

Sister Immaculata shifted in her nearby seat, frowned, and shook her head firmly, but after some pleading from Rosa Maria agreed to take the matter up with the Mother Superior. The next day, when Chaudron called again, another sister informed him that Rosa Maria would not be permitted to leave the grounds for any reason whatever, but she had arranged for the girl to meet with him in the library, for no more than an hour, at exactly one o'clock on Wednesday. She would of course be chaperoned, but the sister in attendance would be instructed to sit on the far side of the room, where her presence would not intrude on their conversation. It was not the arrangement Chaudron had hoped for, but since it was clear that none other was possible, he agreed.

From the school he made his way to the Prado, but found that, like the Louvre, it was closed on Mondays for cleaning. The day was sunny and pleasant, so with no agenda to press him he walked slowly around the area, stopping in front of a small shop that seemed to be part gallery and part emporium for art supplies. He stepped inside and the tinkling bell summoned a short, straight-backed, overstuffed woman with the stern look of someone impossible to please. "Senora Schultz," she announced in the confident tones of ownership. "May I be of service?" Her accent contradicted the origin of both the surname and the honorific. He answered her in French. He had come in, he said, because her place looked interesting.

She shrugged. "As you can see, no one comes here on Mondays. What is it you need?"

Chaudron smiled. There was something about this earnest, saturnine woman he found amusing. "I will not know until I see it."

She stared at him for a moment, not making much sense of that, then shrugged again. With a sweep of her hand she indicated the contents of the store. "There is everything," she said, folding her arms across her bosom. Clearly she would be standing here while he looked.

There were paints, brushes, canvases, and other utilitarian items in much of the shop, and to the right and closer to the window was a cluster of paintings that were copies of what he presumed to be works in the museum. Most of these rested against the wall, but a select few were displayed on easels. It was to these that he was drawn.

"Goya and Velázquez," said Senora Schultz. "Copies made by me."

Chaudron stepped closer to the Velázquez copies. There were

two that caught his eye: a portrait of a bearded dwarf seated with his legs thrust stiffly out in front of him, and a complex grouping of what seemed at first to be children in the foreground, adults standing behind them, and a painter at his easel to the left.

"*Las Meninas*," said Senora Schultz. "The Maids of Honor; The Ladies-in-Waiting."

He stepped closer, trying to make sense of this drama he did not understand.

"Two thousand pesetas," she said.

He nodded absently and continued to stare at the painting.

"In the Prado, it is ten feet tall and nine feet wide," she said. The copy was a modest two feet high. "See how they all look forward? See how the painter does? He is Velázquez and he is painting the King and Queen, who are standing where you are standing. The Infanta watches with her ladies-in-waiting."

Chaudron nodded. He pointed to a figure at the right. "And who is this?"

"Another maid of honor. The dwarf, Maribárbola."

A second dwarf stood to the right, but he, like the normal-sized attendants, had a face of little consequence. It was to Maribárbola that Chaudron was drawn. The strong face. The large protruding jaw. The pride radiating from the firmly held body. *I serve, but I do not disappear.* "What price did you say?" he asked.

"Two thousand. Perhaps less if you buy more than the one."

Chaudron nodded. "It is nicely done," he said. "I have not seen the original, but from this alone I can see you have caught the spirit. Of the time and I think also of Velázquez."

She managed to express her pleasure at the compliment without allowing herself a smile. "Tomorrow when the museum is open, you will see the painting itself. You will see how fine the copy is."

He continued to stare at the painting, gradually incorporating her description into what he was seeing.

"I am working on another copy in the back. I could let you have this one for twelve hundred."

He nodded again and turned to her. "Perhaps I will be back," he said and left the store.

He wandered the neighborhood after that, poking into several similar shops and into the used-book stores that were everywhere. It was in one of the latter that he was led to *El Arte de la Pintura*, a treatise by the man the bookseller described in reverent tones as the father-in-law and teacher of Diego Velázquez.

The newly purchased book in hand, he walked again past the closed gates of the Prado, more frustrated than before at having to wait till tomorrow. Then he retraced his steps to the shop of Senora Schultz, where he disappointed that woman by asking not for the copy she'd hoped to sell, but for chalks and a sketching pad.

"I am, you see, an amateur. Perhaps I shall copy the painting myself."

"I am sure you will do it well," she said with chilly condescension.

Chaudron smiled. "If not, I may return to purchase this one."

"If, indeed, it has not been sold."

The next day he was at the museum just as the gates were opened, carrying his sketch pad and his chalks. A few inquiries set him on the path to *Las Meninas*, and when at last he entered the room that was dominated by its presence he stood staring at the huge canvas, instantly under its spell. Nothing in his conversation with Senora Schultz had prepared him for the work itself. It was as if he'd suddenly entered the very room that held these people; as if he were standing where Philip IV and his queen had stood, posing for the court painter while they were watched by their daughter and her ladies-in-waiting.

He stood devouring the painting as a whole for fully half an hour before stepping closer to examine what for him was its most compelling detail: the prideful Maribárbola.

He set to work at once, quickly sketching the figure of the dwarf, transposing the time-darkened tones of the master's pigments to the brighter, softer colors of his chalks. When he was finished he frowned at what he'd done, then shifted his gaze back to the compact figure in the master's work, unconsciously memorizing the textures and the shades.

The next morning he was back at the Prado again. He checked what he had done, made a few minor changes, and then seemed satisfied he had what he needed. It was not yet eleven and he was due at the convent at one, but suddenly he knew he would not be going.

He put away his chalks and covered his work with a blank sheet of paper. Then he walked to the next room and was beguiled again with more of the work of Velázquez. Suddenly, in front of a large portrait of Philip IV, he realized what he must do.

He sketched the portrait once, then slashed a black line through it and began again. The second time he had what he wanted and spent only a few more minutes on minor changes.

The sun had disappeared when he stepped outside, and rain seemed only minutes away. He crossed quickly to the shop of Senora Schultz, but when he turned the knob the door was locked. It was only then that he noticed the sign that said she would reopen at three. The heavy raindrops began coming down and he stuffed his sketching paper under his coat and started pounding heavily on the door. No answer. He did it again. Still no response. He was just raising his fist for a third try when he saw her coming out from the back dressed in a wrapper, her long hair hanging loose. He pointed to the doorknob, but when she saw him she seemed suddenly angry and pointed to the sign. He banged on the door again and after a moment of uncertainty she shook her head disapprovingly, but reached down to let him in.

"It's raining very hard," he said.

"It is not my function to provide the world with shelter. I am closed till three."

"I came back to buy the picture."

Those were the magic words. She shut the door behind him. "If you promise to leave quickly. I must have my rest."

"May I see it again?"

"It has not changed."

"But I have." He explained where he'd been.

She smiled. "And you made your copy?"

He shook his head. "I am back, you see."

She led him to the small *Las Meninas*. How crude it seemed now that Chaudron had seen the thing itself. The figures were well-enough drawn, but drawn they were, outlined and then filled with color. Senora Schultz had either been incapable of reproducing the master's brushwork or blind to its complexities. Her paint was laid on with workmanlike precision, but each stroke of the master's seemed to begin from somewhere inside its subject and grow outward like the flesh it rendered.

She touched the painting proudly. "It is really quite well done, you see."

He nodded.

"Two thousand," she said.

He was surprised. "Yesterday you said twelve hundred."

She shrugged. "Fifteen. Bargain prices do not last forever."

He sighed, opened his coat and put down his things, and reached for his money. He started counting, then stopped and looked at her. She seemed gentler today, less threatening. He reached out and touched her arm. "Your hair—looks very soft that way." She smiled and as he stepped toward her she seemed to lean his way. He put the money on the table and gently enclosed her in his arms, where she stayed for just a moment before pressing free. She walked to the door and locked it, then came back and took him by the hand.

"It will still be fifteen hundred," she said quietly, and led him to the back.

Pleasantries were exchanged in the spacious kitchen of the house in Clichy, and in a moment a young servant girl came in with glasses of sangria; as she passed them around an astute observer would have seen the half-smile of greeting that passed quickly between her and Mme. Valency. She was in fact the young waitress first seen at the pastry shop around the corner from the Galerie Arlette, Louise Durtal, now rescued from her former situation and in the regular employ of Mme. Valency as part domestic, part secretary, on loan to Clichy for the occasion.

Having been made suitably comfortable, the visiting party was invited to move to the parlor where gauze curtains had been drawn across the large window to soften the afternoon sun. Valfierno had determined at yesterday's rehearsal that at this hour of the day drawn curtains provided the perfect light.

The painting was covered with a red velvet cloth and was propped against the back of a huge armchair. Valfierno walked to it and rested his hand on the covered frame. He turned to Miguel. "I see you have a sense of drama," he said lightly, although of course he himself had been the one who'd arranged every fold of the cloth. Miguel smiled.

"When this opportunity arose," he said to Clara and Thomas Sinden, "Mme. Privas was intrigued, as anyone must be, but it was she who graciously suggested this work might be more appropriate for you.

"Now, as to the painting itself"—he still had not uncovered it—"you will see, it is a portrait of a dwarf; a woman. A German woman named Maribárbola who served as lady-in-waiting to the Infanta Margarita, the daughter of Philip IV of Spain. This same Maribárbola appears in *Las Meninas*, which as you know hangs in a place of honor in the Prado. As you may also know, there were many dwarfs at the Spanish court; they fascinated Diego Velázquez for reasons we can only imagine. Several of his paintings of dwarfs are owned by the national museum, but this exceptional portrait was a gift from the King to Cardinal Almaguer and has remained in the Almaguer family until this day."

The Marquis de Valfierno raised the velvet cloth and Clara Sinden gasped.

"As you can see, Velázquez has painted the dwarf as a hunter," the Marquis went on, "exactly as he often portrayed members of the royal family. Was this done in tribute, or as a kind of mockery? We cannot know, but either way the pose is so completely inappropriate as to enshroud the subject in an air of mystery."

The Marquis said nothing more, but allowed time for the remarkable painting to have its effect. Clara Sinden rose and came closer, as if to absorb more completely the proud bearing, the strong androgynous face, the wonderful grandeur of this diminutive woman standing erect in her manly clothes.

Nothing was said for several moments, and then Thomas Sinden stood. "Well, sir," he said in a voice loud enough to be heard in Marseille, "this is something we might very well like to talk about. Do you agree, my dear?" Clara Sinden nodded. "Mrs. Sinden and I will wait in the car while you and the young man have your discussion."

Later, as they started back, Valfierno reported the Argentinean's asking price as two hundred thousand francs, a figure, he added quickly, that seemed too high. He suggested an offer of one hundred eighty thousand. Thomas Sinden had not been shocked at the high price; he was accustomed to paying for what he wanted. But he suddenly sent the conversation spinning in an unexpected direction.

"Before we make any offer," he said with a broad grin that masked what underlay his words, "I shall ask to have the painting examined by an expert qualified to confirm its attribution." It was said with a warmth that almost masked the fact that this was clearly business; and a special kind of business at that, where the chief concern was not money but something more important: an unwillingness to be embarrassed.

Clara Sinden was horrified.

"But it *has* been examined. The Marquis has no doubt of its authenticity."

Her husband frowned and turned to the Marquis. "I know the Marquis understands I mean no disrespect."

Valfierno nodded. "Of course." But the Marquis did *not* understand. This was not a turn of events he had anticipated. Nothing in his past dealings had prepared him for this, although of course nothing could have. In past transactions the object in question had hung on a wall of honor that provided all the authenticity any buyer could demand.

But this situation was different. *Maribárbola* had a history that even if it were totally believed might lead to uncomfortable questions. A gift from the King to Cardinal Almaguer? Was there a letter to that effect? Valfierno felt foolish for not having had one prepared. He tried to think quickly what corrective steps might be taken, but Thomas Sinden was a step ahead of him.

"I've inquired among my business associates and I've had several dealers and other knowledgeable people recommended to me, any one of whom could probably be helpful. The one name that was on almost every list was that of Lionel Picard, of Picard-Roth. Do you know him?"

"I know the name, of course," said the Marquis, who had never heard it before.

"I know the gallery," said Mme. Valency. "It is around the corner from me, but I've never met the man." She was about to say more but decided not to.

Two days later, Thomas Sinden met with Lionel Picard, who agreed to undertake the evaluation at a fee Sinden found acceptable. As it happened, he explained to Sinden, his father, Alfred Picard, who was no longer fully active in the business, had made a specialty of Titian and Velázquez, and while he himself was fully qualified to make the judgment, the special knowledge available so close at hand could not fail to be useful.

Maribárbola was delivered to Picard-Roth on rue Laffitte and Lionel Picard turned the job over to his father, whose step suddenly regained its youthful spring as he immersed himself in the challenge.

On the following day Mme. Valency began her morning walk up rue Laffitte fifteen minutes earlier than usual. When she arrived at the corner of the Picard-Roth block she stopped to look into other gallery windows as she waited for Alfred Picard to make his appearance in the street. When he did and began fussing with his awnings, she resumed her stroll and seemed pleasantly surprised at their accidental meeting.

"You are especially cheerful today," she said, and the senior Picard explained his new assignment and his pleasure at having something useful to do. When he described the painting, she touched her hand to his arm in apparent astonishment. "Then it's *you* they've come to!" And she began to explain her interest in the painting, then stopped and suggested that since they both had duties to get to this morning they might better arrange to discuss the matter later in the day. He put his hand on hers, hardly able to believe his good fortune, and quickly agreed.

Later, at the small bistro farther up rue Laffitte they sat together sipping port, a habit Alfred had learned from an English customer, he said, who'd insisted that, unlike his countrymen, he was convinced that port was too hearty for after dinner, but exactly right as an aperitif. She smiled her agreement after the first sip, and then marveled at the coincidence that had brought this painting to him and explained the chain of events by which it had come about.

"There is, of course, no doubt of its authenticity. How fortunate we are to have someone of your reputation to verify it."

He took her hand and moved closer, and found himself quite pleased to be exactly where he was. "Perhaps," she suggested, "it might be wise if we said nothing of our discussion."

"Yes," he agreed, "that might be better."

They met often in the next few weeks, and sat close, and she let him hold her hand. He sought nothing further. He seemed content to enjoy her lively company and the warm touch of her responsive fingers.

Meanwhile his efforts with the painting continued and after nearly two weeks of peering at the canvas through powerful magnifiers and visiting the Louvre to examine again other works of the master, Alfred Picard announced his findings to his son, who then summoned Thomas Sinden and informed him that both father and son were convinced beyond any doubt that this work could have been created by no hand other than that of Velázquez, and that the work was of such quality that Sinden should count himself fortunate to have had it offered. "And how did you come upon it?" Lionel Picard inquired.

Sinden smiled. "I'm not sure it would be proper for me to say."

"As you choose," said Picard the elder.

No painting the Marquis had sold in the past had ever been put through this kind of rigorous test. Nor, for that matter, had Mme. Valency. Whether she or the work had carried the day it would be impossible to say. There was, however, one final question that remained.

"I must," said Thomas Sinden, "ask your opinion in one more matter."

Father and son Picard exchanged knowing glances. Picard the elder grinned broadly and turned to Sinden. "What is the asking price?"

"Two hundred thousand francs."

The son's eyebrows went up. "That is high for Velázquez."

Alfred Picard nodded in agreement, but didn't seem as surprised. "High, yes," he said. "As my son says, for Velázquez. El Greco and

Goya have commanded such prices, but not yet Velázquez. I say not yet, because he surely will."

"Then the price is too high?" asked Sinden in a voice so loud passersby on the street turned toward the window.

Lionel moved as if to speak, but then deferred to his father.

The older man smiled. "Let me outline the obvious for you. Works of art are subject to the famous laws of supply and demand, even as everything that is bought and sold. But with art, it is the buyer's attitude that determines both supply *and* demand.

"What do I mean by attitude? Well, if you're a man who collects simply what he calls art, your bargaining position is strong. The world's supply of works of art is vast; if you don't buy one painting, you will buy another.

"But if you define your position more narrowly; if you will buy only *great* art—art that has been defined by the marketplace as great—the supply is very much smaller. Smaller supply, higher price."

At this point Alfred Picard shrugged and smiled. "And how much more difficult it gets when you are set on one particular piece; the supply is now down to . . ." He held up a finger. "One. No other such painting exists in all the world. So if that one is a work you must have . . ." He shrugged again. "Last year Pierpont Morgan paid one hundred fifty thousand *dollars* for a Gainsborough Duchess. Too much? By most standards, yes. But for certain reasons it was a painting he had to have. So in the end it comes down to your own imperatives. To say nothing of your bankbook."

Thomas Sinden nodded thoughtfully, coming closer to a decision, but still not certain. Lionel Picard offered him a glass of something, but Sinden declined. "As you can see," said Lionel, "my father may no longer be fully active, but he remains fully informed."

"Quite so," said Sinden. He turned to Alfred and bowed respectfully. "I thank you for your help."

"Perhaps," said Alfred Picard, "there is one further thing I can say to make my feelings clear. This is the finest Velázquez I have ever seen offered for sale. If for whatever reason you decide not to buy it, I would recommend to my son that we buy it ourselves."

That would have been enough for any man, and it was for

Thomas Sinden. That afternoon he asked the Marquis to resume negotiations with the young Argentinean nobleman. Three days later, the Argentinean having been reported as nearly unbending, *Maribárbola* was acquired by the Sindens for one hundred ninety thousand francs; a high price for a Velázquez, and a record for a Chaudron.

12

*H*ow could he not have noticed before? He smiled at the obvious answer: because there is always a moment of revelation, an instant of awareness, after which nothing else remains the same.

They were lying on the bed in the small apartment on the rue Montalivet. She was asleep and he had just awakened. It was the middle of the afternoon. He had surprised her with a visit because with the wedding still several weeks away he found being without her more and more intolerable. So he'd left the rue d'Aguesseau and the efficient Ramon, busy with his paperwork details, and come to the one place he wanted to be.

The difference was too small to be seen, but large enough to have revealed itself to his familiar touch. He smiled in pleasure and disbelief as he became suddenly aware of this new reality, and he leaned over and kissed her forehead. She stirred and rustled to a new position and settled her hand over his hand still resting on her stomach. It was half an hour before she awakened.

Later, when they'd both dressed and she'd made tea, he asked why she had not told him. She blushed at the idea that he knew and wondered how. He told her and asked again why he hadn't been told.

"I didn't want you to know until our wedding night," she said. "I wanted to be assured that when you married me, it would be for one reason only."

He nodded and remained silent.

The Marquis de Valfierno knew all too well the inexorable logic of simple arithmetic. It was clear that if he assumed for himself the biblical lifespan of three score and ten, he would be dead in thirteen years, or just when his new bride would be turning thirty.

She would not be an impoverished widow, of course, but neither would she be rich enough to be able to live her several remaining decades at the economic level they currently enjoyed.

Till now, he had never spent wakeful nights struggling with moral problems, but this moral problem was cloaked in terms he understood, involving as it did the need to amass huge sums of money.

Whether or not it was right for a man his age to marry someone so young was not the point. The point was that any man who does so has a clear obligation to provide for such a bride so handsomely that the pain of what would surely be her early bereavement would be eased by the knowledge that her only loss would be her husband's company.

These thoughts were constantly in the back of Valfierno's mind these days, and combined with his successful dealings with the Sindens had moved him to believe that this might well be the proper time to embark on what would be the climactic adventure of his life.

He was seated with Mme. Valency in her small office at the back of the gallery, celebrating the sale of *Maribárbola* with glasses of what she had described as a very ordinary sherry. "Great wine should not be wasted on great moments," she said, setting down her glass. "Such celebrations elevate any wine to heights of glory." She raised her glass in another salute and drank again.

Valfierno smiled. "Our friend Miguel presented himself with wonderful style."

Mme. Valency laughed. "That was because he avoided the only possible trap. However, the Sindens must have been famished by the time you returned."

"They are very polite; they said nothing."

"You may take my word that watching Miguel partake of food would have destroyed the illusion."

The Marquis nodded, and she suddenly fell silent. When she spoke again it was slowly and in a voice as low and filled with drama as the lower strings when they embark on something of importance.

"Perhaps the government of France should not be asked to pay ransom."

The change of subject might have seemed abrupt if she had not settled on a topic that had been much on his mind in recent days.

She put her glass down and looked straight at him. "Ransom might not be required. If Thomas Sinden was willing to pay too much for a newly discovered Velázquez, what might he pay for *La Gioconda* herself?"

Valfierno lowered his head and smiled. Then he raised his brows and looked up at her. "I have asked myself that very question."

She reached for the decanter and poured them each a bit more sherry. "Then let's put numbers to it. What indeed might a man of endless wealth be willing to pay for such a prize?"

"A million? More?"

The enormity of the number had its effect on Mme. Valency. "A million francs?"

"Why not?" the Marquis said grandly.

She gasped. "You cannot be serious."

"You are right. Not nearly enough. I would ask a million *dollars!*"

And the two of them dissolved in laughter.

The days until the wedding came down to six, and Bishop Bertrix, chief prelate of the diocese that included most of the Eighth Arrondissement, summoned the happy couple to his offices at la Madeleine ostensibly to review with them the mechanics of the coming event, but really, it quickly became apparent, to try to convince them that even at this late date they might be more comfortable if they decided to move their nuptials to a less prominent venue.

It had been Mme. Privas, of course, who had made the arrangements for the ceremony to take place here, and to be conducted by her friend, Bishop Bertrix.

"We will not consider any change," said the Marquis de Valfierno.

"You do understand," the Bishop continued, his brows drawn so close together the skin between them was pushed into a vertical ridge, "that even an ordinary wedding at the Madeleine invites considerable scrutiny."

"We love your beautiful church," Rosa Maria said in a whisper, relieved that she could summon any voice at all, "and it is our desire to be married here."

The Bishop remained immobile for a few seconds, and then he rose. "Very well," he said, "it shall be as you wish." And in a cold monotone he began to tick off the facts they needed to know concerning their time of arrival and the ways in which various members of the wedding party should array themselves. Then he summoned an acolyte and instructed the pale green young man to show the couple around those parts of the church with which they needed to be familiar. "We will meet again on Sunday," he said brusquely, and left the room.

The Bishop was not the only one to express himself in opposition to the coming wedding, although Clara Sinden's disapproval had to be read between the lines of her regrets. *My husband and I,* she wrote in response to her invitation, *will be unable to attend, owing to previous obligations out of the country.* Those previous obligations were then bustled into reality when she quickly made arrangements for a visit to London.

But the trip to London was postponed three days later, after the Sindens had a surprisingly pleasant evening at a small dinner party to which the Marquis had invited them in order to acquaint them with the bride-to-be. Clara was so thoroughly enchanted by the young woman that the next morning she informed her surprised husband that they would put off the trip to London in order to attend the wedding.

The event itself went smoothly, with Rosa Maria's extraordinary beauty brought to its peak of radiance by the joy of this day and the wonderful secret she carried lightly down the aisle. Later at the small reception at the rue d'Aguesseau, Valfierno raised his glass and declared that no comparable bride had stood at the altar that year in

Paris, or in any other year. Or for that matter in any other place. There was laughter and applause at that, and a loud "Hear, hear!" from Thomas Sinden.

As it happened, the delay in the Sindens' trip worked very much in their favor—Clara's London dealer informed them that Sargent was to be in town at the later date and that he (the dealer) had been assured that an introduction could be arranged. Clara imparted that information to the Marquis at the reception, and Thomas Sinden added that when they returned in ten days' time, he would be eager to discuss with the Marquis the possibility of further acquisitions.

As for the newlywed couple, they would be spending a week at Como, where the Marquis hoped the peaceful surroundings would allow him to sort out several of his recent thoughts.

He stood at the window of their suite on the lake, watching the moon slither over the ripples, and suddenly everything became clear.

He went to the desk and sat, astonished that the obvious had been hidden this long. He quietly opened the top drawer and slid out a sheet of crested hotel stationery. He opened the brass inkwell, picked up a pen, dipped it, and absently began drawing lines and curves. Then he straightened up, dipped the pen again, and in the calligraphic hand his stepfather had taught him, carefully wrote the name *Thomas Sinden*. He stared at it for a moment, then drew a black line through it. Under the crossed-out name he now wrote the number *six*, so slowly that the circle filled with a blob of ink. He stared at the number, transfixed. Then he drew a square around the number and laid down his pen, unaware his hand was shaking until the pen rattled as he set it in the tray.

"I thought you might be here." The whispered voice behind him was Rosa Maria's. She'd entered the room silently and stood now in her nightgown, holding a candle to one side. She was barefoot, as she always was at night.

"You must be cold," Valfierno said quietly.

She shook her head. "What time is it?"

"Almost three, I should think."

"Will you come back to bed?"

"Very soon."

She smiled. "Good. I can't sleep until you do." And she turned and followed her shielded candle out of the room.

The Marquis sat for a moment, still entranced by the revelation of what now seemed so obvious. Then he stood up and put out the lamp, waited a moment for his eyes to adjust to the dark, and, more than normally pleased with himself, retraced his steps to the bedroom.

13

Dismissed!" Paul Rénard hissed the word and leaned toward her, his eyes bulging.

Mme. Valency stared at him and felt her hands go damp with a fear she recognized. But she did not back away.

"Clara Sinden is back in Paris, this time alone. But when I call at the Chanticleer, she will not see me. I leave a note. When I come back the next day, there is an envelope for me, with a check for two thousand francs. My services are no longer needed. If there has been a misunderstanding, she hopes this check will make it right, but she will have no need of my help any time in the future. Do you understand? I am dismissed."

He had appeared at the gallery at closing time, just as Nélie was leaving and Mme. Valency was drawing the blinds. The two of them were alone.

He held her responsible, that much was clear. His florid face was just inches from hers and she could smell the stale odor she connected with other ugly scenes. But her response was calm. "Two thousand francs seems very generous," said Mme. Valency.

His breath caught for a moment as his anger mounted, turning his face the color of fury. Still she did not move back and finally he exhaled and turned away. He picked up a porcelain figurine, a seated shepherd, from a table that held several such miniatures. "A handsome piece," he said.

"Indeed."

"I assume it is valuable."

"Everything here is valued by me."

He looked straight at her and opened his fingers, letting it smash to the floor. She waited a moment before she responded.

"If you intend to do any more of that, I will have to take steps against it."

It was said quietly, but anyone normally perceptive would have heard the underlying threat. Paul Rénard, however, was not such a person; he was a man who had come with something specific to accomplish, and now that his anger was spent he proceeded to explain exactly what it was.

"Here is what must happen," he said. "Since you have deprived me of important income, you will replace it. And if you refuse, I shall write to Mr. Thomas Sinden and tell him the true identity of the woman his wife is dealing with. One thousand francs per week is the amount required. Starting with today."

She looked at him without changing expression. "I do not have that much in cash."

"Your bank draft will be acceptable."

She nodded and went to the small desk in the corner and opened the middle drawer. When she turned back she was holding a small black-handled .25 automatic. She stepped quickly toward him, having been warned by the dealer who'd sold it to her that the pistol was accurate only at close range. "Listen well," she said quietly. "There will be not one penny, now or ever. And if you attempt to destroy the person I have become, I will destroy the person you have always been." He opened his mouth as if to say something, but she stopped him by raising the pistol higher. "Not a word. Leave here quickly or I will do it now. And it frightens me to think with how much pleasure."

He turned at once and was gone.

From the Pont de la Concorde the Skiff sailed south on the Boulevard Saint Germain, leaned to starboard at Boulevard Raspail, then heaved forty degrees to port at rue Notre Dame des Champs. The captain then ordered the vessel slowed to a crawl as he searched for the door to Chaudron's building.

"Number six, did you say, sir?" asked the quondam helmsman, now the uniformed chauffeur whose services for two months had been provided by the Panhard-Levassor Motorcar Company in gratitude not only for the Marquis having purchased their proudest creation, but for his also having been responsible for the sale of a second car to a Mr. Thomas Sinden of the United States for delivery in Newport, Rhode Island, thus encouraging the company to imagine that the sight of their sleek machine in the streets of this fabled enclave might trigger further American sales.

"No, not six," said the Marquis. "I think sixty something. I'll know the door when— There. On the left. Sixty-five."

The driver pulled smartly to the left, urging first his front and then his rear left wheels close to the building line in a firm, gentle maneuver that testified to his expertise. At that moment Valfierno decided he would talk with this man about staying on after the company's largess had run its bounds.

"Wait here, please," the Marquis said grandly as he stood, turned, threw his right leg over the side, missed the tread and tumbled to the ground.

The startled driver vaulted out of the car and came running to him. "Are you all right, sir?"

Valfierno lay still for a moment, stunned not by pain but by a combination of confusion and embarrassment. He raised his head and looked up at the driver, who was bending down to help him. Valfierno waved him off and struggled to his feet, with more difficulty than he'd expected. With a determined effort he reinflated his body and then said with all the dignity he could muster: "I'll be only a few minutes." He turned and strode into the building.

He mounted the narrow stairway, resting on the first landing to clear some unexpected dizziness, then proceeded slowly to the top floor and the door to Chaudron's studio.

His first knock produced no answer, so he raised his fist to knock again when the door creaked slowly open revealing in the middle of the room a full-bosomed woman standing naked, with a steaming kettle in her hand.

He emitted a sound of startled surprise and the woman arched her eyebrows.

The Marquis muttered some inanities, and then suggested he return a little later.

She turned slightly to the encrusted teapot on the table to her right and poured the steaming water. Then she set the kettle down and turned back to him. "You are looking for Chaudron?" she asked.

Valfierno nodded.

She smiled. "You must be the Marquis. The one he speaks of."

"The Marquis Eduardo de Valfierno," he muttered with a slight bow. "At your service." And the stirrings he now began to feel would in another moment, he realized, have him ready to be exactly that. He began to redirect his thoughts.

"Chaudron is there," she said, pointing to the pile of blankets in the corner. "He has not yet awakened."

Valfierno nodded again.

She walked to where Chaudron was sleeping, picked a loose blanket from atop the pile and in one deft swirl wrapped it around herself. "Here is what I think," she said, turning back to him. "I think if you go to the bar at the corner on the right, La Terre Ferme, he can meet you there in five minutes. Maybe ten."

Valfierno agreed to that and was about to apologize for his intrusion when he was interrupted by a knock at the open door. He turned to see the chauffeur standing there with a cardboard box in his hand.

"Excuse me, sir," the man said. "I found this in the street, near where you fell."

Valfierno's hand went automatically to his pocket, which he had not realized till now was empty. "Yes," he said quickly, "thank you."

The chauffeur handed it over, then bowed and excused himself. A moment later Valfierno did the same.

It was nearly a half hour, but finally Chaudron appeared and slid into the chair opposite him. Valfierno frowned. "Your model said five minutes."

"Model?" Then he realized. "Senora Schultz."

It was now Valfierno's turn to be puzzled, and Chaudron's to provide an explanation; but that was something the painter was not eager to do. For one thing, Valfierno knew nothing of his trip to Madrid. Where had the Marquis imagined *Maribárbola* had sprung from? That was not the kind of question that would ever form in the mind of the Marquis. The things he required from Chaudron just magically appeared.

"Marcelline," Chaudron finally said. "Her name is Marcelline."

"Then who is Senora Schultz?"

"That is only a joke between us. Between her and me."

"And what, may I ask, *is* between her and you?"

The painter shrugged.

"Does she live with you?" Chaudron's attachments were always a matter of concern. Even the taciturn Chaudron might find his tongue loosened by the radiance of a pleasant afterglow.

"She stays with me for a while. Who knows how long?"

Farid, the owner, had seen Chaudron enter and he now approached the table with a bottle and a glass. Chaudron shook his head.

"Something else?" Farid asked.

"Some food. Whatever you have."

Farid nodded and left.

Valfierno smiled. "It seems you come here often."

"It is convenient."

"Last night, for example."

"I was here last night."

Valfierno leaned back in his chair and considered how to shape this conversation. One step at a time, he'd determined before he'd set out this morning; but now he wondered if he should not pull Chaudron completely into his thoughts.

"Tell me again about the storeroom."

The Marquis had first learned of the storeroom on a visit to the rue Notre Dame des Champs some time ago, when Chaudron had still been working on his copy of *La Gioconda* and Valfierno had been surprised not to see it in his studio.

Chaudron shrugged. "There is nothing more to tell. It is a storeroom. A big closet where paintings are stored; the paintings students are working on, so they don't have to take them away each night."

"A closet, or a *room*?"

"Big closet. Small room. Is there a difference?"

"How large is it?"

The painter shrugged again. "Large enough. It has a toilet."

"Large enough to contain, say, two men?"

"I would say."

"Three?"

"When you say contain . . . ?"

"Three men. Overnight."

Chaudron thought for a moment. "Three uncomfortable men. Yes, that would be possible."

The Marquis relaxed and allowed his face to form the smile he'd felt all morning. "When our man returns I shall order the best red he has in the house. I want you to drink with me."

If Chaudron was surprised he did not show it.

"Mark this day, my friend. In the future you will remember this as the day you learned you were to be paid the highest price any living artist has ever commanded. More even than Monet." He laughed.

Farid approached with a bowl of something that looked gray and questionable, but smelled good enough to have Valfierno consider ordering one for himself. Instead he asked for the bottle he'd said he wanted.

"Do I have your attention?" the Marquis asked when Farid had gone to get the wine.

Chaudron nodded and the Marquis began to explain. But the normally glib Marquis found himself stumbling over words in his eagerness to tell everything at once. He stopped in mid-sentence, smiling at his unaccustomed clumsiness, and then remembered the cardboard box in his pocket. He took it out and pushed it toward the painter.

"The key we spoke of. It is time for you to make it."

Chaudron picked up the box and put it in his pocket. "It has been so long I'd almost forgotten."

"Yes. As you'll recall, a key is necessary."

Chaudron's nod indicated he understood. But he was more surprised than he appeared. The subject had not risen in so long he'd thought the entire project had been abandoned. Clearly it had not.

Farid approached again with the bottle and two glasses, which he set down. He showed the label to Valfierno: Hospices de Beaune. "I know only two wines," Farid said. "Red and white. But when I bought this place there were two dozen of these set apart from the others, laid aside with care. What is treated with respect sometimes deserves it."

Farid opened the bottle and left. Valfierno poured a glass for each of them, then raised his. "To the extraordinary. To something to be treated with respect."

Chaudron raised his glass and the two men drank, Chaudron draining his glass. "That was very good," he said.

Valfierno filled the painter's glass again. "Leave that on the table until I've finished speaking."

Chaudron pushed his glass to one side. "But all of this can have nothing to do with me. You don't need me to elope with *La Gioconda*."

"I assume you have kept your copy."

Chaudron nodded. "It is there somewhere."

"*Somewhere!* You don't know where?"

"Of course. Be calm, my friend. It is rolled up in a corner. I can find it."

"If not you will have to do it again," the Marquis said sternly.

Chaudron was puzzled. He had thought that making the copy had served no purpose other than to allow him to come and go freely at the Louvre and note carefully the area where the painting hung, the various entrances and exits. The copy itself had not seemed to be of any importance.

"And you were right," the Marquis said, in answer to the painter's question. "But now it *is*."

Chaudron nodded, and Valfierno went on to detail exactly what he had in mind. The painter listened with a growing excitement far beyond the capacity of his placid face to show it. When the Marquis had finished he waited for Chaudron to respond. "Yes," he finally answered. "Everything required can be done."

"Good." The Marquis smiled and leaned back. "You must know that for me this will be the last adventure. After this I will buy a comfortable house somewhere, and I will watch my child grow. *Children,* if God wills it. But there will be no more of this, so you must be well taken care of. Here is what you will receive . . ." The Marquis paused for dramatic effect, and Chaudron leaned forward. "You will be paid," the Marquis said, "half a million francs."

Chaudron's heart leaped inside him, but still his expression never changed.

"Does that please you?" asked the Marquis.

The painter waited a moment before answering. "Yes," he said. "It does."

And so Thomas Sinden was no longer the focus of his plan, and Valfierno was astonished that he'd ever thought he might be. Sinden, after all, while rich enough to pay any price, had never shown himself to be anything but an honest man. While he might, like many such, maintain in his soul the capacity for larcenous behavior under the right (or wrong) conditions, it would be dangerous to assume that possibility. How much simpler it would be to deal with someone who had already demonstrated both the means and the willingness to purchase a stolen work of art.

Why would any man buy a stolen painting he could never display, could never sell, could never even boast of owning? One reason alone: simply to *possess* it; to view it in its secret hiding place and thrill as a miser might, running his fingers through some secret cache of gold. Things beyond understanding are not always beyond belief.

The Marquis de Valfierno never thought of himself as either a good or a bad judge of character; he simply acted on his instincts. And so some ten days after first meeting Farid, he found himself again at La Terre, standing in the street and having to pound at an unexpectedly locked front door. After several minutes, an upstairs shutter flew open and Farid's unshaven face poked out. "Yes, monsieur," he said.

"You are the owner?" Valfierno shouted up.

"Farid. The owner, yes."

"We met the other day."

"If you say we did, then of course we did."

"I must speak to you. Let me in, please."

"We open at noon. Come back then."

Noon was an hour away. "This is important. *You* will find it important. Open up, please."

Either the Marquis' words or his imposing figure proved convincing. Or perhaps it was that Farid now remembered having seen him before. "All right," he said, and he disappeared. A few moments later the front door opened and the Marquis stepped inside.

Farid shuffled around opening shutters and as soon as there was enough light for the Marquis to find his bearings he settled himself at a table. When Farid pushed open the last shutter it flew off its hinges and clattered into the alley. He muttered something about the place falling apart.

Valfierno smiled. "It is like the shoemaker's child."

Farid looked at him uncomprehending.

Valfierno tried to explain. "You are a carpenter, and yet there is disrepair."

"More than you see. One day I will get to it." He frowned. "But what of the shoemaker's child?"

Valfierno shook his head. "Nothing. It does not matter."

"Some wine?" Farid asked.

Valfierno shook his head.

"There is nothing else at this hour."

"Sit down, please." He had suddenly become the host.

Farid scraped a chair into place and sat across from him. "There is much that should be done here. In the beginning I had to have everything just so. But now—the days go too quickly. Sometimes this place is an iron chain around my neck."

Valfierno saw his opportunity. "Perhaps an iron chain you no longer need endure."

Farid stared at him, his dark features drawing tight as he considered the meaning of that. "Is this the thing I will find important?"

The Marquis had not planned precisely this approach, but having seen the chance to explore his man without revealing his purpose, he continued along this line. "Perhaps this is the time for you to sell."

"Are you proposing to buy?"

"There is someone I know who might be interested. What price would you think fair?"

Farid thought for a moment, then rose and went to the bar. He came back with a carafe of red wine and two nearly clean glasses. When the Marquis shook his head, he poured one for himself. When Farid finally named his figure, it was an amount four times what he could ever hope to get. "Sixty thousand francs," he said. "Including every bottle."

Valfierno nodded. "I shall pass that figure to the man I spoke of."

Farid's face relaxed into a surprisingly warm smile. "Why do I think you are not really serious?"

Valfierno shrugged. "We shall see. Chaudron speaks well of you. He was the one who told me you were once a carpenter."

"Ship's carpenter. Yes, I was. Now I have other things to keep me occupied."

"But you still know your craft?"

Farid shrugged. "Such as it is. Or was. Is there something you want built?"

Valfierno smiled. "Tell me, Monsieur Farid . . ."

"Just Farid, if you please."

"Tell me this. Are you a wealthy man?"

Farid shrugged again. "Of course. Just look around you."

"Would the money you got for this place make you rich?"

"I cannot tell you how much money would make me rich. But sixty thousand would make me happy."

The Marquis nodded somberly. "I shall discuss it with the person I referred to."

"Then I shall hope to be greeting you again."

"I think that is more than likely." And Valfierno took out his card case and presented one of the newly minted cards that announced him as Colonel Carlos Almazàn Zamora.

At first he'd thought Peru, or Ecuador, but finally he'd determined it would be Spain. So he explained to Rosa Maria as they took their morning walk past the Elysée Palace and farther west on the Faubourg St. Honoré.

"I've lived in Spain," she said lightly, taking his arm. "Perhaps I do not choose to live in Spain again."

He stopped and turned to her. "Then it shall be somewhere else."

She laughed. "I love it there," she said. "Can it be southern Spain? Or maybe the north, near la Côte Basque, in San Sebastian. There was a girl at school from there." She frowned. "She didn't like me very well."

"She was jealous."

"Of course she was. Or she would be if she saw me now." He smiled, pleased at that. "The south, then," she said. "La Costa del Sol!"

"Yes, yes," he agreed enthusiastically. "Very near Málaga. All perfect children come from there."

"Perfect *sons*. It is to be a son, you know."

He laughed. "I know nothing. It is you who says she knows."

"And you who refuses to believe."

"I shall believe what I see when the time comes."

She pressed his arm and looked at him. "And you secretly hope I am wrong."

"I hope nothing, either way. And yet, how could I not want a daughter as beautiful as you."

"Perhaps next time," she said lightly. "This will be a boy."

"A boy, of course."

She grinned. "I always win."

"Spain, then, is in our future . . ."

She stopped and turned to him again. "Not in a future too far away, I hope."

He shook his head. "Not far at all. By autumn. We will be settled before the child is born."

"The boy," she said.

He nodded. "The boy. But let me tell you of the present. Or the almost present." She took his arm again and they resumed walking. "An invitation arrived in this morning's mail."

She stopped and turned to him excitedly. "From the Sindens?"

He nodded. "We are invited to visit at Newport, toward the end

156

of July." (*The Velázquez hangs just inside the entrance hall. These days, everything goes to Newport! You must not be the exception!*)

She was delighted; surprised the Sindens would be ready to entertain guests so quickly, but clearly pleased with the invitation. Not, however, half as pleased as he. A trip to the United States had already become a definite part of his plan, and this sudden invitation would give that trip a pleasant spin.

His destination was once again La Terre Ferme, but when the Skiff turned into the rue Notre Dames des Champs he decided first to see if Chaudron had, as he'd promised to three days ago, rid himself of Senora Schultz.

He had not. When Valfierno let himself in without knocking the woman was sitting in a corner of the studio, sewing a patch on a pair of trousers. Chaudron was clearly embarrassed. He turned to the woman and asked her to leave while he talked privately with the Marquis. She calmly set her materials on the floor and rose, smoothing her skirt. "I shall be downstairs, with Nicole. I shall wait till you come." And she left.

When the door had shut, Valfierno turned to the painter. "You leave for New York in two weeks. You know the need for secrecy."

The need was clear, and had been clearly explained. Either Perugia or Farid, whom he was about to enlist, might say anything if caught, regardless of promises to the contrary. Valfierno would be secure because he was known to both men only as Colonel Almazàn, a phantom who would be completely untraceable. But both Farid and Perugia knew Chaudron very well, so his only protection would be to leave the country under an assumed name. Toward that end Chaudron had acquired a convincing forged passport, aged and filled with stamps and seals. But if Senora Schultz (or anyone else) ever learned the name on that passport, all the planning in the world would be worthless. "Have you forgotten all this so quickly?"

Chaudron shrugged. "I have my needs."

Valfierno slammed his open hand against the wall. "Impossible! I won't hear of it! Once you are safely in New York, accommodate your needs with anyone you please. But for now there must be no one."

Chaudron nodded forlornly.

The Marquis softened and touched his shoulder. "My friend, if this all goes as incredibly well as we know it can, there may be still more money at the end for you. I promise nothing, but your efforts will not be forgotten. You have dealt with me long enough to know that I know when and how to be generous."

Chaudron brightened at this lure, and promised again to do what he must. Valfierno left.

In the street, he waved off his driver, who climbed back into the Skiff and drove slowly behind him as he made his way the hundred yards down the street to La Terre Ferme. He'd timed it to arrive shortly after noon and when he pushed open the door Farid looked up from his sweeping.

"We have things to discuss," the Marquis said crisply. "I need nothing to eat or drink, but I do need you to sit down." Farid propped his broom against the wall and started obediently toward the table where Valfierno had sat. "And if anyone tries to come in," the Marquis continued, "send them away. You are not open today until we have finished."

Farid nodded and took a seat.

"Now," the Marquis said, all business, "your figure was sixty thousand francs."

Farid nodded, prepared for the much smaller offer he was sure he was about to hear.

"You would sell for less, I know, but no matter," Valfierno said. "Let me come quickly to the point: how would you like *twice* sixty thousand francs, without having to sell your place at all?"

Farid stared at him for a moment, letting the words repeat themselves in his head. Then he asked: "What would I have to do?"

Valfierno told him.

14

*H*is life was divided in two so neatly that it was something he never thought about. Half of him was the doting husband and father-to-be, beaming happily when his young wife guided his hand to where he might feel the joy of fetal kicks, while the other half remained the Marquis de Valfierno, calmly planning the details of a theft so bold it would blare from unbelieving headlines around the world.

The more the planning half reviewed the details, the more convinced he became that an element was missing: his team of thieves should have a captain. And the only man for the job was the man he still thought of as a boy, Miguel. No one was quicker; no one more resourceful.

By the purest chance, Valfierno arrived at the Chateauroux-Privas house at the perfect time. Mme. Privas was upstairs resting, attempting to rid herself of another of the ghastly headaches that seemed to beset her with increasing frequency, and a wildly impatient Miguel was pacing furiously as he complained of having been asked for the fourth time this week to read her into drowsiness.

"I can hardly read Spanish, let alone French," he said, wheeling toward the seated Marquis, whose chin rested on his hands atop his gold-crowned ivory cane. "But my voice soothes her, she says, no matter how badly I stumble. I cannot much longer endure this endless smothering, these humiliating demands."

The Marquis smiled, pleased at the aptness of the opening. "Perhaps it will not be necessary for too much longer."

"Necessary or not, comfortable or not, it cannot go on. What do you mean?" The last was said as the Marquis' words finally made their way through the veil of Miguel's impatience.

A look from the Marquis suggested that Miguel dismiss the servant who had set out the tea things and now stood stiffly by. Miguel did so, amazed at himself for having already said far too much, astonished at how these people became part of the furniture once gotten used to. When the door slid shut behind the exiting figure, Valfierno leaned forward and quickly detailed his plan. Miguel was as wide-eyed as Valfierno had known he would be.

"But how will you sell it?" asked Miguel.

"I expect no difficulty," replied the Marquis. "But in any event, that will not be your concern."

"No, no, of course not. Forgive me. But the concept of what you propose is just so . . . I don't know." Then suddenly he pulled himself together. "How much would I be paid?"

"How much would you expect?"

Miguel responded quickly. "Nothing less than half a million francs."

Valfierno smiled. "Clearly, I should not have asked. I have never known you to be shy." As it happened, Valfierno had planned to pay exactly that amount, but he'd expected to present it as a figure beyond Miguel's wildest dreams. The huge amount had to be quickly put back in perspective. "As you must know, such a figure is out of the question."

"But the task is extraordinary," said Miguel. "You would not be coming to me if you did not think my abilities were, in their own way, as valuable as the painting itself."

Valfierno frowned to mask his amusement at the arrogant comparison. "In their own way valuable, of course, or I would not be here. But I have others to pay who have agreed to far less. And five hundred thousand francs is simply too much money."

"What others? I don't care about others. I will not settle for a penny less."

But he would, of course. And while the Marquis did not in fact intend to pay him less, there was still some work to be done. "I can offer you two hundred thousand."

"Two hundred? I think not." And Miguel turned away and walked a few paces with his hands behind his back. "Three hundred thousand," he said, still looking away.

"Face me," the Marquis said quietly.

The boy turned back.

"We will end this dickering at two hundred fifty. That is what you will be paid."

Miguel thought for a moment, then shrugged. "I could not have resisted the challenge for even less." He smiled. "You counted on that."

"I counted on nothing. I am a businessman, not a mind reader."

Miguel waved his hand, dismissing the subject. "But I must be in charge. I can make no compromise on that. That will be clear to the others?"

Valfierno nodded.

The boy's face suddenly clouded. "And if we are caught?"

Valfierno shrugged. "You will tell the police that you were the one who planned it, you enlisted the other two. And you will be paid as if you'd succeeded. But if I were you, I should take great pains not to be caught."

Miguel grinned again. "There is no chance that will happen. And with my money"—he looked around—"I shall leave all of this." He sobered again. "I must be paid beforehand."

The Marquis sighed. "My friend, that is not possible. A sum that large must come later, after I've received my payment."

Miguel shook his head. "Then I will not risk it. I must know I have my money whether I succeed or not."

"I've promised you would."

"But what if for some reason you cannot. I must know that I'm protected."

Valfierno thought for a moment. "All right, then," he shrugged.

"Your money in advance. And one further thing: I have reconsidered your payment. I will pay you the figure you originally asked; five hundred thousand francs. I will pay that sum because that is what you want."

Miguel grinned and came to him and extended his hand. "You will not regret it," he said fervently.

Valfierno rose and shook hands with him. "I would not have regretted it at the lower figure. This way, *you* will not regret it."

With a length of 883 feet, a beam just shy of 100 feet, and accommodations for nearly fourteen hundred passengers, the White Star *Olympic* was the largest ocean liner afloat. Next year it would share that distinction with its nearly identical sister ship, *Titanic.*

The *Olympic* had completed its first transatlantic round-trip on June 30, 1911, and was due to depart Southampton again on July 3, with the Marquis de Valfierno and his wife aboard, as well as Yves Chaudron.

The two parties would be traveling separately, the men having agreed that it would be better if Rosa Maria had no idea Chaudron was on the same ship. Chaudron booked passage in second-class, where he would be unlikely ever to cross paths with the happy couple.

On the day of departure Chaudron boarded early. He carried a carpetbag suitcase that seemed small for an extended stay, and an antique walnut nightstand that he held with his left arm through the openwork above the shelf. He declined a porter's offer of help.

An hour later, the Marquis and his young bride strode up the first-class gangplank burdened only by a small utility case the Marquis carried, their several trunks having been sent ahead with instructions as to which two pieces were to be placed in their staterooms.

From his spot on the bridge, the Captain looked down through his field glasses and surveyed the arriving first-class passengers, trying to match appearances with the names he'd gone over on the passenger list. When he saw the Marquis and Mme. Valfierno he stopped for a longer look, then handed the glasses to the purser standing beside him. "That handsome pair halfway up—the older man with the beautiful young woman. You see them?" It took the Purser a moment, but then he nodded. "Find out their names. From the look of them I must be attentive." The Purser nodded, handed the glasses back, and started down to the deck.

And thus it was that a pleasant journey was assured, and that at the Captain's table the first night out the Marquis de Valfierno would be introduced to a banker from Chicago who'd just been to London for the coronation of George V; and that later both men would recall they'd once had dealings in Mexico City.

Before he'd left Paris, the Marquis had gone to the Galerie Arlette to seek Mme. Valency's help in selecting the perfect date for the planned theft. It was to be a two-day operation, with the three men entering the Louvre on a Sunday, then waiting till the following morning to remove their prize. Monday was cleaning day, with a security staff one-tenth the normal size.

"But *which* Monday is the question, and for that I turn to you." It was her skills as an astrologer that he sought, and when she realized that she burst into laughter.

"You have me confused with the woman you knew in Mexico City," she said. "I now believe in my own abilities, no longer in mumbo-jumbo."

It was a response he had not expected, and he took it as something of a rebuff. "Well then, since you no longer practice your skills, you are of no use to me." He stood up and started to leave.

She came to him and put her hand on his arm. "Stay a few minutes. You will be leaving the country soon enough."

"And that will matter to you?"

"Of course it will. I will be left with no one to talk to."

Valfierno smiled. "Nonsense. You will have Alfred Picard."

She looked at him reproachfully. "He is a sweet man. And you might thank me for my efforts with him."

Valfierno bowed in mock respect. "Madame, you were magnificent. We could not have succeeded without you."

"You may take me seriously or not. Such things no longer matter to me."

The Marquis sobered at once. "Seriously, of course. You know that in all matters, yours is the one opinion I must have." He leaned forward and kissed her lightly. "Tell me, do you still see him?"

"Alfred?" She shrugged. "From time to time. He is quite fond of me, and in some ways I am of him. But I am careful to offer no encouragement. He knows he and I are friends, and will be no more than that."

Valfierno nodded. "Of course. It could be nothing more."

She stepped back and cocked her head. "Why? Is it his appearance you think a woman finds offensive? What nonsense that would be. Don't you understand how quickly such things become invisible?"

Valfierno found himself deeper into this subject than he'd meant to be. "Of course," he muttered.

"Or could it be his age?"

"He is certainly not young."

"Indeed not. He is sixty-eight."

Valfierno seemed surprised.

"Yes, I know, you thought him older. Not just his goiter, but everything about him makes him seem older. But in fact he is just ten years older than you, twenty-one years older than I am. In fact, if age is to be considered, Alfred Picard and I are far closer in years than you and— What separates the two of you? Some forty years?"

The Marquis picked up his hat from the table and fingered the brim. "I don't know what I have done to anger you. We will talk another time before I sail."

"Yes. Another time," she said stiffly. And the Marquis took his leave, disturbed by the turn the conversation had taken, and unaware as he pulled the door shut behind him of the eyes that noted his departure, and of the man who followed him home.

The Marquis de Valfierno and his bride had been ensconced for nearly a week in the largest guest suite at Belvedere, the Sindens' Newport pleasure dome, by the time the theft occurred.

The theft of a grand object would seem to require a scheme equally grand, a masterpiece of ingenuity well beyond the capacity of all but the brilliant few. And perhaps Valfierno's plan fits that description in some way we lesser mortals fail to understand. But on its surface it seemed simple enough. It involved a key, a storeroom, and three white smocks.

In Paris, the heat wave that had smothered the city for much of the summer had abated by the middle of August, and by Sunday, August 20, the weather was mild enough so that no one perceived anything outlandish in the outer coat worn by each of the three men who entered the Louvre at different times and through different gates late that afternoon.

At a little after three-thirty Miguel came in through the Porte des Lyons along the Seine, nodding pleasantly to the guard at the gate. As he stepped inside, his hands went absently to his pockets, seeking the reassurance of the water bottle in his left-hand pocket, and the ham-filled baguette in his right. Suddenly it didn't seem nearly enough food to last through the night. But it was too late now.

A few minutes later at the Pavillon Sully, Farid entered the museum with what he imagined to be a tourist's saunter, and he, too, discreetly patted his provisions: a bottle of red and some loosely wrapped cheese, meat, and bread.

Perugia, of course, had forgotten his food. He made that discovery as he entered at the Porte Denon. But that concern was quickly forgotten as he felt his false mustache slip badly. He pressed it back into place and held it there to guard against further problems. He was sure he must look foolish with his fingers to his upper lip, but no one seemed to notice.

Miguel and Farid had separately been to the Louvre in the preceding week and walked the route to the Salle Duchâtel, but Perugia's long-time familiarity with the building had made such rehearsal unnecessary.

The arrival time of the three had been staggered so that if there were still visitors in the Salle Duchâtel that near to closing time, the normal turnover would be such that no one would be present to witness more than one of them stepping casually into the storeroom. And if a guard happened to be standing near, a moment's wait would allow time for his normal rounds to draw him elsewhere.

By the time Perugia arrived at four o'clock, the gallery was empty. The museum closed at four.

There was no window in the narrow inside room, and no sooner had the door shut behind Perugia, cutting out the light, than there was a loud clatter as an easel went tumbling.

"Hold still!" Miguel cautioned in a strong whisper.

"I can't see!" said Perugia.

"Be quiet. If your clumsiness isn't heard your voice will be."

"Who will hear? There is no one outside."

"Be still!" Miguel commanded, louder than he'd meant to. He went back to his hoarse whisper. "How do we know who may be passing?"

"We must whisper all night long?"

"Or say nothing at all."

"Or sleep," said Farid.

The sound of the Egyptian's voice coming out of the dark pierced the rehearsed equanimity with which Perugia had determined to greet him. This was the man for whom Sophie had abandoned him, and although she had since been replaced in both his own bed and Farid's, he could not help reacting to the man. His thoughts were interrupted by the unexpected sound of a match being struck, and then the sudden glow of a votive candle in Miguel's hand. Seen now for the first time, the reality of Farid's quite ordinary face seemed easier to accept than the devil who lived in his fantasy. Perugia turned to Miguel and pointed to the candle.

"Will that last all night?" he whispered.

"There are two more in my pocket." And Miguel smiled as he noticed the tilt of Perugia's mustache. "You may remove those ridiculous whiskers."

Perugia's hand went to his upper lip. "Oh." And he removed it. "No one recognized me, I can tell you that."

"Excellent," said Miguel in the whisper all three would use the rest of the night. "Now, we must have some rules. There is the toilet behind you, but it cannot be flushed until at least eight o'clock. By then almost everyone will be out of the building."

"How will we know eight o'clock?"

Miguel opened his coat and took from his vest the handsome Breguet that Mme. Privas had given him for his birthday in June. Without opening the case, he touched the repeater button and the watch chimed gently four times. "Four," he said. Then came the quarter hour signal. "And a quarter." Then two quick dings. "Plus two minutes. Seventeen minutes past four o'clock."

"Let me see that," said Perugia, reaching out.

Miguel pulled it away. "It stays with me."

"Has the watch no hands?"

"Of course it has." And Miguel snapped open the case to show him.

Perugia looked at it admiringly. "Is it not easier to tell the time this way?"

"It is," agreed Farid.

"Perhaps," Miguel whispered grudgingly, "but what if we lose the light?"

"You have two more candles."

Miguel put the watch away. "And one more thing about the toilet. We must agree to use it for nothing but standing business."

The two men nodded.

With their eyes fully accustomed to their surroundings, the one small candle provided a surprising amount of light. Miguel picked up the candle and moved it closer to the toilet.

"It was better before," Farid said.

"I want it away from the entrance. If it's too close, someone passing might notice an edge of light around the door."

Farid nodded, and Perugia slid his back down along the far wall and settled to the floor.

"Yes," said Miguel, "that's good. We might as well get comfortable. We won't eat anything till nine o'clock . . ."

"You said eight," Perugia grumbled.

"At eight we pee," Farid corrected him.

"We must wait till nine to eat?" Perugia had forgotten he'd brought nothing with him.

"Till nine," Miguel insisted. "The night will be too long otherwise."

All three men found something reassuring in Miguel's instructions. A sense of order had been established. Miguel had not thought of it that way, but he sensed it as he heard himself lay down the rules. The three men settled themselves into various positions on the floor, each sprawled in the unique manner his body sought. Nothing more was said for several minutes. Then the whispering began again.

Farid: "I admit I'm excited that it's finally begun."

Perugia: "It doesn't begin till morning."

Farid: "It has *begun*. We're here, inside, and nobody knows."

Miguel: "You make it sound like a game."

Farid laughed. "A game of course, unless we are caught."

Miguel: "That will not happen."

Farid shrugged. "As you say."

Miguel shifted to a new position. There was no escaping the fact the floor was hard. "It will not happen, but if it should, let's say again what we will tell them."

Farid: "We were recruited by you—"

Miguel interrupted. "No, not you. Perugia."

Perugia: "By me?"

Miguel, sharply: "No! I want *you* to tell me what you will say if we are caught."

"If we are caught we will say we were recruited by you."

Miguel: "Was anyone else involved in the plan?"

Perugia shook his head.

Miguel: "Exactly. And after we've split up, if you are caught with the painting . . ."

Farid: "He did everything by himself. Alone."

"Alone," echoed Perugia. "I will say I stole it by myself. There was no one else."

Miguel nodded and the three men fell silent again. This night would be endless; especially these hours before they allowed themselves to pass the time with sleep.

Perugia: "What time is it?"

Miguel, snapping: "I cannot look every second."

Farid: "You don't *need* to look."

Perugia: "No. Let us hear the chimes."

Miguel took the watch from his vest. He pressed the button and all three listened carefully.

"I lost count," said Perugia when the chiming had finished.

Farid, impatiently: "It lacks three minutes of six o'clock."

Perugia nodded and Miguel put the watch away.

By eight o'clock Perugia had fallen asleep and Farid was nodding.

Miguel roused them both. "It is time for the toilet," he said. "But listen . . ."

"I need no instructions," Perugia grumbled.

"Hear me," insisted Miguel. "We will all three use the toilet and then flush only once. Farid first, then me, then Perugia."

"Why must I be last?"

Miguel thought it best not to tell him it was so he would not forget and pull the chain too soon. "Because someone must be."

When they were done Miguel imposed absolute quiet for several minutes, so they could hear if anyone in the building had noticed the noise and come to investigate. Apparently no one had.

There was no more sleeping between then and nine o'clock, when their only meal was to be eaten. As he felt the hour approach, Miguel took out his watch and opened it so they could watch the minute hand creep toward its destination. Just before the hour, Perugia remembered he had no food and he made an announcement to that effect.

"Are you out of your mind?" Miguel shouted. The others shushed him. "Why no food?" he whispered hoarsely.

"I ran part of the way and it fell from my pocket. A street urchin snatched it."

Farid: "That is pathetic."

But Miguel was resigned. "Never mind. We will make do with what we have." He started laying out his supplies on the floor and Farid did the same.

Perugia: "That will go nicely three ways."

The other two looked at each other, and Farid, the experienced restaurateur, divided things up. When he'd finished, the three of them devoured what there was, passing around the bottles of wine and water. Then Miguel announced they would now go to sleep, and would use the toilet only once more, when they awoke.

There was no morning light to wake them in their windowless room, but for Miguel, at least, there was no danger that he'd oversleep. His eyes had popped open every hour through the night, and they opened now just as the last of the candles flickered toward its end. It was twenty minutes past six. There were deep near-snores fluttering from the other two and it took several pokes to wake them and then another moment for them to remember where they were.

Miguel picked up his coat and reached inside the lining where he'd stored the white smocks. He passed one to each of the others and began putting on his own. The smocks were their safe passage through the Louvre, the uniform that every workman wore, the magic cloak that would render them invisible.

Miguel gathered their now superfluous outer coats intending to bundle them when Perugia grabbed his own coat from the pile and retrieved his mustache from the pocket. Miguel took the coat back and laid it on top of the others on the floor. Then he placed the remains of last night's meal in the middle and rolled the coats into as small a package as he could, securing it by tying the sleeves. It had been arranged that this was what he would carry while the other two dealt with the heavy frame-encumbered painting; someone would need his hands free for opening doors and doing whatever else might need to be done, and his artificial leg made him the one.

Perugia's mustache would not stay in place, and Miguel finally lost patience and ripped it off. "If someone recognizes you, you will simply say hello," he said, thrusting the mustache into his pocket.

"But what if it's someone who knows my name?"

Miguel shrugged. "When you leave here, Perugia will have disappeared."

In fact, he already had. For the past two weeks Perugia had been living under the name Ippolito Santana in a newly rented room just off the rue des Grandes Augustin. When the three of them left here and went their separate ways, Perugia would take the painting back to that room, where it would remain until someone came to collect it. That person would identify himself with the code word *Galileo*. Why Galileo? Because it had nothing to do with anything and those were always the best code words; or so the Marquis had explained it to Miguel in the final conversation that had tucked in the last loose ends.

"Now," said Miguel sharply, investing in that one word the crack of a starting pistol. "We will use the toilet one last time, flushing only once, with Perugia last. Then Perugia will step outside, still buttoning his pants. If someone's there, he will do what he must to appear busy until they leave. When no one is in sight he will come back and tap lightly on this door twice." To Perugia: "You understand?"

Perugia nodded and headed for the door. Farid grabbed his arm. "First we pee," he hissed.

When they were finished, Miguel and Farid stayed clear of the door while Perugia pushed it open with one hand as he adjusted his pants buttons with the other. He shut the door behind him and in the darkness Farid let out a sigh. "He will do this right. I know he will."

Minutes went by, or maybe only seconds, until finally there was a tap at the door, followed quickly by a double-tap.

Miguel whispered: "Perugia?"

Perugia: "Of course."

Miguel pushed the door open and the two men came out.

Perugia: "Why could I not simply have opened the door?"

"It's time for work," Miguel replied impatiently, and he turned to his left quickly and took the few steps into the Salon Carré, with the others just behind. But all three stopped when they saw through the archway that led to the Grande Galerie four men in white smocks, one of whom Perugia now whispered was the museum's head work-man, Picquet.

"Don't stand around!" Miguel whispered fiercely. "Perugia, you and I will step to the Lady and look her over carefully. Remember, we are planning to take her to be photographed." Perugia nodded and stepped toward *La Gioconda*. "And Farid, you will stand back and glance at them from time to time. If they should start this way, give us warning. If they leave in the other direction, then tell us that." And Miguel took Perugia's elbow and guided him to their objective.

"But the photographic studio is back through the room we came from. The staircase is the opposite way."

"Be quiet. And if we are questioned, still be quiet. I will do the talking." And Miguel turned to the painting and began examining its frame and its closeness to the wall. He signaled Perugia to do the same. Several minutes went by and they were forced to persist in their dumb-show until finally Farid approached and told them the men were gone.

Now it was Miguel who stood by as Farid and Perugia gently urged the massive frame from the wall, Farid nearly dropping his end as it came loose, with Perugia hissing an Italian oath. Miguel helped them steady the frame and achieve a solid grip, and they started the slow march into the empty Grande Galerie; then they turned right and stopped just inside the Salle des Sept Mètres where the entrance to the staircase was. Miguel went past them and opened the door.

Once inside they put down their heavy load and took a few seconds to catch their breath and adjust their eyes to the dim light that came from the tiny smudged window halfway down. Then it was time to strip the frame from the painting, with Perugia taking the lead in disassembling what he had once helped put together.

Freed from its cumbersome structure, the painting seemed to achieve a kind of purity, a grandeur that came from standing alone. Farid picked up the wooden panel on which Leonardo had painted the likeness that had either captured this woman completely or transformed whatever she had been in life into the image by which she would be known forever. He held it at arm's length, unable to believe what he held in his hands.

"Under your smock," said Miguel, and Farid slid the wooden panel under his smock, resting it on top of his pants, inside his belt buckle. They moved the discarded frame to the farthest corner from the door, where it was not likely to be discovered too quickly, and Miguel led the trio down the winding staircase.

At the bottom they faced the same locked door Valfierno had faced many weeks ago. Miguel took out the key Chaudron had had made from the wax impression but as he brought it to the lock he saw at once it would never fit. The keyhole was not close to the zigzag shape of the key.

He whirled on Perugia. "You said you tried it."

"I did," said Perugia. "They must have changed the lock."

"Step aside," Farid said, impatiently taking a screwdriver from his pocket and stepping toward the door. He stopped suddenly as under his smock he felt the painting slip.

Perugia took the tool from Farid's hand and started to remove the doorknob. No sooner did he have it off than there was a tap on his shoulder and Miguel's whispered voice: "Someone's coming!"

Perugia fumbled the doorknob and almost dropped it, but managed finally to stuff it into his pocket, as he heard from the floor above the sounds of the stairway door shutting and then footsteps descending.

"I will talk," said Miguel. And he raised his finger to his pursed lips, reinforcing the order of silence.

The intruder wore the same white smock as they did. He stopped when he was a few steps above them and grinned broadly. "What's happening? Picked this spot for your morning rest?"

Miguel smiled. "I'm glad you've come. Some idiot has taken the doorknob and we can't get out."

"Sauvet," said Perugia, recognizing the head plumber.

The plumber stopped and squinted. "Who is that?"

"Calabrese," Perugia said quickly, having the presence of mind to give neither his real name nor the name under which he'd rented his new room.

"Yes, of course," said Sauvet, pulling out his ring of keys as he stepped toward the door. "I feel muddled this morning. Slept badly last night." His key turned the bolt easily and he then used his pliers on the shaft to do the work of the missing knob. "There." The door was open.

"Much obliged," said Miguel.

"Glad to help. Don't work too hard this morning."

"We never do," said Miguel with a grin.

The four of them exited into the Salle d'Afrique, Sauvet hurrying off to the right and the other three heading toward the Cour Visconti, an open door, and the street.

15

The blank space on the wall was noticed of course, but not really paid any heed. On Mondays the Palais du Louvre was less an exhibition space than a workplace and it was not at all unusual for a painting to have been removed from its place.

The few workmen who noticed the Lady's absence assumed she was off having something or other done, with the most common guess being that she was having her picture taken. It was not until Tuesday, the day after the theft, that anyone asked any questions.

"How should I know!" the burly guard snapped impatiently. "If you must know when she'll return, go yourself to the studio and ask."

Louis Beroud had come in early on Tuesday morning to resume work on his painting of the whole of the Salon Carré, an item for which the tourist demand seemed never to diminish. But before he could proceed he needed to have the gallery posing for him in its normal condition, with all its residents hung in their accustomed places.

Beroud asked for and received directions, and proceeded straight through the Salle Duchâtel to the closed door that led to the photography studio. There was no response when he knocked and he pushed the door open.

"Be still!" the figure under the hood commanded, and Beroud

obeyed the command. A few seconds later the photographer Fougères emerged and raised his eyebrows to Beroud, questioning the intrusion.

The painting in front of the camera was nothing Beroud recognized, but he assumed the Lady was somewhere present, awaiting her turn. "When will you be finished with *La Gioconda?*" he asked.

The photographer frowned. "Do you see her?"

Beroud shook his head.

"Then why do you interrupt?" And he raised the hood, ready to go back under.

"Wait!" Fougères turned back. "You do not have the painting here?"

"*La Gioconda?* Certainly not."

Beroud returned to the Salon Carré and reported his conversation to the same guard he'd spoken to earlier, who shrugged and started off. "Wait!" Beroud called after him. "Shouldn't somebody know where it is?"

The guard turned back. "You may be certain that somebody does," he answered, and went off to another area.

The frustrated Beroud left his paints and canvas in place and went looking for another guard. When he found someone two galleries away, he approached him waving his arms excitedly and shouted, "Someone has stolen the *Mona Lisa!*"

That did it. The man was jolted to life like Frankenstein's monster. "What? That cannot be!" And he hurried quickly to the Salon Carré, where he saw with horror the empty space and went off to sound the alarm.

The cat relieved the monotony. He welcomed her intrusion and quickly made her the center of his life.

She was small and gray and thin, but instead of letting her inadequacies dictate her personality she carried herself with the confidence of a tiger. She'd followed him up the stairs on the fourth day of his residency, just as he'd returned from his regular walk to get the newspaper. He'd left the door open and she'd slid inside. He managed to find some leftover scraps that she examined with suspicion and then devoured. The following morning he bought a small metal canister, filled it with a dipper of milk, and kept it handy in case she appeared again. She did, and from then on he was a regular stop on her daily rounds. She was not his pet, he was hers. She would eat his food and milk, spend several minutes at her morning scrub, then jump into his lap and run her quiet motor as she allowed him to stroke her for the better part of an hour. Then she'd stretch and be off again, to reappear in the late afternoon, scratch at his door, and stay for only the few minutes it took to check on his well-being. Gone then for the night, to adventures he could only imagine. He took to calling her Cordelia in the conversations he had with her. Their talks not only cemented their bond but also allowed him to hear the otherwise missing sound of his own voice. In the rest of his daily life, grunts and monosyllables sufficed. The grocer had quickly become familiar with his needs and supplied them with a minimum of talk. And the man at the kiosk had his newspapers folded and ready every morning, and handed them over without a word.

His morning walks and the time with Cordelia comprised his only activities. The walks were brief because Ramon had cautioned him to remain out of sight as much as possible. That had been at their first meeting, early in the second week after the robbery.

Perugia had been on his way home with his canister of milk under his left arm and his head in that morning's *Le Figaro* when he'd become aware of an unfamiliar man leaning against the wall at the entrance to his building. Perugia stopped short when he saw him, then continued walking past the building and around the block. When he'd circled back to his entrance the man was gone and Perugia went up to his room. Five minutes later there was a knock at the door and Perugia opened it with an eagerness that was surprising, since he was certain it would be the same man he'd just gone out of his way to avoid.

"Ippolito Santana?" Ramon inquired.

Perugia nodded and Ramon smiled. "I am someone you will be pleased to see."

"Galileo?"

Ramon laughed. "Not Galileo, but someone who knows him well." And he stepped inside. Cordelia scurried out the door before Perugia could shut it.

"Well," said Ramon, looking around. "This does not appear unpleasant."

Perugia shrugged.

"To business, then. I have come with the first part of your payment."

Perugia's face fell. "Not all of it?"

Ramon shook his head. "That is not possible. One third now. A third more in a month. And the final payment when Galileo comes for the Lady." Ramon reached into his pocket and took out an envelope and a slip of paper.

"Please count it, and then sign that you have received the correct amount."

Perugia nodded and took the envelope to the table in the corner, where he counted the money with mounting excitement. One third came to forty thousand francs, more money than he'd ever expected to see in his lifetime. He put the bills back in the envelope, accepted the pencil Ramon offered, and looked at him. "Which name?"

"Perugia."

Perugia signed and handed the paper back, and Ramon gave him the instruction about staying off the streets. "And one further thing," he said. "Remain patient. No matter how long it takes."

"When will Galileo come?"

"When he is ready. Only he knows when that will be. Again I say, remain patient."

Perugia nodded and Ramon was gone.

The newspaper accounts had begun with a small item in the late afternoon edition of *Le Temps* on Tuesday, the day after the robbery, where it was reported that the Louvre had closed to the public early that day because of what officials had announced as a broken water pipe, but what *Le Temps* claimed they had reason to believe was a stolen painting that might well have been the *Mona Lisa*.

By the following morning when Perugia picked up his copy of *Le Figaro*, the story was trumpeted on the front page, with expressions of shock, outrage, and disbelief coupled with pronouncements from assorted officials as to the firm steps that were being taken to assure recovery of the lost masterpiece: checkpoints on every road leading out of the country (was that possible?), elaborate searches of every ship leaving port. In addition, of course, every vessel that had sailed since the date of the theft would be thoroughly examined at its debarkation point, gone over with that fabled fine-toothed comb officials keep handy for these situations. Everything possible would be done; no stone would be unturned. And as for the thieves, the public need have no doubt they would be apprehended and made to suffer for this despicable, heinous, unforgivable crime against the people of France!

Perugia was shaken as he read it; *he* knew who the police were looking for even if they did not. But his calm returned when just as he put his paper down Cordelia gave her face a final wipe and sprang into his lap asking to be fondled, and as he stroked her he could feel the animal's utter confidence flow from her strong body through his hand and up his arm in a warm electric stream that soothed and steadied.

Not all of the newspaper accounts were somber. Four weeks after the robbery the *Paris-Journal* published this suggestion for a public notice to be displayed in every museum in France:

In the Interest of Art
And for the Safeguarding of the Precious Objects
THE PUBLIC
Is Requested to Be Good Enough to
WAKE THE GUARDS
If they are found to be asleep.

And a few days later, the same *Paris-Journal* printed a photograph of the Cathedral of Notre Dame, altered to show one of its towers missing. The caption: COULD NOT THIS HAPPEN TOO?

That same day in the more sober *Le Figaro* Perugia read that the renowned criminal investigator Alphonse Bertillon had been brought into the case; the same Bertillon who had testified as a handwriting expert in the Dreyfus case; had invented anthropometry, the system of identifying criminals through body measurements; and who in recent years had focused his considerable skills on the science of fingerprints. This Bertillon had examined the glass that had covered the

178

stolen painting and had found a thumbprint presumably left by the burglar. Police files would be searched for a print that matched.

That news sent a shudder through Perugia so profound that Cordelia turned to question him. He explained the problem in a low, confiding voice. Twice he'd been arrested for minor offenses by the Paris police: The first time three years ago on suspicion of robbery, a charge the police could not substantiate (they released him after twenty-four hours), and again the following year during a loud disagreement with a streetwalker when he was found to be in possession of an illegal weapon (a knife) and had been thrown in jail for a week. On each of these occasions his fingerprints had been taken, and those patterned loops and whorls now cowered in the files of the Paris police.

But, he reassured himself, the name on his card would be Perugia, and any search for Perugia would end at a blank wall. Still, he was uncomfortable.

As the days went by without the feared knock at the door he slowly began to relax again, and as fear subsided, boredom began. One way to fight it was to draw a calendar on a flattened paper bag and then each morning tick off another day in the march toward the promised second visit of Galileo's friend. That visit occurred exactly as scheduled, and as he later counted his money he found himself pleased with his astonishing financial position. He'd spent almost none of his first payment and now had in excess of seventy-nine thousand francs, an amount he'd never imagined he'd hold in his hand, and there was still another payment to come.

But the feeling of well-being could not alone fill the emptiness of the passing days, and in spite of Ramon's warning he found himself more and more often wandering outside his room, restlessly roaming the streets. He began inquiring about work in the neighborhood shops, but times were not easy and there were no jobs for a man who had no past.

No jobs, that is, that paid. But since money was not now the primary goal he did not hesitate when the perfect situation unexpectedly appeared.

On the rue Christine he had every day passed a long-shuttered gallery on his way back to his room. But one Monday morning the little gallery's front door was wide open and inside a light was on. Curiosity lured him to the doorway and then inside, where his presence startled the tall, black-suited man who'd been standing with his back to him.

Perugia quickly apologized for the intrusion and in the moment's awkwardness introduced himself by the name he'd been born with. Too late to call it back.

"I did not expect anyone," the tall man said.

"I was curious. I have never seen this door open before."

The tall man eyed him coldly. "I hadn't realized I'd left it so."

But Perugia did not really hear him. He was busy looking around. Most of the gloomy paintings displayed around the tiny gallery were dark landscapes, copies most likely, and not even as interesting as the canvases that had been brought to him for framing on the rue Notre Dame des Champs. (That establishment had long since passed from his control. While he'd been away Sophie had simply locked the door and left it when she'd gone off to wherever it was she'd gone.)

The tall man cleared his throat ostentatiously and Perugia looked back at him. "My father was Charles Sellier," he said, as if that explained everything. "I now own this place. As you can see, it is not open for business."

It was an invitation to leave, but Perugia had not been listening; he was too busy staring through the archway that led to a room in the back. A well-lit room; undoubtedly a workroom.

"We are not open," the tall man said emphatically.

"Yes, of course." Perugia nodded. "But as I am here, perhaps I might look around."

The tall man looked at him narrowly. "You are nothing if not persistent. Be quick, then. I must leave very soon." And he went back to examining the contents of the dusty cabinet in front of him.

Perugia started at once for the archway and as he went through he was delighted by what he saw. It was indeed a workroom, brightly lit by a large window. There were tools laid out neatly on shelves above a modest workbench, and panels of wood tucked into bins underneath, arranged by size by someone who cared about such things. He stepped to the bench and reached up for a plane that was lying on its side. Except for its layer of dust it seemed in wonderful condition. Everything did.

He stepped back into the gallery and addressed the tall man standing with his back to him. "Excuse me," he said, and the son of Charles Sellier turned to him. "What will you do with this place?"

"Try to sell it, of course. Although I can't think what there is that would interest anyone."

"Have you thought of opening again?"

He shook his head solemnly. "I could not run a place like this."

The response was exactly what he'd hoped for. "But I could," he said. "I know a little. Perhaps I could run it for you."

Sellier the Younger frowned at that. It had not been anything he'd expected.

"I would not need wages," Perugia went on quickly. "We could arrange some kind of commission."

The tall man tapped his fingers on the cabinet absently. "How do I know you don't mean to steal from me?"

"Do I look like a thief?" Perugia asked, with an indignation to which he was hardly entitled, given his recent activities.

The tall man looked him up and down, his eyes narrowed so as to see through to his very soul. Finally he sighed, either satisfied or convinced he had nothing to lose, and after some further conversation, an arrangement was made.

Perugia rigged a standard shop bell that rang in back when someone entered, and after dusting and sweeping the gallery into presentable condition he spent most of his time at the worktable. First he made, to exacting measurements, a slender slipcase for the walnut panel that had spent the last six weeks under his bed wrapped in old bed linens. Cork runners down the sides of the case would keep the painting pressed firmly in place when the top section was fitted. He stained the outside surfaces and allowed a full week for them to dry before he brought the pieces to his room and fitted Mme. Lisa into her new home. Then he slid her back under the bed.

Next he built himself a modestly sized wooden trunk, again laying out the work with great care and designing it so the slipcase would fit exactly into the bottom; appear to *be* the bottom. There was at this time no plan to take the Lady anywhere. The construction was simply something to keep him busy. Unless of course his inner mind had been spinning fantasies that would only later pass into his consciousness.

His labors in the back room were rarely interrupted by the front doorbell, and when he'd finished with his first projects he went on to others in a constant effort to keep busy: a set of shelves for a corner of his room, on which he organized his clothing; a narrow étagère with carved pillars that he offered for sale in the gallery out front; an elaborate set of library steps that folded into a leather-trimmed stool that so delighted him he brought it home. Then he started on a small house for Cordelia that he knew she'd never enter but that began to take on an importance of its own as he rounded the corners and trimmed them with vertical carvings, much as he'd done with the étagère. He added a chimney with the sides scored to suggest bricks. He cut small windows in the sides and sealed them with tiny squares of beveled glass. He painted the whole a deep brownish-red, then sanded it all down to the wood again and painted it bright yellow. Finally he added her name, not simply painted, or even applied, but painstakingly carved into the side and finished in a yellow paint just slightly darker than the whole.

He brought it home and of course she never went inside. She sniffed around it, fascinated by this addition to the room, and then ignored it. He tried setting her food inside, but she sat outside and waited till he reached in and put the bowl back in its accustomed place.

Meanwhile, almost no one stopped in to the little gallery, and of those who did, fewer still reached into their pockets.

He had of course arranged his working hours around Cordelia's habits, which meant arriving at the gallery no earlier than ten each morning and shuttering the place at four so he'd be back in his room for her afternoon visit, then returning to work for an hour in the late afternoon. But as autumn deepened and stole his light, he no longer went back, so he was fortunate enough to be in his room the evening Mathilde knocked.

Mathilde appeared at his door with streaks of blood running down her bare left arm and both hands full of a squirming Cordelia.

"This cat is yours?"

The knock on the door had been loud enough and angry enough to have prepared him for the strident tone of the question, but he was uncertain how to respond. Was Cordelia indeed his cat? The question seemed especially pointed since an admission of ownership seemed at the moment likely to carry its burden. Still, he could not deny the relationship. He nodded tentatively.

"You see what he's done?"

He looked at her arm, then straight up at her. "She," he said, at which point Mathilde thrust the cat at him and he took her.

"My arm will be scarred!" she said. "What do you plan to do about that?"

Perugia put Cordelia down and the cat, hating all forms of tension, raced out the door seeking calmer surroundings. Perugia led Mathilde to the sink and washed her arm, which when cleaned revealed the source of the bloody mess to have been nothing worse than two quite small scratches. He tore strips from a bedsheet and wrapped them tightly around the wounds, stanching what was now just a trickle of blood, and turning Mathilde into a calmer and much more attractive woman.

Attractive, it must be said, not because of any remarkable physical beauty, but because of a not-unpleasant face and figure, and the fact that Perugia had not been this close to a woman for some considerable time. In a moment, she was seated in the room's only chair and had begun describing her encounter with Cordelia, who she had found tearing apart the bags of refuse Mathilde had left for a moment in front of her door, and spreading the contents all over the hall before Mathilde had grabbed her and suffered her wounds.

Perugia made the proper apologies and the two spent a pleasant hour getting acquainted before Mathilde excused herself and returned to her room upstairs, and Perugia was left with the feeling that Cordelia's attack could not have produced more pleasant results.

The relationship flourished at once, with one or the other spending time, and often the night, in the other's room several times a week. There were moments when they were together in his bed when Perugia found himself wondering how the Florentine noblewoman hiding beneath must feel having such activity going joyously forward no more than a foot above her head. He concluded she'd be pleased.

The three events that triggered his decision did not happen together, but their cumulative effect was nonetheless overwhelming.

First, Mathilde vanished; simply disappeared. His knocks on her door produced no answer, neighbors knew nothing. Each evening, his attention was caught by every set of footsteps on the stairs, but none had the light rhythmic tread he listened for. He continued to listen, past the point of hopelessness.

By now it was midway through 1912, almost a year since the theft, and stories of that incredible event appeared less frequently, crowded aside by the normal tumble of newer events.

For Perugia, no longer having Mathilde to occupy his days made him increasingly impatient with the fact that Galileo had failed to make his promised appearance. True, no date had been given, but a year seemed a very long time.

More months slid by. In January Raymond Poincaré became President of France and in March Woodrow Wilson became President of the United States. On the same day Wilson assumed office, Sellier, the owner of his shop, suddenly announced that he had sold it and was moving to Rouen, where he would wed a second cousin and accept a post in the city administration.

This was the second of the three blows, and much more devastating because it ended the daily routine that had shaped his life for so long. He thought about renting another space, and even examined several, but nothing seemed right and he allowed himself to slip back into aimlessness.

The third and final blow struck in late October when a neighbor brought him the body of the dead Cordelia. She'd been struck by a carriage and had been lifeless when his neighbor found her. Later that night Perugia sealed the body into the never-used yellow house he'd built for her, and the next morning he carried the unlikely coffin to a corner of the cimitière du Montparnasse and quickly dug a shallow grave.

Now he was left with nothing. After two weeks of aching loneliness he began to devise his plan.

He'd begun taking out the painting at night, propping it against the wall, and studying it endlessly. He became familiar with every detail of the murky landscape that swirled behind the glorious Florentine face. She was a daughter of Italy, and he was a son; the fifteen years he'd lived in France had not changed that. There was a kinship between the two of them, and between the painting itself and the land of its birth. He was thinking exactly that one night when there was a sharp rap at his door.

He quickly swaddled the Lady in bed linens and tucked her beneath his bed. The rapping came again, more urgently. "Yes, yes," he said, and he went to the door.

It was the messenger of Galileo. "I hope I do not disturb you," said Ramon.

"Of course not," Perugia assured him.

"May I come in?"

Perugia nodded and stepped aside.

"I know you were not expecting to see me again, but Galileo has been detained longer than he'd expected. He asks you to be patient, and he wants you to be paid the remainder of your fee."

Perugia's face lit up at that, and Ramon took out an envelope and laid it on the table. "This discharges his obligation, but he wants you to know that since this delay has been so much longer than he'd expected, and he will not be able to pick up the painting for at least several more weeks, there will be a fourth payment in the same amount when he arrives. He hopes that pleases you."

Perugia assured him that it did, then took out the money and counted it, nodding as he put it back. Ramon excused himself, and left.

16

*T*here would be no parade. Just a simple ceremony here in the Sig-
noria, on a day as crisp and bright as this one. He would receive a
medal, of course, bending forward gracefully to allow the King himself to drape the bright ribbon around his neck. His acceptance
speech would be brief; he knew he was not an eloquent man. *"This
unknown son of Italy has returned with his country's most famous daughter. Long
live Victor Emmanuel!"* And the band would burst forth, its exuberant
brass blending with the cheers of the adoring crowd.

But on this December morning of 1913 the Piazza was quiet; just
a few early bustlers hurrying to open an office or otherwise impress
some city official. Perugia's train had arrived just after six and he'd
hurried straight here, dragging his wooden trunk with him. A longer
walk than he'd bargained for, but excitement had eased his way.

He set the trunk down and looked around him, drinking in all of
it. There before him was the *David,* and he was overwhelmed by its
magnificence. He was unaware that the statue before him was a
copy, that the original had long since been moved indoors to the
safety of the Accademia; for him, this was the marble into which
Michelangelo had breathed life, and so for him this *David* held all its
power.

He was here to bring home his country's most famous work of art.
She would hang in the Uffizi in a place of honor. It was where she

belonged. He stuck his hand in his pocket to touch the letter again, and lightly ran his finger over the emblazoned crest that spoke of influence, importance.

The journey had been simple. His wooden chest had been opened for a cursory look at the border and he'd been waved right through, his appearance having seemed nothing unusual: an Italian working man returning from a stint in France. Even his brand-new passport raised no questions; undoubtedly a replacement for one whose pages had been filled with official stamps that recorded many such comings and goings. Whatever special security precautions had once been in place at the border had simply dissolved in the current of time.

He inquired at the desk of a hotel just off the Piazza but found the rates too high for his liking. The desk clerk did not seem surprised. Perugia started to leave, but the clerk called him back and wrote something on a slip of paper—the name of a hotel across the river. Perugia listened as the clerk gave him directions, and ten minutes later he was checked in to the modest Tripoli-Italia in a room that faced away from the Arno, but otherwise suited his needs.

He had not slept all night, but when he sat on the bed it was not to rest, but to look again at the letter from Alfredo Geri, the letter that had brought him here.

The sequence had begun in November 1913 when Perugia had stumbled on a small advertisement in the *Paris-Journal*. Alfredo Geri of Florence, dealer in art and antiquities, offered to purchase art objects at reasonable prices; respondents should describe in detail the item or items being offered, and could be assured of a prompt reply. A thrill had rippled through him as he'd read the notice.

There had been no writing materials at hand, but he'd gone out at once to buy what he needed, and then in a frenzied few moments wrote and posted the only letter he'd ever written in his life.

He was an Italian living in France, he'd written, who currently had in his possession the missing *Mona Lisa*. This masterpiece must be restored to its proper place in the country of its birth! The Louvre was filled with works stolen from Italy by Napoleon, and to remedy this wrong he had stolen *La Gioconda* from its place and was now prepared to escort the Lady back to her home in Florence. An urgent reply is requested. He'd signed the letter *Leonard* and put down the address that until now he'd taken such pains to keep secret. He would watch daily for the postman and claim any reply addressed to *Leonard*.

That reply might never have come if Alfredo Geri had not discussed his strange letter with his friend Giovanni Poggi, the director of the Uffizi. Both men were convinced the writer was a madman who was in possession of nothing more than a lively imagination, but Poggi was a firm believer in the logic of nothing to lose, and urged Geri to respond with the letter that drew Vincenzo Perugia to Florence.

So the Italian patriot walked happily into the trap he'd set for himself. He made his way to Geri's gallery, the location of which well-dressed Florentines had no trouble pointing him toward, introduced himself to the proprietor, escorted that gentleman back to his hotel, where to Geri's considerable surprise Perugia removed from its false-bottomed hiding place a painting that the hairs on the back of Geri's neck signaled him was genuine.

"Of course," said Perugia, "I think a reward would be only right."

"Yes. Yes, of course," said Geri, thinking ahead to his next step.

"Five hundred thousand lira would be acceptable."

Geri cocked his head and looked at him, unable to believe that any man could be so far from understanding the true nature of his own situation. "You are a remarkable man," said Geri, and Perugia felt himself filled with the kind of pride that only honor can bring.

Geri's visceral reaction to the painting was quickly confirmed when Giovanni Poggi compared it with photographs of *La Gioconda* that he'd had brought to his office at the Uffizi, and which he now examined with a large magnifying glass as Perugia and Geri stood silently by.

Finally, Poggi set the glass down. "There is no doubt of it," he said to Geri. Then he turned to Perugia. "I am grateful you have brought this to us. Wait here for a moment, please."

Perugia smiled with what would soon turn out to be inappropriate pleasure as Poggi stepped outside. It was only a moment before the museum official returned, accompanied now by three rather large policemen.

"Your passport, please," said the largest of the three.

"Mine?" asked Perugia, pointing to himself in total confusion.

"At once," the policeman said sharply.

"But I— It is back at the hotel."

"You should have it with you at all times. But no matter, we will send someone for it. Understand that as of this moment you are under arrest."

Perugia was shocked. "What for?"

"You are detained. Those are my only orders. Come with us, please."

And the other two policemen grabbed him firmly by the arms and marched him quickly out of the office, leaving Geri and Poggi standing there shaking their heads in disbelief.

And thus it was that the newfound patriotism of Vincenzo Perugia earned for him the prison cell he might well have avoided forever if he'd followed the instructions of those far wiser than he. The Italians tried him, with the agreement of the French; perhaps with the *relief* of the French, who might well have been pleased to be spared this final embarrassment. He had done the deed alone, he insisted to the court, and he was not pressed on the point. Nor was he pressed on his reason for waiting twenty-seven months to complete his act of artistic repatriation. The crime had its confessed villain, and no one wished to tarnish the triumph of his capture and the recovery of the world's most famous painting by excessive concern for loose ends.

And so Vincenzo Perugia and the most important woman in his life both wound up where they seemed to belong: the former in a prison cell in the country he professed to love, the latter back on the wall in the country she'd called home for four hundred years.

But what of the others in all of this? Till now we've followed the stolen painting, but more than two years have gone by and in that time the others have not been idle.

17

By the third day out of Le Havre, the Marquis de Valfierno had begun his negotiations with Milo Gallagher, president of the Cook County Mercantile Bank & Trust Company.

The weather had cleared that morning after two days of steady drizzle, and the Marquis and his young wife were taking advantage of the sunshine with a stroll on deck when they encountered Milo and Faith (the two couples had achieved first-name intimacy last night when both had dined at the Captain's table) stretched out in deck chairs. The polite Milo surrendered his chair at once to the pregnant Rosa Maria and was about to find a steward to set out additional chairs when the Marquis suggested that the ladies might enjoy relaxing and getting better acquainted while the two men strolled the deck on this beautiful day.

Rosa Maria and Faith exchanged confirming looks and announced themselves pleased with that arrangement, so the two men went off together toward the rear of the vessel. Once there they leaned against the rail and watched the swirling white patterns being carved in the ocean by the ship's giant screws.

Milo Gallagher inhaled great gulps of the pungent, surely salubrious morning air, and let go of each slowly, reluctantly. "I declare myself cured of diseases yet to be discovered," Milo intoned.

Valfierno smiled and Milo looked at him steadily, as if waiting for him to go on. When he didn't, the banker said quietly, "You are aware that you and I have met before."

Valfierno smiled. "I am. And I am pleased that you remember."

A steward had slid beside them and asked if he might get the gentlemen something. Milo turned toward Valfierno, who shook his head, then turned back. This was a steward he had not seen before. "You are new," he said. The man nodded. One of the regular stewards had come down with severe stomach cramps last night and the ship's surgeon had had to remove his appendix.

"And they dropped you down out of the sky?" Milo asked.

"I am a machinist. I do two jobs now."

Milo nodded. "American whiskey for me. Jack Daniels, a generous portion, in a large tumbler, mixed with an equal amount of distilled water." The steward bustled off and Milo turned his gaze back to the churning wake. "British ship or not, I see no reason to change my habits. But understand, I do love England. We were in London for the coronation. An impressive show, glorious and silly at once, like weddings and lawn parties. But I suppose I can understand why they love it. And, who knows, perhaps that's the secret of their greatness. Something is, and it might as well be nonsense as anything else."

He turned back to the Marquis. "Now my dear fellow, what about you? What excitement occupies you these days?"

He'd opened the door partway, and now it was up to Valfierno to enter slowly, preferably through a wider opening if Milo could be encouraged to provide it. He lived now in Paris, Valfierno explained, where he'd been fortunate in several areas of business, still of course dealing in works of art.

Milo nodded appreciatively. "If your success in business has been as fortunate as your choice of a wife, then you are to be congratulated."

The Marquis bowed. "She will be pleased with the compliment."

"When is the child due?"

"November."

"Your first?"

Valfierno nodded. "And a reminder of my need to provide for the next generation. And for the one after that."

Milo laughed and the steward appeared with his drink and proffered a slip of paper and a pencil. Milo held up his hand in a stop sign. "I am not to be bothered with that sort of thing. The purser should have told you."

The steward nodded in some confusion and put the offending slip of paper in his pocket. Then he clipped a holder over the rail and set Milo's glass in it. "Sorry, sir," he said. "Will there be anything else?"

Milo shook his head and the man hurried off, not sure he understood this arrangement but hardly prepared to challenge it.

Milo took an appreciative sip of his whiskey and set the glass back in its holder. "Tell me," he said, "are you still in the business of providing the unattainable?"

"When I can."

Milo reached into the breast pocket of his blazer and took out his card case. He handed a card to Valfierno. "You know I would always be interested in hearing from you if the circumstances warranted it."

Now the door was opened wide.

"What if I told you," the Marquis began slowly, "that your interest comes at a fortunate time."

"I would encourage you to explain."

The Marquis looked at him, having already decided how much to say, but preferring to seem unsure. Milo reached again for his drink and took another sip. "You seem to have some reluctance . . ."

Valfierno shook his head. "Just a bit of hesitation. Unnecessary with you, I know. I must, however, ask for certain—how do you say? Promises, I suppose."

"Such as?"

Valfierno shrugged. "If you are interested in what I am about to tell you, I know I can count on your discretion. But if you are not, I must have your word that what I say will go no further; will not be spoken of, even to your wife."

Milo Gallagher took another sip, a rather large one this time, and his face seemed flushed. It seemed to the Marquis that this was not Milo's first taste of alcohol this morning. "I can promise that."

Valfierno nodded. Even without this reassurance he knew he had no reason for concern. Milo Gallagher had already bought one stolen painting (or one he *thought* had been stolen). That made him vulnerable enough to guarantee discretion.

Might there not be some risk in Milo's obvious fondness for the bottle? Valfierno had quickly weighed that possibility and dismissed it; drink might be Milo's habit, but it would never be his undoing. The Marquis had watched him drink steadily last night at the Captain's table and had observed no change in either his speech or his demeanor.

So Valfierno went ahead, explaining in a few brief sentences what he planned to do, and the fact that he had been on his way to New York to find a buyer. But if Milo chose to be that buyer Valfierno's stay in America could be as relaxed as that of any tourist.

Gallagher said nothing at first, just nodded his head and pursed his lips as he drummed his fingers on his glass. He then raised the glass and drained it in one long and satisfying draft. When he finished he returned it to its holder on the rail.

"You say it all so simply, as if it were just waiting to be lifted from the wall. What if your plan fails?"

Valfierno shrugged. "The risk is not yours. If we fail, we fail at something that can never point to you. The venture involves risk. But for us, not for you."

Milo shook his head. "You do astonish one." He looked around. "Where is that steward?"

Valfierno shook his head.

"Yes, well. I'm sure he'll be back. How much do you expect to realize from the sale of this stolen treasure?"

The steward appeared and Milo handed him his empty glass. "Another," he said, and the man nodded and left.

"A very high price, I am afraid," said Valfierno.

"My dear fellow, if you're afraid at all, which hardly seems possible, it's not because of your price. In fact, I suspect that part rather pleases you. Tell me what it is."

Valfierno reached in his pocket for his card case and a pencil. He turned the card facedown on the rail and on the back drew an American dollar sign, and then the number one with a comma, and nothing more. Milo Gallagher nodded slowly and Valfierno crumpled the card and threw it in the ocean.

* * *

The Chicago banker had promised to deliver his answer before the *Olympic* reached New York, and the afternoon of the final day at sea the two men arranged to meet at the swimming pool, Milo having thought it essential that they explore this dazzling feature before the voyage ended.

The pool turned out to be of modest proportions, spare and utilitarian, a rectangular wonder whose claim to fame was not its grandeur, but the fact that it existed at all; it was the only pool to be found on any ocean liner anywhere.

The room that contained it was not much larger than the pool itself and designed only for what had been assumed would be its principal activity. The two men took their obligatory plunge and then managed to find two camp stools on which they sat facing each other as they toweled off. Milo came quickly to the point.

"I am interested, of course," he began.

"But you still have a question."

"The question is the one you might imagine. The question is money. The *question* is what a million dollars is simply out of."

Valfierno looked confused.

"It is far too much," Milo said emphatically.

Valfierno leaned back as an attendant brought them fresh towels. Milo looked up at the man. "Is anything served here?"

"I can get you gentlemen whatever you would like."

But not quickly, it was clear. Milo shook his head and the attendant left.

Valfierno dried his face again with the fresh towel, then draped it around his neck and smiled. "I think the price is really very modest," he finally said, and when Milo started to speak the Marquis held up his hand. "If the work in question, the most famous in the world, were to be sold by the Louvre on the open market it would fetch not one million, but five."

"And that five would be gladly paid; by me, by any number of people. Because that five million would buy a prize that could be owned freely, displayed in any way its owner chose, shown with pride. In one stroke it would transform its owner into a collector of international importance. It would be like having the world's most beautiful woman not as your mistress, to be visited only in secret, enjoyed only in stolen moments, but as your *wife*." Milo smiled. "Surely that is something you of all people can understand."

"Ahh, but is not the mistress sometimes the more exciting?" The Marquis carried the thought no further. He watched the unreadable face behind which yes or no was forming. Finally Milo looked at him and sighed.

"You know of course I must have it." He stuck out his hand and the two men shook. "Now, sir, the last time we did business you wanted a check in advance, with certain understandings."

Valfierno shook his head. "This time there is no need. When you read of the Lady's abduction, be prepared to write your draft within two weeks."

"You will come for it yourself?"

Valfierno shrugged. "If not me, then someone else."

"How will I know this person is from you?"

"He will have his package, of course. And you will know him because he will say he has been sent by Galileo."

Milo smiled. "Such wonderful intrigue. It almost justifies the price."

Faith Riordan Gallagher had never been a sound sleeper, but she had learned to keep her eyes shut and her breathing deep whenever her husband rose in the middle of the night. That would give him his chance to get to the bottle he kept hidden among his underthings and have his way with it in secret. His drinking had never been a threatening problem, and her averted eye, she'd convinced herself, had helped to keep it from becoming one.

He had three swigs in quick succession, then put the bottle away and went into what on shipboard he insisted on calling the head for a sip of water. Then he slipped back into his bed (there were two doubles in this enormous stateroom) and was quiet enough so he might have been asleep, she wasn't sure. Moments later he suddenly laughed out loud. Then he sat up quickly.

"Milo?"

He turned to her, confused. "Yes?"

"Were you asleep?"

"I'm not sure."

"You were laughing."

"Was I? Well then, yes. I suppose it was a dream."

"It must have been very funny."

Not all that funny, he was thinking. And not really something he wanted to discuss. "I can't remember exactly. It was all . . . I don't know. Confusing. Time to go back to sleep."

They said good-night and he lay back again and recalled the dream. It had centered on the cottage just off Lakeshore Drive that he'd bought for Faith in the days before their marriage, when their meetings had needed to be secret. Later, of course, he'd managed to arrange for the annulment that had freed him from one marriage and quickly propelled him into another. The new couple had moved into their imposing Federal home in Cedar Grove, but he'd held on to the cottage, at first because the housing market had been too soft, then simply because it was something he still wanted.

In his dream, he was back at the cottage. He'd forgotten his key, so he climbed in a living-room window and then worried that if he'd been able to do it so easily, so could anyone else. Something would have to be done about that. Then he'd gone to the kitchen, opened the cupboard, removed all the dishes, and pulled the cupboard's bottom panel toward him along its concealed tracks, revealing beneath it his hidden treasure. He'd lifted it out gently and propped it against the wall, where the softness of the late afternoon sun deepened the Lady's glow. Then suddenly he'd laughed aloud in pleasure. And awakened.

Lying here now, he realized that's where he'd hide it, and in just that way. He'd visit the cottage whenever he could, just as he had in the past.

The letter from Clara Sinden to Rosa Maria had narrowed the choice to two. *There are now so many wonderful hotels in New York that it is impossible to choose badly. But I should be happiest to think of my friends in one of the two places that have meant the most to me.*

When I was very little (five, I think) I took tea one Sunday with my parents and their friends the Brinkmans (who brought along their ten-year-old Adonis son) at what was then the brand-new Holland House, and it has forever remained for me a palace of enchantment. And of course there is the wonderful St. Regis, which had just opened its fabulous doors when I was eighteen, and so was chosen for my party. What an unforgettable evening that was!

They are personal associations, I know, but for that very reason I offer them with affection.

Their trunks had preceded them, whisked off the *Olympic* the second the ship had docked and hurried ahead. So when the Marquis stepped down from the carriage that had been sent for them he carried only his small utility case, and that item was swiftly taken from his hand by a smiling attendant so that he and his young wife might be unencumbered as they entered the flawless St. Regis Hotel. A rustle of turning figures followed the striking couple as they crossed the wide lobby in their regal parade to the enormous marble desk. The marked differences between them seemed less to set them apart than to define them as a pair: the remarkably lovely young woman who bore herself and her budding child with the pride she'd learned from the humble sisters of St. Ursula, and the much-older man whose confident smile and careless stroll seemed almost contrived to serve as counterpoint.

From behind the desk, the tall clerk smiled down. "The Marquis de Valfierno," he said, with never a doubt that this was the man he was greeting. "And Madame," with a cursory nod toward Rosa Maria. "You may sign later, if you choose, or we will send someone to your rooms."

In response the Marquis took the pen from its inkstand and the clerk turned the register toward him.

"Approximately two weeks, I believe," the clerk said, and the Marquis nodded. "I am sure you will find your stay even more pleasant than you imagined." With that the clerk stepped off the unseen box that had provided him with several extra inches and took a diminished step to his right, where he snapped his fingers toward the attendant who held the couple's utility case. As the attendant approached, the clerk turned back to the couple. "When you are ready, please pick up your telephone and we will send someone to see to the unpacking."

Rosa Maria's unpracticed English muddied the details, but the tone was unmistakable and she could not keep herself from glancing toward the Marquis with a tiny smile that broke through her efforts to contain it. It did not escape the clerk, who bowed toward her again. "Unless you prefer to do it yourself."

"Oh no," Valfierno answered on her behalf. "That will be agreeable."

The clerk smiled and bowed, and the attendant led the way to their penthouse suite.

The Marquis and his wife would be spending two weeks at the St. Regis before traveling on to Newport. Despite his unexpected good fortune on board the *Olympic* there was still a great deal of work to be done, and New York was the place to do it.

For his less visible associate, Yves Chaudron, the stay in New York would be longer, six weeks at least, and in rooms far removed from Fifth Avenue. The painter had promised to contact the Marquis as soon as he was settled in suitable quarters, which would of course be quickly. Events had been set in motion and time was important now.

As it happened, those suitable quarters had already been chosen, although Chaudron had not indicated as much to Valfierno. The chooser had been Senora Marcelline Schultz, that multinational woman with the German surname, the Spanish honorific, and the tongue that wrapped itself most comfortably around what was clearly her native French. She had preceded Chaudron by several weeks and had found both a flat and a studio on nearby streets just off lower Broadway, and had sent him both addresses.

Chaudron's driver now pulled up to the second of those addresses, the studio on Lafayette Street, where the driver helped him set his things on the sidewalk. Chaudron paid the man, then added some extra coins to the tip when the driver seemed less than satisfied.

Chaudron had come here to examine the studio first, so that if it proved suitable he might leave some essentials here without having to explain their uses. He'd always viewed explanations as tedious, and in this case they were clearly unwise.

He was still on the sidewalk juggling his baggage for the trip upstairs when a small boy of perhaps ten or eleven appeared and offered to help. "You can help by staying here," said Chaudron, in the French he suddenly realized was useless. Then, in a kind of sign language that seemed to him quite clear, he indicated that the boy should stay and watch his things while he went upstairs alone. And he did.

The studio was large and comfortable, with an enclosed bathroom—Marcelline had chosen well. It was large enough so that if need be he could stay here overnight, or even move in permanently if that later proved advisable. And the place itself was as bright as he could want.

Through the large south-facing window, he now discovered to his pleasure, he could see the Statue of Liberty. He walked to the window and took in the view with a sudden appreciation for the work that in photographs had always struck him as clumsy, and in miniature in the Seine had always seemed ridiculous. But seeing it now in the proper scale to its surroundings, standing in the spot where it had been meant to stand, there was no question that it commanded the harbor with majesty. He was admiring this view, altogether pleased to be in this new environment, when his calm was shattered by a deafening clatter from the stairwell. The meaning of the noise was instantly clear.

He rushed from the room, flew down the two flights of stairs, and came upon the sight he'd feared: the young boy who'd been meant to wait on the sidewalk watching his things was sprawled on the bottom landing, covered with the contents of his ripped carpetbag. Nearby were the remains of the walnut nightstand Chaudron had so carefully carried both on and off the *Olympic*.

The flood of oaths that sprang from Chaudron were shouted in the language the boy could not understand, but the anger behind them caused the boy to burst into tears. Chaudron sprang at once toward the scattered pieces of the nightstand and examined them quickly. Some were as splintered as he'd feared, but several, though shaken loose, were still intact. Somewhat relieved by that, and therefore calmer, he addressed himself to the boy's situation, helping him to his feet.

"I was bringing it upstairs," the boy said meekly.

"Your eye is cut," said Chaudron. The boy understood the sign language that accompanied the foreign words and his hand went to the spot above his eyebrow where Chaudron was pointing. He could feel the sticky blood, and then see it on his finger. He accepted the pocket cloth Chaudron handed him and held it against the cut, and then listened apologetically as Chaudron scolded him in French, pointing out that if he'd waited on the sidewalk as he'd been told this never would have happened.

No matter, Chaudron's gestures seemed to say, just leave, and the unhappy boy did so quickly, disappointed at not having earned the tip he'd hoped for, but consoled by the fact that even if he had it would have been in unspendable coins.

Chaudron gathered the scattered pieces of the nightstand and carried them upstairs, leaving his clothes strewn all over the staircase. For the moment, it was not the clothes that mattered.

The walnut nightstand had been painstakingly crafted by Chaudron, fitted together from panels he'd cut to size from the large walnut headboard that had finally turned up after a long search at a used-furniture store near the Church of Notre Dame de Bon Secours. He had been thrilled to find it and had willingly paid a delivery fee equal to its purchase price to have it carted to the rue Notre Dame des Champs.

He'd sanded and trimmed the old wood (unlikely to be from the sixteenth century, but a hundred years old at least), then cut the thin boards into precisely measured rectangles, laminated them into sets of three, and wound up with six sturdy finished panels. On each of these he would later paint his copy.

Examining the panels now, Chaudron determined that only one could not be salvaged, and he put that one aside. The others could be trimmed and sanded back into shape, and if any of them lost a half-inch here or there it would never be noticed by any of the six buyers, who in any event would have nothing to measure it against, or indeed any reason to do so.

The secret was kept from Senora Schultz for a little over a week.

He had immediately established a routine of coming to the studio by eight o'clock each morning, working until nearly two, then eating whatever lunch she'd bagged for him and going out to scour the neighborhood for a replacement piece of walnut for his final panel. He finally stumbled on a sideboard whose doors seemed close to right, and after several trips back to this same store persuaded the Armenian shopkeeper to sell him just the doors, having finally convinced him that he could easily replace them with some other fabrication.

It was with these large doors in hand that Chaudron reentered his studio late one afternoon to discover Senora Schultz standing in front of his easel, palette in one hand, brush in the other, working away on his second copy, which he'd barely begun.

He stood there for a moment open-mouthed, unable to believe what he was seeing. The canvas copy he'd made at the Louvre was on an easel to her right and she referred to it frequently as she blithely added highlights to *La Gioconda*'s left sleeve, which, unaccountably, she seemed to have decided to finish first. Then suddenly she stopped as she sensed him behind her and turned happily to greet him. "See what I've done while you were gone!"

There followed a brief shouting match during which he made clear his feelings on the subject in words and gestures rude enough and loud enough to reduce even the doughty Senora Schultz to tears. Tears worked their frequent magic and he ended up with his arms around her, comforting her and assuring her that her efforts had not only done no harm, but had in fact been worthy, and thus restored to favor she slid her hand inside his thigh and in a matter of just a few seconds managed to turn one emotion into another.

Afterward, as they lay entwined on the floor, he agreed that of course he respected her ability and of course he would let her finish the copy and keep it as her own. She thought his enterprise was simply making copies, to sell as such. Only several weeks later, after the theft in Paris, did she manage to put it all together.

The Marquis de Valfierno concluded his business in New York in less than the two weeks he'd allowed for it. It had gotten off to a shaky start when the first two men on his list had not only turned down his extraordinary proposition, but made it clear they wanted no further contact with him. "Not under *any* circumstances," the second man had emphasized. That last had been unsettling, but he'd spent a lifetime doing work not designed for the easily wounded so he quickly shrugged it off and proceeded down the list, successfully lining up the next five in order. Added to Milo Gallagher, that brought him to the magic goal of six, with each eager buyer believing that if the abduction of the Lady went off as planned, his would be the hands into which she'd be delivered.

They'd planned to go to Newport on Sunday, but as soon as the Marquis announced to his wife that his business was concluded she was eager to leave at once. A telegram to Clara Sinden quickly brought a return wire assuring them that their early arrival would be not just welcome, but an unexpected treat.

18

The words were tumbling out in a too-rapid mixture of Clara Sinden's delight in seeing them and embarrassment at having kept them waiting. But the gist of it seemed to be thus:

Thomas had tried and failed to get Frederick Law Olmsted Jr., whose father had designed thirty-five acres of formal gardens at George Vanderbilt's Biltmore in Asheville, but young Olmsted's teaching schedule at Harvard was too demanding to allow for commissions. So Thomas was now in the library, from which she'd just come, seeking to enlist Beatrix Jones Ferrand, who had done so much to soften the splendid gloom of Wakehurst, the forbidding Elizabethan manor owned by the Van Alens, less than a mile from here.

Clara laughed. "But of course all that must seem nonsense to you." Rosa Maria laughed with her and reached out to hug her friend again.

"But let me look at you," Clara said stepping back. "Why you hardly show at all."

The three of them were standing in the grand entrance hall at Belvedere. Clara had been informed as soon as her friends had arrived, but it had been several minutes before she'd been able to extricate herself from the discussion in the library, for which she now apologized again.

The Marquis indicated the area around them. "It allowed us time to absorb this much splendor before moving on. And of course to greet an old friend." He pointed to *Maribárbola*, who hung on the wall to the right as one entered this hall, in a cluster of works that included two Sargents and a Theodore Robinson landscape.

"Yes," said Clara. "I must find some other place for her. She shouldn't be here with the Americans, but she is a fascinating woman, and Thomas' favorite, and he wants her here, where visitors will see her at once." She laughed. "And now I must agree she has made the space hers alone; I would fear her wrath if we tried to move her. But come, I want to show you your rooms myself."

And Clara did, taking their arms and guiding them through the entrance foyer and up the right side of the huge arms-akimbo marble stairway, and to the apartment that would be theirs.

In Rosa Maria's room a maid was unpacking and started to excuse herself when the two women appeared, but Clara stopped her. "No. That's fine, Lydia. Finish, please." She turned quickly to Rosa Maria. "If you don't mind."

Rosa Maria nodded and Clara embraced her again. "You cannot imagine how glad I am to see you," she said.

Dinner was in the family dining room, with its mantel of Wedgewood jasperware, a near-replica of the one at Biltmore.

"At first I resisted the idea," said Thomas, spraying crumbs from his dinner roll as he spread it open. "It has never seemed right to copy anything. But then Tavolara explained it as being a tribute rather than a copy, an acknowledgement, really, and I rather liked that." Tavolara, Thomas explained, was the Italian sculptor engaged by Clara to see to the trim.

"We were fortunate to get him," Clara said.

Thomas laughed and turned to her. "We have been fortunate with all our people, haven't we, Clara?"

Clara straightened and smiled slightly. "Yes, I believe we have," she said firmly.

Thomas extended his hand toward her in a gesture that carried the warmth of his affection despite the length of the table between them.

"Oh," he said suddenly remembering. "I must tell you what I've just learned from Mrs. Ferrand. In the banquet hall at Biltmore there's a portrait of Olmsted, senior of course, done by—well, I imagine you can guess."

"Tell me."

He smiled at her. "Who must the artist be if I ask the question?"

She smiled. "Sargent, of course."

"Of course. Your very own Mr. Sargent. So it occurred to me that if Mrs. Ferrand accepts our commission we should engage Mr. Sargent to raise her to immortality in just the same manner." He turned to the Marquis. "We met him in London, you know."

Rosa Maria sat stiffly on the edge of the bed in the dark, her body trembling, her voice a whisper. "God would not allow his greatest miracle to drive apart the man and woman who helped him to create it."

"This has nothing to do with God," the Marquis said, more sternly than he'd meant to.

She'd been unable to sleep and at two in the morning had come into his room and slipped into bed alongside him, her gentle touch moving him closer as he drifted in the half-dream of her warmth. Then suddenly he'd awakened and pulled back in alarm.

In Montevideo there'd been the boy with the stunted, misshapen arm hanging uselessly from his shoulder. The young Eduardo had asked his stepfather what could have caused such a thing. The Librarian's usual twinkle had disappeared as he'd soberly explained that such grotesqueries were the result of ignorance and foolish behavior. This was what happened when husbands and wives failed to curb their appetites during pregnancy; the fragile fetus was susceptible to intrusion, with deformity the frequent result, or sometimes a damaged brain. It was a lesson that must never be forgotten.

The Marquis draped his robe around the shaking Rosa Maria, and she pulled it tight, not so much for warmth as to cover the body that now embarrassed her.

"We must be strong," the Marquis whispered.

She nodded, yielding as she knew she must to the strength of his conviction, but knowing in her heart and soul that he was wrong. She stood and turned to him. "I do not believe that love is a weakness, or that it can harm the life it creates." And then she was gone and the door between their rooms was shut again.

He was awake the next morning with the first bright streaks of light and he slipped down the back stairs and outside, where he was greeted by Otto, the large German shepherd whose enthusiasm for two-legged creatures made him a useless watchdog but a wonderful companion. The dog was delighted with the early company and half led, half followed Valfierno the quarter mile or so to the beach, where he happily chased the stick that was flung for him again and again as the Marquis watched the morning sun raise itself out of the ocean and begin its journey across the sky, as it had yesterday and would again tomorrow; as it had for Philip of Macedon and his son Alexander, for Caesar, Charlemagne, Euclid, Galileo, Napoleon, Simón Bolívar, for the cleverest, most powerful men of history, all of whom had left their mark on this planet, and all of whom had reached a time when, no matter their superior natures, they no longer could survive.

When the time was right he would send a cable to Miguel.

The waiter in the Gentlemen's Lounge of the steamboat *Priscilla* was surprised to see the large, familiar figure. "Mr. Sinden. I wouldn't have expected you to be with us today."

Thomas Sinden lowered himself into one of three leather chairs around the low table and grunted his response. "A break in the routine," he said. The other chairs were empty, as was most of the lounge. "A chota peg, if you please." The waiter nodded and came back a moment later with a tray holding a net-covered pressure bottle of sparkling water and a small tumbler with very little whiskey at the bottom.

"Shall I?" the waiter asked, and when Sinden nodded he picked up the glass and carefully sprayed the inside till the glass was almost half full. "Will there be anything else?" the waiter asked.

"No, not a thing," said Sinden. "And if I should fall asleep, wake me when we pass Block Island."

The waiter nodded and left.

Till now he'd spent all of August at Newport, but a complication in a long-planned utilities merger had brought him back to New

York on Monday, where two days of work had finally put things back on track. Now it was Wednesday afternoon and he was headed back to his beloved Belvedere, where he'd arrive in time for dinner.

He sipped his drink, then put it down and opened his briefcase to take out his still-unread copy of that morning's *New York Times*.

"Impossible!" said the Marquis as Sinden pointed to the headline on page one.

"What is?" asked Rosa Maria. They had both just joined the Sindens in the drawing room before going in to dinner.

Clara turned to her. "The *Mona Lisa* has been stolen. Yesterday."

"Monday morning, actually," boomed Sinden. "They didn't discover it till yesterday. Damned inefficient, I should say. If they'd discovered the theft sooner, they might have it back by now!"

"But how could such a thing have happened?" asked Rosa Maria.

Sinden tapped the paper contemptuously. "How indeed! No one has any idea, but that doesn't keep them from inventing theories."

Rosa Maria turned to Valfierno. "I wonder if Mme. Privas knows of this."

Sinden laughed. "My dear, you may be sure everyone in Paris knows!"

"Everyone in the world, I should think," the Marquis said slowly, carefully, in a near-monotone that put a smooth surface on the turbulence he felt underneath. *It had happened. They had not been caught. The plan had worked.*

He turned to Rosa Maria. "But of course you're right to think of Mme. Privas. New security measures may well be in order. I shall write her this evening and present my thoughts."

He wrote a note that evening, but not to Mme. Privas; instead he composed his cable to Miguel. The message called on him to come to Newport as quickly as possible. He was needed here.

And a week later, when Miguel responded to these new instructions, he completed the circle for Paul Rénard.

Paul Rénard's surveillance of the Galerie Arlette had begun the day after his astonishing confrontation with Mme. Valency. The humiliation of that incident had coursed through him in recurring waves as he'd tried to sleep that night and left him convinced he could find no peace until he exacted retribution. What form that retribution might take he had no idea, but it was clearly important for him to learn a great deal more about what went on there.

This search for information might have been accomplished more simply by questioning Louise Durtal, whose position in Mme. Valency's life had become more important and whose importance in his own was such that in the average week they spent a good many hours together, especially on Wednesday nights, her one night off. But since Paul Rénard entered every involvement with the certainty that it would end and the likelihood that it would end badly, it did not seem prudent to question Louise about someone to whom her loyalties might prove stronger.

So if he needed information, he would be wiser to get it for himself, and he determined to watch the gallery every minute of the day and learn who came and went with any frequency. Every morning he took up his post before the doors were opened and, except for necessary breaks (which he varied daily), remained on watch until after the place was locked for the night and the rolled-up shutters clattered into place.

Paul Rénard was no stranger to anger, but it was a rage such as he'd never felt before that focused his every faculty on the task at hand. His attention never flagged, his eyes never left the door. He saw with clarity through mist and rain, noting every face that came and went, every expression with which his former wife greeted every caller. Not knowing what he sought, every shard of information was examined and saved to see how it might later fit into some sort of pattern. Nothing could be dismissed as unimportant.

The Marquis had been the first regular visitor to be observed. The man's connection with Mme. Valency's enterprise was, of course, unknown, but Valfierno's formidable presence was enough to stimulate interest, and at last one night Paul Rénard followed him home.

A series of discreet inquiries in the area of the rue d'Aguesseau provided Rénard with several scraps of information about his subject, including his name and the fact that he had recently been married to someone exceptionally young and beautiful.

But at that point the Marquis' gallery visits suddenly stopped and he was nowhere to be seen. When Rénard returned to his informants in the rue d'Aguesseau a few well-spent francs bought him the information that the couple had left on what promised to be, judging from their considerable luggage, an extended vacation.

Exit the Marquis, enter Miguel, whose visits to the gallery had been noted before and who now seemed to turn up more often; often enough for Rénard to enlist an assistant, a sixteen-year-old boy, so the two of them could keep constant track of him. This very quickly produced the surprising fact that Miguel seemed to live in the mansion on the Boulevard Haussmann that belonged to that possessor of legendary wealth, Mme. Jacqueline Privas.

Whoever these people were, they clearly did not lack for funds. But what enterprise, if any, tied together the two men, the gallery, and the Privas mansion, Rénard had no idea. Until, that is, Miguel suddenly broke his pattern.

On Sunday August 20, Claude, the boy who'd been assigned to keep tabs on Miguel, had seen him exit the Privas mansion just before three in the afternoon, and had followed him to the Porte des Lyons entrance to the Louvre. Once his quarry had disappeared inside, Claude had returned to his normal post across from the Privas mansion and waited for him to return. And waited.

He stayed through the night, and still no Miguel. At seven in the morning, Paul Rénard, anxious at not having received his nightly report, appeared and remained with the boy, who despite having been given permission to leave was at this point too curious not to stay. Finally, at almost ten in the morning, Miguel appeared, still dressed as he'd been the afternoon before and wearing the rumpled look of someone who'd been up all night. He stopped in front of the entrance and looked back to see if he'd been followed, then quickly slipped inside.

Paul Rénard dismissed Claude with instructions to get some sleep and be back by nine that evening. From now on they would watch the entrance day and night, twelve hours apiece. This young man, whoever he was, was becoming much more interesting.

On Wednesday, when the newspapers blared their stories of the theft of the *Mona Lisa*, Rénard instantly made the connection. There was no way he could be sure, of course, but the hours of his absence surrounded the time of the theft like a perfectly fitted frame.

Paul Rénard saw at once that at the very least this information could provide a solid fulcrum for the prying loose of considerable sums of money. He found himself covered with a light sweat as the pleasure of these potential numbers became increasingly entertaining.

Since Monday, the day Miguel had returned, he had remained inside the mansion. Finally, on Friday morning, with Claude on duty outside, he came out, turned left on the Boulevard Haussmann, and with the unnoticed Claude behind him made his way to the Mexican Consulate.

Claude entered behind him and busied himself with some pamphlets while Miguel stopped at the reception desk and was pointed toward a man at the counter. Miguel nodded and stepped to the counter with his passport in hand and after a few moments of conversation, during which the official flipped quickly through the pages, Miguel was handed back his passport with a reassuring nod, and he put it in his coat pocket and left.

Claude followed him outside, then crossed the street and hurried ahead, and crossed back and walked toward Miguel, brushing against him as he passed, excusing himself and rushing away. A suspicious Miguel reached at once for his money and was reassured when he felt his wallet, but seconds later he checked for his passport and realized it was gone. By then, Claude was nowhere to be seen.

"Yes, now we know his name," said Paul Rénard, with the touch of annoyance that kept anyone in his employ mired in incompetence. "But the price of learning his name has been showing him your face, which means you are no longer of any use to me."

Claude looked down. It was not the reaction he had expected, but of course he could see that perhaps his judgment had been faulty.

Another boy was hired the next morning and his first job was to return the passport by the simple expedient of slipping it under the front door of the Privas mansion with no note, no explanation. It had to be returned at once so as not to impede whatever journey Miguel Acevedo, a citizen of Mexico, had planned.

This second boy now divided the watch with Paul Rénard, and

with Rénard on duty, two days later Miguel left the mansion and walked to the Champs Elysées offices of the Hamburg-Amerika Line. Rénard waited for Miguel to conclude his business and then approached the same clerk and with a few adroit questions managed to learn that the young man's destination was New York, that he would be sailing in three days on the *Amerika,* and that, to the clerk's considerable surprise, he would be traveling first-class.

Paul Rénard reacted to that information with a laugh and the comment that first-class was too rich for him, but that oddly enough he too would be sailing on that ship. He booked third cabin and paid in cash.

Thus did Miguel lead Paul Rénard to New York and then to Newport, where both men booked rooms at the modest Neptune Hotel, a comfortable place two miles inland from the grandeur of the Cliff Walk and Bellevue Avenue.

The next morning Rénard followed Miguel to Belvedere, where, from his hidden vantage point outside, he once again caught sight of the Marquis de Valfierno.

19

The driver, doing as he'd been asked, looked again at the piece of paper. "Nine-eighteen Cloverfield Drive. Yes, sir, this is it."

Valfierno looked around at the flat land that stretched all around him, a view broken by just the house in front of which they were stopped, and two others nearby; all equally small, neat, unprepossessing, spread out in a kind of architectural yawn. "It cannot be. Might there be another street with this name?"

The driver shrugged. "None's I know of. Anyways, you said near Lakeshore Drive."

The front door of 918 swung open and a smiling, waving Milo Gallagher stepped out. "Right here!" he called. "I am here!" Valfierno relaxed and asked the driver to wait for him, then stepped down carrying his package.

"Well, my friend," Milo Gallagher said when the two men were inside, "I can hardly believe this day's arrived." It was mid-afternoon but the front drapes had been drawn. Through an archway Valfierno could see into the kitchen, where the lights were on and an empty glass sat on the counter. "You're confused, I can see. This is not what you expected. I should have told you it wouldn't be. This is not my home, you see. It's—well, it doesn't matter. Sit down." Valfierno sat and leaned the package against his chair. Milo picked up the envelope that had been lying on the table between them. He opened it, extracted the check, and handed it to the Marquis. Valfierno looked at it and nodded.

"There are funds in that account to cover it," Milo said. "But of course you know that." Then, quietly: "And I will tell you that this is the most astonishing day of my life. May I see it?"

Valfierno stood again and propped the package against the back of his chair. He gestured to it. "It now belongs to you. You may see it any time you like."

Milo didn't move. He seemed unable to. In fact his normally heightened color had suddenly drained, leaving him a ghastly white. "Open it," he whispered. His hands were shaking.

Valfierno quickly removed the twine, then slid the painting from between the layers of corrugated cardboard that covered it and laid it flat on the table, in the light of the chandelier.

For a few moments neither man spoke as Milo stared at the remarkable image. He was unable to move, unable to believe what was here before him, what he now possessed. Finally Valfierno reached out and touched him. "I will say good-bye," he said.

Milo nodded, his eyes never leaving the picture.

He took the sleeper back to New York and sat fully dressed in his compartment, missing dinner, a thin smile set in his immovable features as he stared out the window and saw but didn't see the countryside slip by. There was in his pocket a check for one million dollars.

Non, merci, he called out when the porter knocked to see if the gentleman wanted anything. Then quickly the Marquis realized there was something and he pulled the door open to ask if he might have a table. The porter smiled, entered the compartment, and pulled out the small dining table stowed flush in the wall beneath the window. Valfierno tipped him and he left.

Now he was smiling because he'd regained his sense of purpose. He switched on the compartment lights and picked up the slim envelope-briefcase he'd bought in Paris because it would be just big enough to hold the few things he needed with him. From inside he withdrew one of the six envelopes he'd already stamped and addressed, and laid it on the table. Then from his wallet he removed the check, put it on the table facedown, and on the back wrote quickly and firmly: "Only for deposit. Account LRS 57-6918-4771." And he signed his name. He took a loose sheet of paper from the briefcase, folded it in thirds, cradled the check inside the folds and slipped the whole thing in the envelope and sealed it. He turned the envelope over and checked the address. It was, of course, correct: to Ramon, at the rue d'Aguesseau. He would mail it in New York, and within the next several days there would be five more envelopes heading to the same address.

His work in New York could easily be accomplished in a matter of days but he planned to stay longer; he had told Rosa Maria that business would keep him away for at least two weeks. That would allow time for her to have a leisurely visit with Miguel in his absence.

At not-yet sixty the Marquis de Valfierno foresaw many years ahead for himself, but since the inevitable had earned its name for good reason he was determined that Rosa Maria's inevitable loss would, when the time came, be no more painful than it had to be. And so he planned for Miguel to be more and more in their company, and later he would find a reason to invite him to live with them on the southern coast of Spain. It would be Miguel who would complete the raising of his son.

She was a tall, slender woman, dressed simply in a striped shirtwaist and light flannel skirt that, combined with her intense brow and slight forward tilt, gave her a sense of purpose, as if she'd just been interrupted at something she needed to get back to. The attraction was immediate.

"Sit down, please," she said, doing so herself as the Marquis did. She swept back a wisp of light brown hair with the back of her left hand in a practiced gardener's move. It might have been gardening that she'd come from. "Now, I assume you haven't heard about my husband."

"I . . . don't know. From the way your butler looked when I asked to see him, I assume there is something . . ." Valfierno let the sentence end in a puzzled shrug.

"He died a month ago." Simply stating the fact. "Almost six weeks, to be accurate."

The news was not entirely surprising, given the strangeness of his reception. "I am . . . sorry, of course. If I had known, I would not have come." Instinctively he rested his hand on the package alongside his chair.

"It was in the newspapers, of course," Edith Schuyler said briskly. "Rather prominently. But perhaps you've been out of town."

Considering his unmistakable accent, she should more likely have assumed his absence to have put him in another country; but even if she'd thought that, her comment would have been the same. If you'd been somewhere other than New York it didn't matter if that somewhere was Amagansett or Katmandu—you'd been out of town.

"In Newport, in fact," Valfierno said, and the young Mrs. Schuyler (maybe thirty-five or forty) was suitably impressed.

"You have a place there?"

Valfierno laughed. "We are guests of the Thomas Sindens."

Edith Schuyler's eyebrows raised a little, hoisted by a tiny involuntary twitch. "Oh? At Belvedere? I am told it is magnificent."

"You may be sure it is everything you've heard."

"I've never been to Newport. I mean, not even once. For some reason, Harry disliked the place." *Harry.* Henry Schuyler. "Raised a different objection every time an invitation arrived. Soon enough they stopped arriving." She shifted in her seat, leaning slightly toward him. "But clearly you're here because you had business with Harry. Something to do with that package, I'd suppose."

Valfierno put his hand on it again. "Yes. But of course now it is of no consequence."

"A picture he had bought?"

"Let us say he'd planned to buy."

"Something for his . . . Hideaway Collection?"

Valfierno frowned, not understanding.

Edith Schuyler laughed. "Oh, come now, Don Valfierno, you cannot imagine I don't know about that. I've never actually seen any of the pictures; that kind of thing doesn't amuse me. But it wasn't because he hadn't asked me to. Often. So you were one of his suppliers. What naughty item had you brought him this time?"

Valfierno shook his head. "It is difficult to describe. But it is not what you imagine."

"My dear sir, I imagine nothing. My imagination does not run in those directions." She stood and stuck out her right hand. "Thank you for stopping by, and I'm sorry Harry was thoughtless enough to die and cheat you of your sale. I'm sure you'll find another buyer."

The Marquis smiled and shook her hand. "Perhaps. In any case, let me assure you the picture is not what you think. Nothing of the sort."

Edith Schuyler shrugged. "I am pleased to hear that. And even if what you say is not true, I thank you for having the courtesy to say it." She withdrew her hand. "Good-day."

The Marquis bowed and left.

Two days later he was back, again presenting his card to the surprised butler, who asked him to wait and was back a minute later to lead him into the front parlor, where Edith Schuyler was seated.

After the usual amenities, Valfierno sat. "There were some questions I had," he explained, "about your husband's . . . What you called his *hideaway* collection." It had occurred to him, he continued, that if Mrs. Schuyler wished to divest herself of these pictures, he might be able to help her find a buyer.

She frowned and thought about that, and promised to give it further thought. "And I must say it was kind of you to return with such an offer."

"Not at all," Valfierno said. "I was pleased to have a reason to see you again."

She laughed and pulled the bell cord to her left. "How very gallant. I was just about to have tea. Let me ask Cummings to lay another place."

He stayed for two hours and they told each other all about themselves, or all each wished the other to hear. She scolded him gently for having married a woman, girl really, so much younger than himself. But then, she admitted, she was hardly one to talk, having been twenty-six years younger than Harry Schuyler.

Whatever kind of mourning she was in was clearly not demanding, and he saw no reason not to ask her to join him for dinner two evenings hence, an offer she accepted without hesitation. Their evening together went so well they dined a second time two evenings after that, after which he introduced her to his suite at the Holland House.

The soft knocking at the door did not belong in the context of Geraldo's open treehouse where the two boys had been playing, so he whisked himself with split-second accommodation to his bed at home and heard his father's soft voice at the front door. "I do not have to count it," the Librarian said quietly, in that voice whose whispers carried across vast rooms. "And I have asked you not to come to my home. Sign? Yes, of course." And the young Eduardo waited for the scratchy sounds, but before they could come the fully grown Marquis was bolt upright in his bed at the Holland House.

"Thank you," the distant female voice said, followed by an awkward *"thank you"* from a man. Then the door shut quietly and a moment later Edith Schuyler was in the room.

"You're awake," she said.

Only fully awake just then, and back firmly in the present.

She walked to the dressing table and sat facing the mirror. She took a squat jar from the paper bag, set it on the table, and unscrewed the top. "I sent the boy for some cold cream. I see he didn't get what I asked for, but it will do." She dipped her fingers in and scraped a precise dollop to apply to her face. "I can't imagine what took him so long."

"What time is it?" Valfierno asked.

"Just past ten. In the morning. I've already called home. I didn't want them panicking." She applied the cold cream deftly, in small amounts that quickly disappeared. "My skin is so dry. I must do this every night. I'm sure I'll pay the price for being so late this time."

Valfierno smiled. "What did you tell them?"

"At home? That I broke a heel on my shoe and stayed overnight with friends."

"Did you tell them which friends?"

She turned and stared at him. "Of course not. What difference does it make? They don't believe me anyway." *They*—the servants. "This will give them something to gossip about."

"And that doesn't disturb you?"

Edith Schuyler threw her head back and laughed, a deep, pleasant sound. "Terribly, of course."

She was in a dressing gown of his that seemed to suit her perfectly. He got up and stood behind her, and caught her eye in the mirror and smiled. "Good-morning."

She looked at his naked figure in the mirror and then returned to her task. "Yes, of course, good-morning."

He slid his hand inside the dressing gown and gently cupped her breast. She put down the jar of cold cream and sat stiffly for a moment.

"Aren't you taking a lot for granted?" she asked quietly.

"That you would feel this morning as you did last night?"

She turned and looked at him, looking up, beyond the sign of his arousal. "No," she said quietly. "That I'd be willing to wipe my face clean after all the effort I've just put into it."

"Perhaps you are not."

She looked at him for a moment, then smiled and touched him in the one place that would make her intention clear, then turned and quickly toweled her face free of its shiny layer.

"Yes," she said later as they lay there. "Of course you're surprised." She turned from her back to her side to face him, and he gently traced the curve of the small breast that had reappeared. "Why would a woman like me, so soon after her husband's death, spend the night with a man she barely knows; a man who will disappear in a matter of days?"

He nodded. That had indeed been the meaning of his one-word question: Why?

"There are simple answers that I think would make things very clear, but they are also very long, and besides, I'm not sure I know you well enough. Or myself. But perhaps the simplest answer is this: What makes you most attractive is that you *will* disappear. You're the purest lark, the first ever of my life. No wonder I find you so attractive."

He tried not to change expression, but apparently he had.

"Oh, come now, that does not wound your vanity."

"Certainly not," he insisted.

"You are of course a most attractive man or I wouldn't be here."

"And you are," he said, his smile back in place, "a most attractive woman."

"How wonderfully well we go together," she said lightly, and not knowing how to take it he leaned forward and kissed her forehead.

"Umm, very sweet," she said briskly, and with a quick, athletic move she was out of bed, back in his robe, and seated at the dressing table reapplying her cream, this time a little faster.

Alone later in his living room he finished the breakfast that had arrived in silver-domed splendor, patted his mouth with the impossibly soft royal-blue napkin, and smiled contentedly in appreciation of what had been a splendid string of pleasant hours.

He arose and looked at himself in the full-length mirror, still trim at almost sixty. He turned to the right and to the left in the handsome dressing gown that she had so recently worn, examining the man she had seen, and finding himself not at all displeased.

He stepped closer for a better look at his face, and saw and touched the stubble just above his beard. That sent him to the telephone where he asked for the barber shop. "What time is it?" he asked the man who answered.

"Almost noon, Don Valfierno," came the reply.

"I would like Nicholas to come to my suite at twelve-thirty."

"Certainly, twelve-thirty," the voice confirmed.

The Marquis clicked down the telephone hook, then released it and told the operator he would like to send a telegram. When she connected him with Western Union he dictated a message to Rosa Maria at Belvedere in Newport, Rhode Island, in which he explained that his business here would probably drag on longer than he'd expected, but he'd be back in no more than three weeks.

That done he leaned back in his armchair and let himself drift into a pleasant nap that was interrupted by the arrival of the man he knew to be the finest barber in New York, who curried and trimmed his spirits back to the high level they'd been at earlier this morning. When Nicholas left, he was ready to turn his attention to the work that remained.

He went to the desk, set a sheet of stationery in front of him, dipped the pen in ink, and wrote the number six with a square around it, as he had so many months ago. How perfect that number had seemed. Six copies, six million dollars.

He put the pen down and reached under the desk for his utility case. He opened it, laid back the satin lining that covered the bottom, and lifted out two folded sheets of paper. He spread them on the desk, pressed them flat with the edge of his hand, and reviewed again the list of names.

Six had been checked, with a double check now next to Milo Gallagher's, and a line through Henry Schuyler's. It was time to choose the replacement name, the one that would bring the list back to six.

But as he looked slowly down the names it became clear there could be no sensible replacement. His approach to each of the original six had had about it a sense of drama, even romance: *Here is the offer: if you wish to possess the world's most beautiful, most famous painting, I will steal it for you. If I am successful you will read of the event, and you will be hearing from me within the month. And from the day I hand it over, only you and I will know the Lady's new address.*

But to find a buyer now, after the event, would be entirely different. In the first instance, each buyer had become a co-conspirator who would eagerly await first news of the theft, and then his call. To approach someone now would be entirely different; nothing more or less than peddling stolen goods.

He picked up the pen and dipped it again. Then he crossed out the number six and after a moment of final reflection, reluctantly wrote beneath it the very much smaller number five.

He delivered two paintings that afternoon, propelled by the robust good spirits of his half day with Edith Schuyler. When he returned to his rooms he put a second check mark next to those two names on his list, copied the remaining two single-checked names and addresses onto a separate slip of paper, slid the master list back under the satin at the bottom of the utility case, and returned the case to its place under the desk. From his slim briefcase he then took out one of the envelopes pre-addressed to Ramon, endorsed the two checks for deposit, and enclosed them with a short note, the purpose of which was less to communicate than to keep the checks from showing through. When he was done he called down to the desk and said he had mail to send. A moment later someone was at the door to collect it.

Now the unplanned evening stretched before him and he toyed with the notion of calling Edith Schuyler, but as he reached for the telephone there was a knock at the door—a bellman delivering a telegram from Rosa Maria. She was disappointed of course that his stay in New York would be longer than planned, but she was pleased that it would afford him more time to explore the fabulous city; if, of course, he could find the time for that. She signed with love from her and from the Person Within, "who would express it himself if only he knew how (or she)."

When he put the message down he found himself missing her acutely and he dressed quickly and went down to the dining room for an early dinner.

The next morning he arrived at Chaudron's studio at just past ten to pick up the first of the two remaining paintings. As always, it took insistent twisting of the bell and pounding on the door to be heard two floors up, but when the Marquis finally gained entrance he found the two paintings waiting for him; the final two, wrapped for delivery and leaning against the wall. He picked up the first and told Chaudron he would be back before lunch for the second, and both men exulted that their project was nearing completion.

His first call went smoothly enough, despite the fact that the grateful buyer was so filled with nervous excitement he botched his check and had to tear it up, and then on his second attempt had had to pause halfway to allow his racing pulse to settle before he could finish. But finish he did at last, handing it over with effusive expressions of gratitude.

The second call did not go so smoothly.

20

*I*t was a moment before Paul Rénard realized that the dapper little man clicking toward him in the bar was the desk clerk he'd talked to this morning at the St. Regis; in his native habitat the man had seemed a good head taller. How this illusion had been accomplished, Rénard had no idea, but there was no doubt that the person sliding into the seat opposite him was indeed the same fellow.

"Am I late? I think I am late."

Rénard shrugged.

"Not to you it may not matter, but to me it does. I cannot abide being late, with a duke or with a plumber. Not, of course, that you are either."

Paul Rénard shifted in his seat. His English was not nimble enough for this kind of chat, so he jumped quickly to the matter at hand.

"Do you bring the name of the hotel?"

The desk clerk smiled. "How eager you are to learn it."

"Do you bring it?"

The desk clerk tilted left and reached into the right pocket of his jacket, from which he withdrew a small envelope. He put it on the table, waited a dramatic second, then slid it across. Paul Rénard picked it up and opened it quickly, his body slowly relaxing as he read what was inside: Holland House, Fifth Avenue and Thirtieth Street. "Yes," Rénard muttered automatically as he read the note again.

"I am sure," the desk clerk said slowly, to be sure his point would float across the language moat, "you are grateful for this information."

Rénard looked up at him, then reached into his own jacket pocket where he had stored a folded ten-dollar bill in preparation for this moment. He handed it to the desk clerk, who examined it without pleasure.

"I had hoped your gratitude might be grander," he said coldly. Not being a man of charm, he sought to bully his clients in these matters, but in Paul Rénard he was dealing with someone who cared nothing about meeting anyone's expectations. Rénard put the piece of paper in the envelope and slid it across the table. "If you have not be happy with my money, then please to return it to me, as I return your information."

The desk clerk rose and stared at him. "You are an amusing fellow," he said with an icy edge, "but I ask you never to call on me again." And he pocketed the ten-dollar bill and left.

The St. Regis had been the second hotel Rénard had wandered into that morning, the Plaza having been the first. *"Yes, the Marquis always stays with us,"* the desk clerk had said from his invisible perch, *"but he is not here now."*

"Is there somewhere else he might be staying?"

"Impossible!" the clerk had huffed. *"If he is in New York, then he is here!"*

But further conversation had elicited from the lofty clerk the promise to inquire at other likely hotels, at all of which he had important contacts, and to meet with Monsieur Lemâitre at six. Lemâitre was a name Rénard had frequently used in the past.

The Marquis had been absent from Newport for three days before Rénard had realized he was gone, a sudden awareness that had produced something close to panic. Where had he gone to? Had he taken the painting with him, or had Belvedere been the stolen *Gioconda*'s final destination?

Two drivers from Thomas Sinden's staff were regulars at the Neptune bar, and that night Paul Rénard befriended them by a method no more complicated than standing a couple of rounds. He elicited the seemingly trivial information that early Tuesday morning the Marquis had left by steamer for New York. This was Friday.

Before going up to his room he stopped at the front desk and asked the unsmiling clerk for paper, an envelope, and pen and ink. After a deep sigh at having been troubled, the man began looking slowly through drawers and the requested items were finally produced. Paul Rénard sat at a dimly lit table in a corner of the lobby and composed a short letter, which he folded and put into an envelope. He sealed it and faced the blank side for a moment, still surprised at the unexpected emotions that had prompted him to write. Then he carefully wrote her name and his own address and brought it to the desk where he asked to buy postage.

The clerk shook his head.

"You have none?"

"At the railroad station. There's a window."

The next morning Paul Rénard bought his postage, affixed it to the envelope, and stopped himself as he was about to drop it in the slot. Then he tore the letter into tiny bits and threw them away. He hadn't told Louise where he was going—not even that he was leaving the country. The postmark would reveal that much, and without knowing why he didn't think it wise. The whole letter had suddenly seemed unwise.

His train for New York was on time, and he boarded it not knowing that his quarry had already made a trip to Chicago and returned, or that the Marquis would be making several deliveries. He assumed there'd be only one, and that once he'd seen it made he'd be in position to act.

The pleasant, unhurried atmosphere at the edge of the park made it easy to watch the entrance to the huge marble mansion while attracting no attention. He sat on a bench across from the house, pretending to read the newspaper he'd bought from a passing newsboy, and drew no more attention than any of the scattered readers, talkers, loungers, and sleepers, arrayed all around.

He could scarcely believe his good fortune; he'd managed to catch up with Valfierno at what was clearly the critical moment.

Rénard had overslept that morning (a frequent problem) and had not spotted his man until the Marquis returned to the Holland House at close to noon. Rénard had then waited near the main entrance and when Valfierno came out again followed him in a taxi down to a shabby building on Lafayette Street. It was several minutes before Valfierno reemerged, and when he did he carried under his arm a wrapped package of the size and shape of the stolen painting; it could be nothing else. The Marquis climbed back into the automobile that had been waiting for him, and Rénard followed in a cab to Fifth Avenue and Sixtieth Street. He watched as the massive entrance doors to the mansion swung open and the Marquis was welcomed inside. Then Rénard crossed the avenue, sat, and waited.

Inside, Valfierno was shown to the library, where he sat alone and waited for what must have been half an hour before the polished wooden doors (mahogany?) eased open and Pearson Beck strode into the room behind his bristling mask of hair: steel-gray eyebrows, full sideburns, impasto mustache, and a porcupine beard that seemed to precede him by several inches.

Valfierno started to speak, but Beck held his hand up for silence and lowered it only when he heard the solid click of the double doors closing behind him. Then he beamed. "Now, sir," he said, "what liquid refreshment may I offer?"

"None, thank you," said Valfierno.

"An abstemious fellow. All right, then, I shall abstain along with you and we'll get directly to business. Please let me see what you've brought me."

The Marquis nodded and set his package on the low table that separated him from Pearson Beck. He faced it toward himself and deftly, swiftly stripped the wrappings. Then his body went stiff in surprise and a chill went through him as he looked in horror at a painting he had not expected.

The *Mona Lisa*, yes, but unlike any copy he'd either seen or imagined. This version was so clumsy in its proportions, so bold in its thick black outlines, so garish in its blatant contrasts, it seemed more the work of a ten-thumbed dauber than of the Florentine master. It

225

was crude to the point of caricature, to the point of embarrassment, and for the first time in his life the Marquis de Valfierno found himself dumbstruck, left without the slightest notion of what to say.

"Well," said the still-beaming Beck to the frozen Marquis, "I should like to see my purchase."

There was no alternative. Slowly Valfierno turned the frame in his direction, wondering how he would deal with the outburst that would surely follow. But to Valfierno's complete surprise the smile on Pearson Beck's face, instead of twisting into fury, deepened into a look of pure ecstasy and when he spoke his words came softly, cushioned in tones of awe and reverence. "I cannot believe what I see before me. I have waited for this moment, and now she is here and she is mine."

Beck said nothing more, and when Valfierno tried to speak no voice would come. He cleared his throat, croaked something inaudible, cleared his throat again, and finally managed a "Yes, indeed." A third clearing of the throat, and then: "The most famous woman on the face of the earth. *La Gioconda*, in all her splendor." With a deep breath he was suddenly back in command. "Obtained, I might add, with no little difficulty."

Pearson Beck stood and smiled at him. "Yes, indeed. No little difficulty, I'm quite certain. For which, I'm sure, you'd like to be paid." He crossed to his desk and pulled down the writing surface. "Difficult tasks can lead to whopping paydays." He took out his check ledger, flipped it open, and began to write. "And none, I'll wager, as whopping as this." He stopped and turned to the Marquis. "Spell your name for me, please."

"You think this is a joke!" It was not a question, but an accusation flung angrily at the half-smile that had escaped Chaudron's best efforts to contain it.

Chaudron waited a moment before answering, and when he did the remnant of the smile remained. "You say he *liked* it?"

The Marquis was breathing heavily; the effort of returning himself to normal. "I say he saw no difference. It was to him the masterpiece itself. He accepted it completely. I suppose that is what you see as funny."

Chaudron shook his head, then shrugged. "How can I fail to?"

Valfierno leaned toward him. "What I must know is *why?* What possessed you? Anyone with half an eye would have seen through it at once."

Chaudron stood up and stretched. Valfierno had found him resting on the cot he kept at the studio. He stepped to the window and gazed out, toward Bartholdi's Liberty, partially shrouded in low-hanging clouds. "She can barely be seen today. Sunshine suits her better."

Valfierno's eyebrows came together. "What are you talking about?"

Chaudron shrugged. "Nothing that would interest you."

"What interests me is why you did this. Don't you realize what could have happened?"

Chaudron thought about that for a moment. "I wonder," he said. Then he shrugged.

"Damn it man, I want an answer!"

The painter slowly smiled again. "Have you not considered I might be as surprised as you?"

The Marquis had not, and the question derailed his thoughts for just a moment.

Chaudron walked back toward him and slumped on the cot. "Perhaps not *quite* as you." And Yves Chaudron told him about the copy Senora Schultz had made, and how she had been the one who had readied all the copies for delivery, wrapping them in butcher's paper, and how she must have substituted her own for one of his.

"But *why,*" the Marquis wanted to know.

Chaudron lay down full-length on the cot and crossed his ankles as he rested his hands in his crotch. "Who can say? And what would it matter? The man believed what you delivered. That is all that matters."

The Marquis was furious. "And if he'd called the police?"

Chaudron shrugged. "To tell them what? What could he say to the police?"

"You are a fool. Sometimes I think you don't understand our position. Where are the other two?"

"The other two what?"

"You painted six."

Chaudron nodded.

The Marquis counted them on his fingers. "Four were delivered. One was not because Henry Schuyler died. Another was not because of your Senora Schultz, who should never have been here in the first place."

"Yes, then there must still be two." He indicated a kind of tall broom closet. "They are in that narrow closet. I thought just one was left, but I cannot quarrel with your arithmetic."

Chaudron's torn carpetbag tumbled out when Valfierno opened the closet door, and behind it were the two panels and the rolled canvas master. He took them out quickly. "Get a saw," the Marquis hissed. Chaudron looked at him blankly. "A saw. At once!"

One was finally produced and the Marquis snatched it from the painter's hand and began hacking away at the painted panels.

"What are you doing?"

"These must be destroyed! We will cut them up and burn them."

"Have you lost your mind? You'll cut your hand off." He stared at the Marquis, who handed him the saw.

"Here. You do it. I cannot accomplish this sort of thing."

The argument persisted through several more heated non sequiturs, and then the tone slowly cooled as Chaudron began to see that the existence of the copies could do them no good and might in fact do considerable harm. He took the proffered saw and set to work unhappily (the panels had been made with meticulous care), using it to reduce them to narrow strips, which he then cut in half and wrapped in paper along with the canvas and brought out to the back of the building. As the package burned in the rubbish bin, Chaudron's pain increased as he watched the smoke curl skyward in billows no more distinguished than those from any burning trash.

For the Marquis the destruction of the paintings brought the enterprise to an unexpected but nonetheless definite conclusion, and as he took his leave he was overcome with a sense of victory so strong that he hugged Chaudron in a surprise gesture (to both of them) of warmth and triumph and skipped down the front steps with the rhythmic bounce of a twelve-year-old. At the curb, he dismissed the hotel car that was still waiting for him and directed his stride north-ward, determined to cover the considerable distance to the Holland House on foot, and possibly in record time.

He hadn't walked ten yards when he heard the sharp voice be-hind him.

"Stop! At once!"

Valfierno froze at the sound of the voice that seemed to carry the ring of authority. He turned slowly, as if to delay a confrontation that was not likely to be pleasant. But the source of the command was not what he'd expected. Ordinary. Average height. Street clothes. An official?

"I must talk to you," the man said brusquely, and Valfierno was now aware he was being addressed in French.

"About what?"

"Do you know me?"

Valfierno's eyebrows rose as he stared at his questioner. "I do not."

"If not me, then perhaps my name. I am Paul Rénard."

Valfierno nodded. "If you claim to be."

"You and I have a great deal to talk about."

"Nothing that I am aware of."

"I intend to make you aware."

"Yes, that seems to be your purpose. Continue, then."

"Here?"

Valfierno shrugged. "If privacy is your concern, we are likely to have a good deal more of it right here than almost anyplace you might suggest."

"What about your hotel room."

"I think not."

Rénard smiled. "I see. For that I would have to be either rich or a beautiful woman. Or perhaps both."

Valfierno stiffened. "Monsieur Rénard, if that is indeed who you are, I am pressed not by time but by my desire to rid myself of your company as quickly as possible. If you have anything to say to me, do so at once."

After a moment's hesitation Paul Rénard said, "As you wish." And he made known his purpose.

Would the Marquis have reached the same conclusion if curiosity had not led him inside the grand, newly opened building of the New York Public Library that morning? Impossible to say, but wander in he did. And once inside memories were triggered, associations made, a day recalled.

Through its fourteen years of construction, passersby had viewed the library's scaffolded modern French facade with head-shaking skepticism, convinced the enormous job would never be finished. Then late in May the metal braces had been peeled away and the building was seen to gleam with the radiance of a teenager's smile.

He entered through the main entrance on Fifth Avenue—a Porte des Lyons, but of another sort. Grander, wider, but white-marble cool, with its recumbent lions more bored royalty than feral guardians. Inside, he was suddenly aware of why he'd come. He asked for the reading room.

He walked up the two flights of stairs and as he entered the enormous room he was overcome by the memory of a smaller, similar room he'd been taken to so many years ago.

His stepfather, as the Librarian of the National University, had been invited to attend the retirement ceremonies of the Adjunct Librarian, a frail gentleman who had served a succession of superiors "with diligence and devotion" for some fifty-three years and was to be presented with a Scroll of Appreciation signed by President Batlle Y Ordóñez, or at the very least by someone skilled at approximating his hand.

To the elder Valfierno it had seemed an opportunity to impress upon his nine-year-old stepson the magnitude of his official position, and so he agreed to attend. And on the day he brought with him the young Eduardo.

The Library staff responded to the presence of their chief with great enthusiasm, bowing and beaming in their freshly pressed best, the warmth of their greeting reflecting not an ounce of affection, but rather the mysterious respect commanded by the rarely seen.

The speeches began and slowly oozed on as each minor functionary rose and having nothing to say took forever to get it said.

The elder Valfierno leaned toward young Eduardo. "Are you listening to this?"

Eduardo nodded vigorously.

"Then you are wasting your time. Listen to me instead, and I will tell you something about libraries that you have never heard. Do you know what's all around you?"

"Books," Eduardo said, sure of the answer this time.

"Of course books. But what's *in* the books."

Eduardo shrugged. "Stories. Words."

"Yes, stories, words," the Librarian said impatiently, "but also ideas, n'est-ce pas?"

"Ideas, too." Eduardo nodded.

"Exactly!" the elder Valfierno said. "And tell me about these ideas. Do they lead to wisdom?"

The path of the conversation was becoming clearer now. "They do *not*," Eduardo said emphatically.

The Librarian smiled and stroked his head. "Of course they do not. And do you know why?" He didn't wait for an answer. "Because of their very profusion. Do you know what an expert is?"

Eduardo thought he did, but the risk seemed too great, and certainly unnecessary. He shook his head.

"An expert is someone who has read just one book. Think about that. Complete absorption in *just one book* provides absolute clarity, a path to be followed with confidence, a path from which one need never swerve. The Bible of course is the greatest example. But examples abound. Look around you."

Eduardo did.

"Shelf after shelf, room after room. Devotion to any one of these can make you a clear-eyed fanatic; certain of everything, grasping nothing. What then is the solution? Reading everything in sight?"

"No." This was sure to be right.

"No, indeed. Because taken together all they can do is produce argument, disagreement. A cacophony of contradiction. What can one learn from shelves of books when each is in conflict with its shelfmate, when each idea leans against its refutation?"

"Nothing."

The elder Valfierno beamed. "You are quick to comprehend. Then if nothing is ever to be learned, what is one to do?"

Eduardo shook his head.

"One must recognize that since any collection of the ideas of others seethes and writhes in endless conflict, it is useless as a source of guidance. One's only resource can be found in oneself." He paused dramatically. "But therein lies a danger." He paused again, this time waiting for his prompt.

Eduardo provided it. "And what is that danger?"

On the platform, the speaker had concluded and there was polite applause. The Librarian leaned toward his stepson and cupped his hand to the boy's ear. "Too fine a regard for the feelings of others."

Eduardo nodded sagely and whispered: "How much longer must we be here?"

"Patience."

"May I help you?" The voice that jolted him back to the present came in a sprayed whisper from the tall, bespectacled man before him, who now repeated his question.

"Yes," the Marquis responded, realizing he had no idea how long he'd been rooted to this spot. "I should like to know where I might find the box for the Book Fund."

The tall man seemed puzzled; it was a question he had not heard before. He walked the few steps to the main desk and quietly inserted the inquiry into the ear of the attractive young woman behind it, who shook her head, then leaned forward and imparted an answer that, close as Valfierno was, he could not hear.

"We have no such box," the tall man informed the Marquis.

In Montevideo there had been such a box, installed by his stepfather on taking office. The older students had ignored it, but each year's crop of freshmen could be counted on for modest contributions before acquiring their inevitable worldliness.

The Marquis thanked the man for his trouble and left.

Blackmail's bad name is compounded by the payer's knowledge that payment may not end the matter. It is no great news that the blackmailer's appetite, instead of being sated, is too often aroused by the pleasure of that first bite.

Just such concerns had kept Valfierno delaying his meeting with Paul Rénard. But finally he was ready, having devised, he was sure, the right way to deal with the matter. The genesis of this plan was too tangled in wisps of memory to be traced exactly, but it was rooted in the further thoughts of his stepfather that had followed him back from the library.

The incident he recalled had occurred when he was fifteen and had asked for an increase in his monthly allowance, which like all allowances fell just below the level that comfort required. The Librarian had promised an answer the following morning, and after breakfast had announced that since the fairness of the current amount was in question, he would cut it in half for the next two months. Eduardo was of course aghast and deeply hurt. But when the two months went by and in a dramatic ceremony the Librarian restored the full amount, it seemed, as he'd known it would, a wonderfully adequate sum.

In the matter of Paul Rénard there was no question that payment would have to be made, but what amount would end the matter forever? Did such an amount exist? Slowly he came to realize what must be done, and marveled at the simple solution to which his memories had led him.

Unaccustomed sums of money disappear quickly, and in their wake new needs are created. But money doled out with clockwork regularity creates dependency; life without it cannot be imagined.

A meeting was quickly arranged, Valfierno calling Rénard at the hotel whose number he'd given him. The meeting was at the south corner of the New York Public Library, where people flowed past the two, unaware that they were ignoring a conversation between the man who stole the *Mona Lisa* and his extortionist.

"Write down your Paris address," Valfierno said brusquely, handing him a small piece of paper and a pencil. Rénard stared at him. "Write it down!"

Rénard started writing.

"Every month for the rest of my life . . . not your life, but *mine* . . . you will receive a check in the amount of twelve thousand five hundred francs, which in the course of a year is one hundred fifty thousand francs."

Rénard finished writing and looked at him for a moment, then started to speak.

"Your thoughts are not significant! Give me that."

Rénard handed over the piece of paper.

"That amount each month, and never another franc. Not *ever*. And if you fail to keep your end of the bargain, which of course is total silence, then let me explain what will happen.

"I have not lived this much of my life without making the acquaintance of several people who have always been ready to do *anything* for money. You will be found, and you will be dealt with." Valfierno let his face relax and reached into his pocket. "So I suggest you congratulate yourself on being a clever fellow." He drew out a folded slip of paper. "Here is the first payment. In the future the check will arrive each month between the first day and the tenth. Assuming this address is accurate."

Rénard assured him it was.

"Good. And just one more thing: Let me never see your face again."

Paul Rénard nodded and was gone.

21

It is the second birthday party he's attended in two days. This one is outdoors—a picnic for two on an unusually chilly November day, a modest spread that has been set out on a slope that rolls a gentle half mile to the rushes of foam that scallop the edge of the sea.

Edith Schuyler is thirty-nine today. She has gone to a great deal of trouble to put this picnic together herself. With some help, it's true, but mostly by herself. Which makes it disturbing that his interest in it seems to be minimal.

"It occurs to me," she says, leaning back on the blanket and drawing a second blanket across her legs, "that I am exactly in the middle: twenty years younger than you, and twenty years older than *la princesa*. Do you find significance in numbers?"

Valfierno shrugs. His mind is on himself, on what for some time now he's thought of as his malaise, and what he's planned to do about it. The steps have been taken. There is at this point no turning back. Why should he have felt this discontent surrounded as he is each day by endless perfection? He had invented a series of reasons, each of which held some element of truth, but it had not been until this morning when the early sun pried his eyes open that he'd seen his situation with perfect clarity. It was this endless living in the present tense. In other places, other times, each day had been driven by the tension of tomorrow: plans, objectives, calculations. Since Málaga all tomorrows have shrunk to nothing more than extensions of today.

She taps the place beside her, inviting him to sit there.

"In a moment," he says. "I must stretch first." And he stands and does.

She lies back and shuts her eyes against the sun. "Are you avoiding contact with me?"

He turns to the sun and presses his face against it. Nothing is said for what seems to her too long.

Edith: "Is this the last time I shall ever see you?"

The question is unexpected and he does not answer.

It is November 8, 1913, exactly one month before Vincenzo Perugia will embark on his lunatic journey to Florence and his ultimate imprisonment. Yesterday, a joyous Francesca Angela Maria celebrated her second birthday, painting her face with glazed frosting and flinging bright ribbons around the parlor of the hillside house in Málaga her parents had bought the month before she was born. A great deal has happened since.

And hasn't.

The thieves have not been discovered. Not even Perugia, at least as far as Valfierno knows. (He is late getting news.)

Other things have not happened.

Edith Schuyler has not been discovered. At least not the truth of why she is here. The widow Schuyler had arrived in Málaga four months ago, appearing at the home of the Valfiernos one afternoon breathless with the story of an astonishing coincidence. She had taken a villa nearby, just for a change of scenery, and had arranged with a local farmer for deliveries of fresh vegetables and dairy products. This farmer had mentioned the unusual couple who lived not two miles from her, and from his description she was sure it must be the Marquis and his family, and of course it was! She and Rosa Maria became fast friends at once.

The Marquis made his way to the rented villa with frequency, on two occasions inventing important trips to Granada that kept him there a week at a time. But for the Marquis the renewed ardor he'd felt at Edith's arrival slowly cooled. So much for paradise. Again.

The boy with the withered, useless arm had indeed existed in Montevideo exactly as the Marquis had described him that night in Newport. But the young Eduardo's question to his stepfather had drawn not the stern warning Valfierno had intoned to his wife, but rather a simple shrug and a shake of the head; a who-knows-the-answers-to-such-things, a such-is-life.

The Marquis had imagined that his lack of interest in his then-pregnant wife would disappear with the birth of the child, or at the latest when her body returned to something close to normal. But that did not turn out to be the case. Fortunately, Rosa Maria ascribed his lessened ardor to his age, for which she had the deepest respect.

And how did Ramon, the girl's father, accept the startling request that was made of him? Whatever emotion he might have felt could not have been discerned by the most sensitive observer. His response had been a nod and a promise the matter would be attended to.

It had been on his visit three months ago, when he was on the Costa del Sol to do his annual accounting with the Marquis. When they'd finished the books, which Ramon had prepared with his customary thoroughness, the Marquis shut the door to the study and warned him the subject to be raised would be a delicate one under any circumstances, and would be especially so as things stood with all of them. Ramon nodded and listened expressionlessly as Valfierno outlined what needed to be done. Ramon was quiet for a moment, his face showing nothing, then he gravely explained that of course the Marquis was aware that he had no experience in matters such as this, and in fact had no notion of where to begin. To which Valfierno responded that the only experience that counted was his own with Ramon, which made him certain there was no miracle the barber could not accomplish. The flattery took some of the sting from Ramon's pain.

Now Ramon was back, presumably to attend his granddaughter's birthday party (which he did) but more importantly to put into Valfierno's hands the annulment from the Office of the Holy See.

Edith Schuyler sits up and brushes her skirt. She's been crying behind the arm that has been across her eyes and she makes no attempt to hide it. "When are you leaving?"

"In two days."

"But we'll not see each other again."

He shakes his head.

"Have you told her?"

"I will tell her in two days, in the morning. I will tell her and leave."

Edith stares at him for a moment, then rises and brushes some leaves from her skirt. "You've planned this from the beginning. That's what the boy is doing here."

The boy is, of course, Miguel, who has been living in the guest house since the Marquis and his young wife began their residence here.

He shrugs. There is no point in trying to explain what is at best a fine distinction between what he'd planned and what was happening now.

Edith: "I'll tell you something strange. She's the one I feel sorry for, not me. I have a bargain for you: I'll promise to leave if you'll promise to stay."

He bends over and starts to fold things to be put away. She comes to him and stops his arm. "Will you?"

"Impossible," he says.

He travels first to Rome, because it's a city he's never seen and he knows no one there. But in the first forty-eight hours the freedom he's sought turns from goal to burden. It has been half a lifetime since he's been without the mirror of another person in which to admire himself.

He is dining alone in the hotel dining room one night when he's invited to join the table of two couples with men his age and women much younger. The conversation is lively and pleasant and afterward the men invite him to join them in a round of cards, and they lead him to a card room on the balcony floor where he sits down at a table with them and others to a game of chemin de fer.

He wins, in American dollars, twenty-six thousand, and for an hour afterward he feels the heady joy of the winner who knows he's been touched by God. But by morning sobriety returns. He will not gamble again because he is not comfortable exposing himself to chance; in everything he's ever done his objective has been the *elimination* of chance.

The next morning, early, he goes on to Venice, where his stay is longer than he'd planned as he allows himself to be pillowed in the comfort of the place. Then back to Rome to try to revive his spirits. It is while in Rome that he reads of Perugia's arrest.

"When in Rome, do as the travelers do." The table laughs. "Not the tourists, you understand," continues the Frenchman Gagnon, "but those to whom travel is a way of life; the pleasure nomads who understand business."

It is late at night and the table is full of men and their perfect cigars and pot-bellied glasses bottomed with brandy. Their women have gone to bed.

"What *kind* of business?" Gagnon is asked.

"Whatever is in the wind. These people have no special expertise; unless it is an understanding of money that goes beyond the mere selling of goods and services. They sniff the breeze and know which way to jump."

"And what are they sniffing now?" asks another. "If it is safe to ask."

Gagnon smiles. "Aside from the usual things, the sweetest smells come straight up from Africa. *French* Africa."

"Is that what they say in Paris?"

"You've missed the point. That is what *I* say, in Rome."

Another murmur of laughter.

Gagnon goes on and talks of land speculation in Morocco, "in spite of all that sand." There are wise nods around the table.

"Who will buy this land?" a Dutchman asks with a frown.

"The coming flow of colonists, and indeed there will be one.

There is already a trickle. Losers must begin again somewhere, you know."

So must winners, the Marquis thinks. It's the one shared thread of failure and success—each requires a new beginning.

Later that week the persistent cold weather plaguing southern Europe turns colder still, and Valfierno puts together the two things he now knows about Africa: first, that it reeks of opportunity, and second, that it's warm. He books a steamer for Casablanca.

The land-buying frenzy he finds there is even wilder than his information had advertised, and the lure of the unfamiliar fills him with new energy. Within a remarkably short period of time he is in the middle of it, organizing a company to buy hotels in Morocco and laying plans to sell what Karl Decker describes as bales of stock throughout Morocco and France.

Karl Decker.

Karl Decker is a reporter for the Hearst organization. He's been in Morocco for three months covering a tribal rebellion and has just made his way to Casablanca from Fez, his party having been shot at, and then having their trucks stopped dead by axle-deep mud. Finally they were forced to continue in the only way possible, on foot through that very same mud.

Decker is cleaned up now and refreshed, seated alone with a comforting drink on the terrace of a small restaurant in the center of town. It is chilly here, the temperature lowered by the cold breezes that have reached this far south from Europe. Here the temperature is in the fifties, a level to which no one is accustomed and which indoors seems even worse, since there are no heaters. Which is why he sits outside.

He sips his brandy to maintain the comfort of an inner glow, and as he sets it down he is startled to see a familiar face coming from the street that leads to the Arab quarter; the Marquis de Valfierno.

A greeting is shouted, and after a puzzled frown the Marquis recognizes him. The two had met several times in the past, and spent some pleasant evenings together. They had last met in Buenos Aires, where Valfierno had shown him the factory where they turned out their Murillos, having first extracted a promise that Decker would not print a word of it.

As Valfierno seats himself, Decker reminds him of that night, and of the fact that he has kept his promise, and the two of them laugh at the memory of what now seem ancient days. Then the Marquis sobers and looks at Decker, trying to decide. Perhaps the sight of an old acquaintance has softened the Marquis. Or perhaps the story is something he wants to tell.

"Would you be willing to give me that same word again?"

Decker sighs. "My friend, why must your stories come with the price of enforced quiet? Tell me something I can use. It's how I make my living, you know."

"All right," says Valfierno, "I will ease my demand. Only because this is a story you will enjoy; you especially, because of what you know of me already. I will give it to you as something you can print, but you must promise you will not do so until you have heard of my death."

Decker smiles. "I don't know that I want a reason to be glad when I hear of that unhappy event."

"I don't expect you will be."

"Fair enough. And given the difference in our ages I should outlive you by some twenty-five years, I suppose. But what if I'm shot by a jealous husband?"

"Your loved ones will be no less saddened than they would be otherwise."

Decker was silent for a minute. "I must have something for myself. How about this: I'll give you my word, but only if you promise to buy the next drink, and the next one, and the one after that for this entire evening, and on any other evening we might ever spend together."

Valfierno laughs. "You drive a hard bargain."

Seventeen years later, Karl Decker learned of Valfierno's death and wrote his story. It was published in the *Saturday Evening Post*, June 25, 1932.

One wonders who might have read it. Did the readership include the survivors, if any, of the small group of five collectors, each of whom had received his first shock some twenty years ago when the stolen painting had been recovered and restored to its place in the Louvre?

Each of these gentlemen, being unaware of the others, might well have been able to convince himself that the bizarre circumstances of the painting's recovery made it likely that the version in the Louvre was a copy, and that he possessed the masterpiece. But now self-deception was shattered as each learned that the painting had not been stolen for him alone, but that his panel was one of five copies, and that someone had laughed at the eagerness with which he had paid a fortune.

Or in the cases where death had preempted embarrassment, might the Decker piece have been read with some bewilderment by the buyers' descendants? Each member of this group, you see, would already have been puzzled by his or her discovery of this magnificent panel on which had been painted what he or she would know to be a copy of the masterpiece, since the original is where it's supposed to be. But doesn't it seem strange that this piece is stored away so carefully? If the wooden panel is significant in any way, why was it not displayed in a place of prominence? And now this Karl Decker says it's one of many such copies. But still, a limited number. Might Decker's piece give to the item a valuable provenance? Inquiries must be made.

Ruggiero Nicola had not read the Decker story. And if he had, it's unlikely the evaluator from Christie's would have connected it with the near-cartoon of *La Gioconda* he discovered among several paintings hidden in a corner of the Pearson Beck mansion. Beck had died and the family was planning to offer a few choice pieces for sale. This surely would not be among them. In fact, Nicola could not imagine what it was doing in the home of a man with discernment enough to have a particularly fine Murillo hanging in his sitting room.

But the question that looms the largest takes us back to that restaurant terrace in Casablanca.

The story the Marquis told covered the basic facts and certainly provided Decker with everything he needed for his piece. But what if the urgencies of the two men's respective lives had not limited their contact to that one evening and the Marquis had had the time, and the attentive audience, to enable him to be more expansive, to tell his story in all its detail? Would he have told it as it is written here?

Very likely, I imagine.

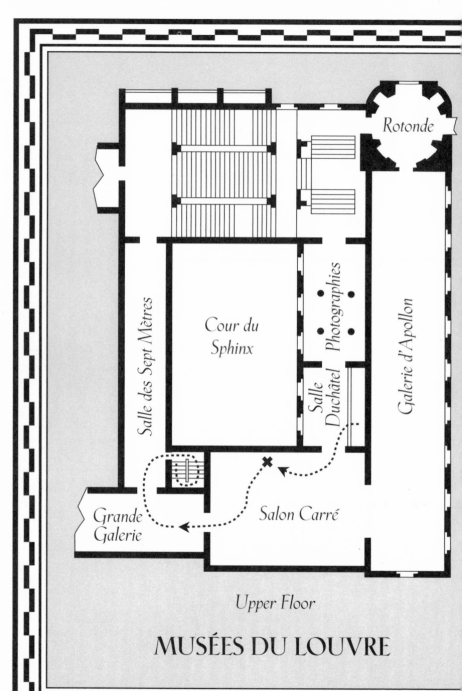

Rotonde

Salle des Sept Mètres

Cour du Sphinx

Photographies

Salle Duchâtel

Galerie d'Apollon

Grande Galerie

Salon Carré

Upper Floor

MUSÉES DU LOUVRE